2/10

The sheer physical strength of the man was impressive—the wide shoulders, the muscled thighs—she had felt this for herself as he had carried her up those stairs.

But there was more than mere strength here. Yes, it was most odd. It was there in his eyes... This evening Emma would swear she could put her life in his hands and rest easy.

But he is a Norman!

Pointedly, she made a show of looking about his bedchamber. It was furnished with royal extravagance. There were two braziers— comforting glimmers of heat. Adding more coals to one of them, Sir Richard waved her towards it. 'Warm yourself, my lady.'

My lady. Tears pricked at the back of her eyes. How long had it been since anyone had done her the courtesy of addressing her by her title? But he would soon stop doing so once he learned about her son...

RUNAWAY LADY, CONQUERING LORD

Carol Townend

First published in Great Britain 2009
Large Print edition 2010
Harlequin Mills & Boon Limited,
Eton House, 18-24 Paradise Road, Richmond, Surrey TW9 1SR

© Carol Townend 2009

ISBN: 978 0 263 21147 4

Harlequin Mills & Boon policy is to use papers that are natural, renewable and recyclable products and made from wood grown in sustainable forests. The logging and manufacturing process conform to the legal environmental regulations of the country of origin.

Printed and bound in Great Britain
by CPI Antony Rowe, Chippenham, Wiltshire

Carol Townend has been making up stories since she was a child. Whenever she comes across a tumbledown building, be it castle or cottage, she can't help conjuring up the lives of the people who once lived there. Her Yorkshire forebears were friendly with the Brontë sisters. Perhaps their influence lingers…

Carol's love of ancient and medieval history took her to London University, where she read History, and her first novel (published by Mills & Boon®) won the Romantic Novelists' Association's New Writers' Award. Currently she lives near Kew Gardens, with her husband and daughter. Visit her website at www.caroltownend.co.uk

Recent novels by the same author:

THE NOVICE BRIDE
AN HONOURABLE ROGUE
HIS CAPTIVE LADY

Author Note

In the eleventh century heraldry
was in its infancy—the devices of the
various noble houses did not start to develop
properly until the second quarter of the
twelfth century. However, flags and pennons
may be seen on the Bayeux Tapestry.
They were used in the Battle of Hastings to
convey signals as well as to reveal identity.
Count Richard of Beaumont's crimson
pennon is similar to these.

To Lucy and Mike with love
and much thanks for supporting
historical research in *la belle* France

Chapter One

Winchester—1070

Emma was halfway to the wash-house just outside the city walls when the fluttering of a red pennon caught her eye. Up there, on the road that led to the downs, a squadron of Norman horse soldiers had crested the rise. With a scowl, Emma gripped little Henri's hand. She was late, but this she had to see. Was it him? It had to be. Sir Richard of Asculf, commander of the Winchester garrison, was finally returning from campaign in the North.

Emma stared past the row of cottages and some field strips up the hill, squinting in the bright spring sun while the March wind tugged her green veil and skirts. One knight looked much the same as another in full armour, hence the importance of his pennon. And, of course, more than one knight had a red pennon. Since William of Normandy had come to wrest the crown from King Harold, Emma had seen several such. Sir Richard's had a silver line running through it, but the *conroi*, or squadron, was still too far away for Emma to make out the device.

'Mama, you are hurting my hand!' Henri said, trying to slide his small fingers out from hers.

'Sorry, sweetheart.' Emma slackened her grip, but she stayed stock-still, waiting while the column drew nearer. If it was Sir Richard, and her instincts told her it was, he had been away for several months near York. The rumours were that it had been a particularly bloody campaign; already some were calling it the Harrowing of the North. Many Saxons had been put to the sword, and not just warriors—women and children had been killed, too. *Murdered* was perhaps a more accurate word. Some said even the ducks and pigs had been slaughtered, and the grain had been burned to ensure that anyone left standing would have neither the will nor the wherewithal to contemplate rebelling against King William. Up around York, the Saxons that had been left alive would be battling merely to survive, exactly as she was.

But Sir Richard would be all right; his kind always were. A strong, handsome face lit by a pair of penetrating grey eyes hovered at the edge of Emma's consciousness. Sir Richard was Norman, and while he might be a friend of her sister, Cecily, he was likely as ruthless as the worst of them. Those eyes…so cold.

Anger churned in Emma's stomach as the line of horse soldiers snaked over the rise, chain-mail gleaming like silver, shiny helmets pointing to the sky. Doubtless they were eager to return to their quarters. Everything that had gone wrong in her life was their fault, she thought, homing in on the great grey the lead knight was riding. Sir Richard had a grey destrier. If the Normans had never crossed the Narrow Sea, her life would have proceeded as it should have done. Her mother and father would still be alive, her brother, too. Lady Emma of Fulford would be happily married and Henri would be legitimate…

Normans. Apart from her mother, God rest her soul, Emma loathed them.

Yes, it was Sir Richard sure enough, that warhorse gave him away.

'Sir Richard.' Muttering the name as though it were a curse, Emma turned back to the river path.

Sir Richard was no doubt returning to a comfortable feather bed in the castle while, thanks to the likes of him, she—Emma glanced at the washhouse that sat by the river shallows, smoke gushing through the open side—must pound linen from dawn to dusk simply to put bread in her belly.

Emma sighed. Her morning's work lay ahead and if she wanted to eat, she had better get to it. Releasing Henri, she set about unpinning her veil and kilting up her skirts. Since daybreak, she had been dreading this moment, but there was no escaping it. Today was her turn in the river at the washing stones. No matter that the spring sunlight had little heat in it, no matter that the Itchen was colder than melt-water from an ice-field, it was her turn at the washing stones.

Aediva was already in the river up to her knees, energetically bashing a twist of linen against the stones.

'Good morning, Aediva,' Emma said, tugging off her boots and setting them down by a twiggy hawthorn.

''Morning, Emma.'

'Mama, may I play with my boat?' Henri waved a crudely shaped wooden off-cut under Emma's nose.

'Yes, but not until I come down to the water. Wait there.' She pointed at the hawthorn bush. It had not yet unfurled its leaves. 'I have to see Bertha first.'

'Oh, Henri's all right.' Aediva looked up with a smile. 'I will keep an eye on him while you collect your washing.'

At Emma's nod, Henri skipped towards the washing stones, blond hair—just like his father's—shining in the sun. *Where was his father?* Emma wondered, unable to suppress a shiver of fear. Shortly after the arrival of the Normans, Judhael had told her that he was going to take refuge in the North. Anything, Judhael had said, rather than submit to a foreign invader. *Had Judhael gone north? Had he been involved in the recent fighting?* Emma bit her lip. *Had Judhael been killed?* Emma's love for Judhael was entirely gone; he had destroyed it in the days after the Conquest and Emma hoped—indeed, she prayed—never to see him again. But she did not wish him dead.

She smiled at the son she and Judhael had made when a Saxon king had sat on the English throne. Illegitimate or not, Henri was the light of Emma's life. He would soon be three. She forced herself to sound cheerful. 'Mind you stay clear of the water.'

'Yes, Mama.'

The Winchester wash-house was a three-sided wattle-and-daub barn, open on the river side. That morning, three of the fires inside had been lit, and steam billowed out from several kettles. Bertha, who ran the wash-house, was supervising a girl stirring a frothing cauldron with a wooden paddle and a boy was lifting wood from a stack to feed the fires.

The moment Emma set eyes on Bertha, her blood ran cold. Bertha's face, normally red from the steam and the heat of the fires, was as white as snow and the skin round her mouth was pinched and tight.

'Bertha, are you all right—what's happened?'

Bertha caught her breath. Her round brown eyes were small with worry and when she made a point of stepping sharply backwards, *away* from Emma, cold fingers touched Emma's neck. Something terrible must have happened for Bertha to look at her like that. 'Bertha?'

Bertha swallowed. 'I…I am sorry, Emma. There's no work for you today.'

'No work?' Several willow baskets were stacked up round the side of the wash-house, as they were every morning. A number of them were quite clearly overflowing with dirty laundry. 'What's that, then?'

Bertha moved behind one of the cauldrons and, ridiculous though it might be, Emma could not shake off the idea that Bertha was afraid of her. But why on earth would Bertha look at her like that?

Deep furrows appeared on Bertha's brow. 'I am sorry. Truly. But I have no work for you.'

Emma blinked, unable to believe what she was hearing. Bertha was a good friend, one who always made certain to save her plenty of work. 'I don't understand.'

'It is quite simple. I have no work for you, not any more.'

Emma looked pointedly at the laundry baskets. 'No?'

'No.' Bertha took a small step towards her. It was then that Emma noticed the bruising on Bertha's wrist. Lord, on *both* her wrists. 'I am sorry, Emma. Some old friends have returned to Winchester. I…I only have so much work to offer and they are desperate. *Desperate.*' Bertha almost spat out the last word, but for the life of her, Emma could not grasp what she was being told.

Emma frowned, her eyes kept returning to those bruises. 'Your friends have demanded work?'

'N-no, not exactly.' For a moment Bertha would not meet her eyes, then she looked Emma straight in the face. 'I mean, yes, *yes*, they do need work.'

Bertha was hiding something. Those bruises had not been there yesterday and they were in some way connected with Bertha's ominous change of heart. *No work?* She must keep calm. 'Bertha, I *need* the laundry you give me. How else can I earn food for Henri and myself? I also need to pay Gytha for our lodgings at the mill.'

Bertha spread her hands. 'There is nothing I can do. You will have to find work elsewhere.'

Emma blinked. 'I shall come back tomorrow. Perhaps then—'

'Don't do that. No point.' Colour flared on Bertha's cheeks. 'I won't have work for you tomorrow, either.'

A cold fist gripped Emma's insides. 'No work— Bertha, you are saying…never?'

Bertha nodded. 'That's it, never. You will have to go elsewhere.'

Dazed, Emma walked blindly into the March sunlight and came to a dead halt just outside the wash-house. *No work. Saint Swithun help her, what could she do?*

Henri was jumping about on the riverbank,

screaming with laughter as Aediva pulled faces at him, but their laughter seemed a long way off. Overhead, some rooks were cawing as they flew over the city walls towards the castle and the woods beyond; they, too, seemed very distant. *What will become of us?*

Moving as in a dream, Emma forced her legs to move. She made it as far as the riverbank, and sat down next to the hawthorn where she had left her boots and her veil. Drawing up her legs, she leaned her head on her knees.

Bertha had no work for her. What else could she do?

Minutes ago Emma had been dreading her turn in the river. She wiggled her toes; they were already blue even though she hadn't been in the water and wasn't likely to enter it, not today. Right now she would kill to be in the Itchen alongside Aediva. *What was she going to do? However was she going to pay Gytha?*

Lifting her head, Emma looked back over her shoulder. Through a gap between two cottages, a couple of ploughboys were visible, hard at work in one of the field strips. One was pulling on the ox's halter, while his companion steadied the plough. In their wake seagulls dived and mewed.

And there, past the field strips, on the road beyond was Sir Richard of Asculf, the most powerful man in the district, riding back to his garrison at the head of his squadron. A couple of wolfhounds were loping alongside him, and a small white dog she was unable to identify.

The most powerful man in the district.

They were almost back in Winchester. Richard's *conroi* had crested the rise overlooking Eastgate when his shoulder gave another twinge and his fingers tightened involuntarily on Roland's reins. It was a mere twitch, but nonetheless it had Roland tossing his head. Richard suppressed a smile. For all that Roland was such a big-boned piece of horseflesh, these years in England had seen him become highly sensitised to Richard's slightest movement.

'Is your shoulder paining you, sir?' his squire, Geoffrey, asked. 'You rode like a demon back there. We almost lost the hounds.'

'What, are you worried you might have to re-stitch me?' Richard said, with a grin. There had been no surgeon handy when they had removed the arrow and his squire had proved to be a little squeamish when it had come to sewing him up.

'It seems quite possible, you ought to take more care.'

'Geoffrey, it was only a scratch. Best to keep moving. Don't want to seize up.'

'No, sir.'

Richard turned his gaze back to the road. In between Richard's squadron and the city walls a row of cottages followed the course of the river. Some lads were doing some late ploughing, scoring the earth with dark furrows. Crops were being seeded in other holdings, apples trees were being pruned.

'The city looks idyllic from here, eh, Geoffrey, the clear skies, the bright sunlight?'

'Aye, just like home.'

Richard shot his squire a startled glance. 'You think so?' Winchester would *never* feel like home to him. He longed to return to Normandy, but King William had ordered him to remain in Winchester and command the garrison. And, as a loyal knight, Richard would obey.

As they approached Mill Bridge the road took the *conroi* past the wash-house. One of the laundry women was knee-deep in the river, talking to her child as she beat linen against the rocks. Another, a young girl with a thick blonde plait, sat to one side, hunched by the riverside in an attitude of exhaustion. She must have heard their hoofbeats though, because at their approach the girl rose. Setting her hands on her hips, she stared as they rode by.

There was a certain belligerence in the girl's stance for all that she was a slender little thing. Her feet were blue with cold. Shapely legs, what Richard could see of them. Geoffrey had seen her, too; he nodded at her as they passed, but the girl didn't respond. Richard doubted she even saw Geoffrey for she was, he realised with something of a jolt, staring at him with that narrowed gaze he had come to recognise in many Saxon eyes. Blue eyes, gleaming with hostility. And yet behind the hostility, if he was not mistaken, there was fear, too. Such a shame. She might be pretty, if ever she lost that scowl.

Just then the boy by the riverbank gave a shriek; the hostility vanished from the girl's face and her head whipped round.

'My boat, *my boat*!' the child wailed.

The stick he had been playing with was drifting beyond his reach. The woman in the water tried to snatch at it as it floated past, but missed.

'*Mama!*' The child's distracted wail drew the

bare-legged laundry maid to his side, concern in her every line.

Shaking his head, Richard looked towards Eastgate and wondered if, after what had happened at York, Normans and Saxons would ever learn to live in peace.

Some half an hour later, when Emma had calmed Henri about the loss of his boat and the shock of losing her work had begun to ease, her green skirts were neatly back in place and her veil was securely covering her hair.

'Gytha will help us, Henri,' she said, pushing through the crowd on Mill Bridge.

Henri glanced up and nodded as though he understood what she was talking about. Sometimes, it seemed to Emma that Henri really did understand everything she said to him, but that was ridiculous. Her son was not yet three, how could he? She paused to smooth a stray lock of his hair back into place. There was no trace of the tears brought about by the loss of his boat, thank goodness. Henri was smiling his normal sunny smile.

Emma's nose wrinkled. Smoke! The smell of smoke was not in itself unusual, but great acrid gouts of it were hanging over the bridge, stinging her eyes, catching in the back of her throat. Henri began to cough. Someone's cooking fire must have got badly out of control.

'Mama, look!'

Emma waved her hand in front of her face to clear the smoke and her jaw dropped. The mill! Some fool had set a fire in the mill yard. Gytha was running to the river with a bucket in either hand and her husband, Edwin, was tossing water onto a smoking fire set all too close to the wooden wall of the mill.

Someone yelled, 'Fire!'

An excited babble broke out among those on the bridge, but no one was running to help. Picking up her skirts, clinging to Henri, Emma elbowed through and into the cobbled yard.

'Here, Henri, wait by the wall.' Eyes round, Henri stuck his thumb in his mouth and went to stand by a couple of grain sacks.

Emma raced to Gytha's side, grasped a bucket handle and set to work. The fire was not large and a few bucketfuls later it was reduced to a hissing black mass.

'Lucky it was small,' Emma commented, as she, Gytha and Edwin frowned down at the smouldering remains. 'But what fool would light a fire so close to the mill?'

Silence. Gytha was biting her lips. Edwin refused to meet her eyes. Indeed there was something in his stance that put Emma in mind of Bertha. *Oh, no, what now?*

'Gytha?'

Gytha's throat worked. She glanced at the onlookers blocking Mill Bridge and Emma followed her gaze. A great bear of a man stood in between two nuns from the nearby convent. The hood of his cloak was up, but Emma could see that he wore his brown hair and beard long, in the Saxon manner. Emma sucked in a breath; she must be dreaming, but she thought she knew him.

Azor? In Winchester?

It couldn't be. But for a moment it was as though Emma was wrenched back four years in time to 1066. The man had a long brown beard, just like Azor's. She must be mistaken—many Saxons wore such beards. Even as Emma looked, he ducked back into the crowd, leaving the nuns staring avidly over the handrail at the goings on at City Mill.

Gently, Gytha touched her arm. 'Emma, you had best come inside.'

Edwin exchanged glances with his wife. 'I'll make sure the fire is right out,' he said, 'and then I'll shift the grain sacks ready for the carter.'

Usually when in the mill, Emma found the familiar rattle and rumble of the mill wheel calming, but today it seemed too loud. Perhaps because her nerves were jangling even the rush of the river under their feet seemed deafening.

'Was that Azor on the bridge, Gytha?'

Gytha made her way to the hopper and scooped in some grain. Henri followed, settled himself on the floor by Gytha's skirts, and began drawing patterns in the flour dust.

'Gytha?'

Briefly, Gytha closed her eyes. 'Yes, that was Azor.'

Emma felt as though the mill had been tipped upside down. Azor was Judhael's most staunch supporter; he was also another champion of the lost Saxon cause. 'Sweet Mother.' Mouth dry, she swallowed hard. 'Does that mean that Judhael has returned?'

'I am afraid so.'

Emma's nails dug into her palms. 'You have seen him?'

'Yes.'

'Oh, Lord.' Emma drew a shaky breath. 'You spoke to him?'

'Yes.'

'And…?'

Gytha smiled sadly at Henri and shook her head. 'It doesn't matter what he said. I think you should forget it.'

'He is still bitter? He knows that I live here?'

'Yes to both questions,' Gytha said.

Emma felt the blood drain from her face. 'I thought I could escape him here, that I would be safe among all these people. If I had gone back to Fulford, Judhael would have found me in a moment. How did he find me?'

Gytha lifted her shoulders, her eyes were wide and concerned. 'I have no idea, but it wouldn't take much to discover your whereabouts. A question here, a question there.'

'I have prayed and prayed that he would never come back.'

'Well, Judhael and Azor have both returned and somehow Judhael has learned that you live here.'

'Gytha, he said something else, didn't he?'

Gytha dropped the grain scoop back into the sack and dusted down her hands.

'Gytha?'

Gytha pursed her lips and something clicked in Emma's mind. Crossing the floor in two strides, she took Gytha's arms and looked at her wrists. Mercifully, they were unmarked. 'He threatened you, didn't he? And Bertha—Judhael must have been to see her, too.' She scrubbed at her forehead. 'What was it Bertha said—something about desperate friends having returned…?'

'Emma, what are you talking about?'

'Judhael! He must have threatened Bertha, which is why she has stopped giving me work—'

'Bertha had no work for you?'

'Apparently not. There were several baskets of linen lined up to be washed, but I wasn't allowed near them. Judhael must have paid her a visit, don't you see?'

'I am beginning to. He certainly wants you back.'

'The man is mad! After what he did up at Seven Wells Hill, the way he beat Lufu when he learned it was she who told Cecily the location of the rebel camp. Lufu was only trying to help get my baby brother to safety.' Cold sweat was trickling down Emma's back. She looked at her son, at Judhael's son. If Judhael got hold of Henri— It didn't bear thinking about. 'I'll never go back to him, never!'

'Of course not. Never fear, we shall pay him no mind. We managed to put out the fire and—'

Emma's blood turned to ice. 'Judhael set the fire?'

'We are not sure, but it seems likely. It happened shortly after his visit. I think it is meant as a warning. He suggested we throw you out.' Gytha grimaced. 'Lord, I hadn't meant to tell you that. Emma, we shall pay him no mind.'

'Pay him no mind? Gytha, the man tries to burn down the mill and you say pay him no mind! What if he had set the fire at night and no one noticed until it was too late? We might have been fried in our beds!'

'Hush, Emma, you are alarming Henri. And anyway, no one was hurt.'

'Henri and I shall have to leave.'

'Nonsense, that is exactly what he wants!'

'What do you mean?'

'Judhael wants you back.'

'If he thinks threatening my friends is going to make me go back to him, then the war with the Normans had damaged him more than I realised.' She sucked in a breath. 'Do you think he knows about Henri?'

Gytha shook her head. 'I doubt it, he didn't mention him.'

'That at least is one mercy. But I won't have him threatening you. God help us. I *like* being here with you and Henri does, too. Don't you, Henri?'

'Yes, Mama.'

'Emma, it isn't right that Judhael should be threatening you. You are a lady—'

'Not any more I'm not.'

'Yes, you are. Your father was Thane of Fulford. Judhael was only a housecarl.'

Emma sighed. 'Be that as it may, I won't bring trouble to your door. Henri and I must leave.'

'Judhael said he would return tomorrow.'

'I shall be gone by then.'

'You can't go to Fulford.'

'No, I can't, Judhael is doubtless waiting for me to do just that.'

'Where then? Where will you go?'

Chapter Two

Sir Richard of Asculf was in the castle stables when the messengers arrived.

Richard was stripped to the waist and his broad shoulders gleamed with sweat, for he himself was personally grooming his destrier, the grey he had in a whimsical moment named Roland. Outside he could clearly hear the *chink, chink, chink* of a mason's chisel. Work was being done on the gatehouse.

Since he had taken up the reins of command again in Winchester, Richard did not expect to get as much exercise as a man in his prime needed, and he enjoyed grooming Roland. He was fond of the great beast; they had been through much together. Outside, his two wolfhounds lounged in some loose straw that had escaped into the bailey, eyes closed as they drowsed in the sun. He had no idea where the white mongrel was—scrounging a bone from the kitchens, perhaps? That dog was always hungry.

The rattle of hoofs on the cobbles alerted Richard to new arrivals. Glancing up, he shoved back his glossy brown hair and almost immediately four riders trotted into view, framed by the doorway. Their horses were flecked with foam, almost blown.

A crease formed in Richard's brow. 'Geoffrey!'

His squire's head popped up from the next stall, where he was at work on his own horse. 'Sir?'

'See what those men want, will you?'

'Yes, sir.'

'Make sure they are offered refreshments and if they have dispatches, tell them I will meet them in the solar in half an hour when I've finished here. Oh, and pick out good grooms for those horses, they have been ridden too hard.'

'Yes, sir.'

Geoffrey went out into the bailey and Richard resumed brushing Roland's coat. Roland snorted and snuffled and pushed against his hand. 'Easy, boy. You like that, do you?'

A shadow fell over him. 'Sir?'

'Geoffrey?'

'It…it is not dispatches, sir. They have a personal message for you, and they say it is important.'

'From the King?'

'No, sir, but I think you need to hear it.'

'Not this minute, surely?'

Geoffrey's eyes were alight with excitement. 'I am afraid so, sir.'

Sighing, Richard straightened and emerged from Roland's stall. 'If they are envoys,' he said, grimacing at his half-naked state, 'I'm not dressed to receive them.'

'You'll want to receive me, my lord.' A man pushed past Geoffrey and extended a hand in greeting. 'You are Sir Richard of Asculf, garrison commander?'

My lord? 'Indeed, but who the devil are you?' Snatching his *chainse*, his undershirt, from the partition, Richard wiped his face. The man, a knight to judge by his costly armour, wore a grim expression. Judging from the growth on his chin, he had not shaved for some days.

'Sir Jean Sibley, my lord, and at your service.' The man's gaze flickered briefly to the wound on Richard's shoulder.

Richard gestured that they should move outside. *My lord?* Out in the bailey, the other knights who had accompanied Sir Jean had already dismounted. Richard felt their eyes rest curiously on him.

'My lord.' Sir Jean pressed a bundle of crimson fabric into his hands.

A knight's pennon? No…

A betraying gleam of gold had ice skittering down Richard's spine. 'My cousin,' he managed, 'something has happened to my cousin.'

'Yes, my lord.'

Bemused, scarcely able to credit what was happening, Richard watched as Sir Jean and the other knights bent their heads in respect. 'My lord, I regret to inform you that your cousin, Count Martin of Beaumont, died a week since and—'

'Martin? What the hell happened?' Richard unfolded the crimson fabric. Martin's pennon. It was almost the twin of his, the only difference being that the *pale*, the line through the centre of the Beaumont pennon, was gold rather than silver. A count ranked higher than a knight. Face set, Richard opened it out, and swallowed. This would be hard to accept. He had not seen his cousin in over a year, but as boys they had been fostered together. They had been as close as brothers.

Martin is—was—too young to die, Richard thought, though he knew full well that many younger than Martin had died since King William had come to England. That poor mite he had seen cut down in the North was but one of many—even now that child haunted his dreams....

Putting the child out of his mind, Richard focused on the man in front of him.

'It was an accident, my lord,' Sir Jean was saying. 'The Count was drilling the men and his horse threw him. You know how he was.'

Richard nodded. 'He would have to take part.'

'Exactly so, my lord. The Count fell and dislocated his shoulder. At first we thought that was the sum of it. But sadly...' Sir Jean spread his hands '...sadly it appears there were other, hidden injuries.'

'Internal ones?'

'There must have been. The Count died a week since. And in the absence of heirs, you, my lord Count, have inherited the title.'

Gesturing for Sir Jean and his men to follow, Richard strode across the bailey, the Beaumont pennon crushed tight in one fist, his tunic and *chainse* in the other. 'No children? I would have thought it possible that he and Lady Aude—'

'My lord, they were not yet married.'

Richard blinked. His cousin and Aude de Crèvecoeur had been betrothed since she was still a child and Martin had worshipped her. 'He never married Lady Aude?'

'No, my lord.'

'Why the delay?' Aude de Crèvecoeur was not to Richard's taste, and if it had been he who had been betrothed to the woman, then he *would* have delayed, till Doomsday. But, *chacun à son gout*, Martin had adored her... It made no sense.

'I do not know, my lord. The Count did not confide in me regarding his marriage plans.'

'It happened at Beaumont?'

'My lord?'

'The accident happened at Beaumont?'

'Yes, my lord.'

'Are you certain no foul play was involved?' Entering the hall, Richard lowered his voice. 'Both my lords of Alençon and Argentan have long had their eyes fixed on Beaumont.'

'The thought crossed our minds, too, my lord. But, no, the Count died of injuries from the fall, there was nothing more sinister.'

Reaching a trestle, Richard dropped the pennon on the table and dragged on his *chainse*. Geoffrey busied himself with serving wine. 'It's a damn waste,' Richard said. 'Martin was a fine man, a fine count.'

'Yes, Lord Richard. But I am sure that you, as heir to your cousin's estates, will also make a fine count.' Sir Jean gave him a direct look and spoke with a new intensity. 'If I may speak plainly, you are needed in Beaumont. As you say, Alençon and Argentan are on the prowl. How long will you need to settle your affairs in England?'

Richard took a cup of wine from Geoffrey. 'That will depend on King William. As Duke of Normandy he will have to approve my inheriting the Beaumont estate. It is his right.'

'Of course, my lord, but surely he is bound to agree? William needs good men in his Duchy, as well as in his kingdom here.'

'That may be so, but in the past he has shown a marked reluctance to let me leave England.'

Confidentially, Sir Jean leaned closer. 'That must change, my lord. Beaumont's position is of strategic importance to him, which is why both Alençon and Argentan would like to get their hands on it. The Duke *must* agree to your accession and *soon*. Delay could be disastrous for his interests in

Normandy. We have tried to keep news of Count Martin's death from both Argentan and Alençon, but it is only a matter of time before they hear the news. And then...' His expression darkened.

'I understand. Nevertheless, I need King William's permission before I can leave England. And until then, I remain Sir Richard of Asculf.' He lifted his wine-cup to his lips.

'Of course, my l—sir. And I must mention a further pressing matter. May I ask, will you now take the Lady Aude as your wife?'

Richard all but choked. 'Marry Aude de Crèvecoeur? Lord, man, why the devil do you ask me that?'

Sir Jean cleared his throat. 'Her brother, Count Edouard, may expect it.'

'Expect it?'

'Lady Aude was betrothed to your cousin some years ago. She has been brought up to be Countess of Beaumont. Since you will be Count in your cousin's place, her brother may hope you will honour the arrangement.'

'He can hope away,' Richard spoke bluntly. 'I do not wish to marry her.'

'There may be trouble, L—Sir Richard. At home there are pressures...'

Holding up his hand for silence, Richard stared blankly into his wine-cup. He didn't need to hear any more. Truth be told, he needed time to think. Martin was dead, dead. And if King William agreed, *he* would indeed be Comte de Beaumont. It was hard to credit. 'I have long wished to return home,' he murmured, 'but not this way, not at the cost of my cousin's life.' And he would be damned before he married Aude de Crèvecoeur.

'No, sir, of course not.'

Gathering his wits about him, for it would not do to appear indecisive before these men, knights of Beaumont who had been loyal to his cousin and would soon, he hoped, swear fealty to him, Richard gestured Geoffrey over. First, the King must be informed of events in Normandy. 'Geoffrey, be so good as to fetch a quill and ink to the solar.'

'Yes, sir!' The boy was beaming from ear to ear. There was a world of difference in being squire to a knight and being squire to a count, and this unlooked-for promotion clearly delighted him.

Richard shook his head, but he could not find it in his heart to blame him. Geoffrey had scarcely known his cousin—how could he be expected to mourn him?

Halfway to the door, Geoffrey turned. 'Shall I fetch a scribe, too, my lord?'

'No, this is one letter I shall write myself.' Sir Jean was in the right; until they reached Normandy, the fewer people who knew about his cousin's death, the better.

'Very well, sir.'

Richard fixed a smile on his face and turned back to Sir Jean and the knights who had travelled from Beaumont to bring him this news. 'It is time, I think, for some introductions,' he said, indicating a fellow with a crest of fiery hair who stood at Sir Jean's elbow.

The following day, Richard was back in the castle stables rubbing Roland down after an early gallop through the water meadows and around the city defences.

Richard was uncomfortably aware that tending to a destrier clad only in one's chausses and boots was perhaps not an undertaking for a count. However, at the moment the company of animals was preferable to the company of people. Neither Roland nor the hounds minded how much exercise he took, nor did they think any the less of him if he took time to think and plan. Besides,

Richard was damned if he was going to break the habit of a lifetime, caring for his animals himself, simply because poor Martin had died. And in any case, only a handful of trusted men knew of his elevated status.

His letter to King William had been despatched, but no reply had been forthcoming. Yet. He was impatient to be back in Normandy.

The regular *tock, tock, tock* of chisel on stone told Richard that the masons' work on the gatehouse was not yet completed. He heard the occasional shout from the overseer and the creak of their hoist.

In the orchard just outside the city, a cuckoo was calling, its voice floating clearly over the castle walls. Spring, thank God. It had been a hard winter. Perhaps this year he would be celebrating Easter in Beaumont....

A shadow fell across the stable floor. 'There are two women to see you, sir.'

Richard glanced up with a grin. He was expecting one woman, Frida from the Staple. '*Two?* Geoffrey, you flatter me.'

Despite the exercise Richard had been taking, sleep remained elusive. Which was why he had decided to add another, more pleasant, form of exercise to his regime. It had been too long since he had had a woman, perhaps that was what he needed; it certainly could do no harm. And the entire garrison knew that the best women available locally were to be found at the Staple, the inn past Market Street. With the news from Normandy added to Richard's daily responsibilities, Richard had not had time to visit the Staple himself to pick one. He had sent Geoffrey along in his stead, with orders to look out for a suitable girl.

But *two* women? Lord. If that didn't do the trick, nothing would.

Of late, Richard's dreams had been filled with disturbing images, bloody images that centred on a Saxon child whose death he had been unable to prevent. Richard hoped the girls were pleasing—another wakeful night would drive him insane.

Geoffrey cleared his throat. 'No, sir, you misunderstand. These women are not from the Staple.'

'Oh?'

Richard heard footsteps. More shadows darkened the doorway as a young woman and a small boy stepped forwards, both with that fair

Saxon colouring. An older woman stood close behind. Richard's eyes narrowed; they were familiar, but he could not at first place them. The woman who had come forwards was comely, with large blue eyes and honey-blonde hair that she had twisted back beneath a threadbare veil. Her clothes were unremarkable, a faded green gown, a thin leather belt with a worn purse hanging from it.

The boy clung to her skirts and eyed the great wolfhounds warily. Richard's other dog, the mongrel, was not around. Slowly, the boy stuck his thumb in his mouth. And then Richard had it—this was the bare-legged laundry maid he had seen by the river. With her veil on and her clothes set to rights, he had not known her. Her face was shadowed with tiredness, but she had lost that scowl she had been wearing by the river. And, yes, she was all the prettier for it.

His *chainse* over his shoulder, Richard came towards them. He was irritated not to see Frida, and no question but the laundry maid was about to disturb his morning with a petition.

The fear in the boy's eyes as he stared at Richard's wolfhounds made him set his irritation aside. 'They will not hurt you,' he said softly, in

English. Richard's command of the tongue was weak, but when pushed he could generally make himself understood. 'They like children, just do not startle them. They have been asleep, you see.'

The laundry maid's companion stepped closer and held out her hand to the child. Of course, this was the child's mother, the woman who had been in the river when they had ridden in. 'Henri, come here.' The boy went to her slowly, eyes on the hounds, and the two of them backed out into the bailey.

The pretty laundry maid remained. Her smile was nervous; yes, she was definitely about to ask a favour of him. Best get this over with, and then he could see if Frida might suit. From Geoffrey's description Frida had much to offer. It would have to be a temporary liaison, of course, since he hoped to be leaving for Normandy soon. 'Your name?'

'Emma…Emma of Fulford.'

Merde, this was Cecily's *sister*? Lady Cecily of Fulford had married his comrade Sir Adam Wymark, and Richard counted her among his dearest friends. He took a closer look. Yes, the resemblance was there if you searched for it. So this was Lady Emma of Fulford—a lady washerwoman! Her father had been a Saxon thane, her mother a Norman noblewoman. Richard had met Lady Emma before, albeit briefly, but he knew her by repute.

It was not lost on him that she had not used her title, nor that she had chosen to ignore him yesterday by the river. As he recalled, despite her Norman mother, Emma of Fulford had been singularly unhelpful in the days immediately following the Conquest. For that reason alone Richard was disinclined to like her, never mind that she had obviously divined that he had an assignation in the stables, and was currently trying to look down her little nose at him. He bit back a laugh. Since the woman only reached his shoulder, looking down her nose at him was, of course, impossible.

But, by St Denis, the years had changed her. Emma of Fulford's clothes were little better than a beggar's. Gone was the finery she had once worn to flounce around her father's mead-hall. Gone were the thane's arm-rings she had called her own. Briefly, Richard wondered what she had done with them. They had been jingling on her wrists the day he had met her, barbaric Saxon bangles with the soft gleam of gold. When had that been—three years ago, more? He couldn't recall. Had she lost the arm-rings, or sold them?

She always had been a stupid wench. Why else would she have run off with that Saxon hothead? The whole of Wessex knew they had been lovers, and for her, a noblewoman, to have taken a man out of wedlock—it was almost unheard of. She was lucky not to have had a child.

As Richard looked at her, his gut tightened and for a moment he thought he saw pleading in those large, dark-lashed eyes. But, no, he must have been mistaken. Her nose lifted, her lips firmed.

'Sir Richard.' She inclined her head, eyes flickering briefly, haughtily, to his naked chest. He could almost see her thoughts—why was he, a knight, grooming his horse? What would she say, Richard wondered, if she knew he was soon to be Count of Beaumont?

More was coming back to him. In the winter of 1066, hadn't Emma of Fulford been persuaded to abandon her rebel lover on Beacon Hill? Richard hadn't liked her haughtiness then and he didn't like it today. Striding past her, he went to the water trough, sluiced himself down and dragged on his shirt. Gritting his teeth, he reminded himself that this was Cecily's sister, and that she had been brought up as a thane's daughter. A laundry maid! He wouldn't mind betting that her status as a fallen woman meant she was shunned by half the town. What was that Saxon word for nothing—*nithing*? Did the people consider her *nithing*? Whatever her past mistakes, this woman deserved better. There was breeding and beauty there, and, of course, she spoke fluent French.

'You need my help?' he asked, reverting with relief to that language.

'I… Yes, please. My sister, Cecily—she married your friend Sir Adam—'

'I know who your sister is.' The woman before him was perhaps an inch or so taller than Lady Cecily, but she was not tall. Richard seemed to remember that her figure had been fuller when he had met her, but it was hard to judge it today, hidden as it was beneath that hideous gown. Her waist seemed slim. He found himself recalling the daintiness of her feet and the exact curve of her calves. He hoped Frida was half as attractive.

'Yes, of course. Well, I do remember Cecily mentioning you were a good friend—'

To Richard's horror, her voice broke. Abruptly she turned her head. 'I… That is… Oh, Lord…' She blinked rapidly, but not before Richard had seen her eyes glaze with the swift shine of tears. When she looked up a moment later, she had herself in hand. 'I would like to work here in the castle. I thought—since you know my family— you might be able to put me in touch with the castle steward, and perhaps…perhaps a recommendation…' Her voice trailed off.

Richard could tell by the set of her lips that she loathed asking this favour of him. Emma of Fulford might have been stripped of her finery, she might have lost her reputation, but she had kept her pride. 'Work? You mean washing linen?'

The nose inched up. 'Yes, I…I have experience. I have been working at the wash-house. But I would prefer to work in the castle. Clothes, household linens, fine silks…anything. I know how to handle the most delicate imported fabrics. Nothing will be damaged. I am also a competent seamstress.'

How the mighty had fallen. It was hard not to smile, but Richard managed it. Something in her proud posture touched him. Let her keep what dignity she had left. 'There are competent seamstresses aplenty here.' He rubbed his chin while he thought. Lady Emma might have been foolish in the past, but this was Adam's sister-by-marriage, and he wanted to help.

'I see.' Emma of Fulford's shoulders slumped;

she began to turn away. 'I…I thank you for your time, sir.'

Richard took her arm gently. 'Don't be so hasty, I have not said I will not help you, merely that we have no need of seamstresses.'

The arm beneath the cloth was slighter than he had expected, fine-boned. It crossed his mind that she might not be eating enough. Releasing her, Richard knew a moment's confusion. Sir Adam Wymark had married this woman's sister. Adam was the best of comrades and amenable to Cecily's every wish, so why had Emma not been given houseroom at Fulford?

He opened his mouth to ask before it occurred to him that the less involvement he had with this woman, the better. He would be leaving soon. And while he did not know much about her, what he did know told him that she was—complicated. Richard already had more complexities than he could cope with. But there was something in her manner and person than held his admiration. Add to that the loyalty he felt for Adam and Cecily and he had to help her.

'Geoffrey will make an appointment for you to meet our steward. Geoffrey?'

'Sir?'

'See to it.'

'Is she to work in the laundry here?'

Richard shook his head. 'I think not. Lady Emma needs something more suitable to her station, you understand me?'

'Yes, sir.'

'Very well, take her to the steward, and if he has nothing for her, let her make enquiries in the ladies' solar. In the meantime, pass me my tunic, would you?'

'Thank you, sir,' Emma of Fulford said, bowing her head. Geoffrey handed Richard his tunic and he dragged it on. 'Thank you very much,' she said, curtsying gracefully.

Richard was buckling on his belt when a movement across the yard caught his eye. A smiling woman waved and started making her way slowly towards them, hips swaying as she walked. This must be Frida from the Staple.

Frida was wearing a tight-laced yellow gown that emphasised her generous curves. The deep slash in the front revealed more than a hint of bosom, and the full skirts frothed about her ankles. Yellow suited her and that undulating walk was calculated to draw the gaze of every man in the bailey. Frida's walk had the power to halt the tocking of the masons' chisels. It even reached the cookhouse—through the open door came a clang as someone dropped a pot.

Richard grinned and wished that he had shaved. This was the sort of woman for him. His relationship with Frida would be uncomplicated, a brief business affair unencumbered by guilt or messy emotion.

Emma of Fulford had seen Frida and with a slight tinge to her cheeks was edging away. 'Your…lady…is here, I see.'

Face flushing for no reason that Richard could point to, he cleared his throat. Frida was a whore as everyone knew, but she was said to be a faithful whore who kept to one lover at a time. If they suited, she would be his and his alone—for as long as he was in England, and for as long as he kept supplying her with the trinkets and coin that she would doubtless require.

Nevertheless, as Richard watched Frida slowly make her way towards him, he found that the graceful, slight figure of Lady Emma of Fulford had a tendency to linger at the back of his mind.

Chapter Three

'More fitting?' Emma stormed out of the bailey with Henri in her arms. Aediva was no longer with her, having gone back to the wash-house immediately after Emma's interview with Count Richard. Earlier, when Aediva had heard where Emma had been going that morning, she had insisted in coming along—bless her—to give Emma moral support. Emma had good friends, and for that she was grateful, but this morning it seemed to Emma that what she needed were *powerful* friends.

Crossing the drawbridge, Emma stalked into what was left of Golde Street after King William—with typical Norman arrogance—had had half the street pulled down to build his castle.

'More fitting?' Her steps were brisk and jerky and Emma was unaware that she was still mut-

tering to herself until Henri patted her cheek and tried to make her look into his eyes.

'Mama? Mama angry?'

'Yes, sweetheart. Mama is *very* angry.'

Henri's face fell, his hand dropped.

'Oh, not with you, sweet, not with you.' Emma made her voice light. 'It is that man I am angry with, that bone-headed, patronising man.'

'Sir Rich?'

Emma gave a humourless laugh. 'You are not daft, are you, my lad?' Saints, she must guard her tongue with Henri; he might not have seen three summers, but he understood far too much of what went on about him. 'Sir Rich about sums him up.'

'Mama? Smile?'

Sir Rich, indeed. But as far as she was concerned he was singularly unhelpful. Forcing a smile, Emma marched down the street. What next? Where next? Panic was churning inside her.

'We need work,' she said. 'Somewhere to live.'

'Yes, Mama.'

Sir Richard must have known his steward would not have any work for her, he must have known she would be turned away. He had humiliated her. Clearly, Sir Richard disapproved of her working as a laundry maid. Not fitting for a lady, oh, he had never stated it quite so baldly, but he thought it. She had read it in those cold grey eyes. Not fitting, indeed. And here she was leaving the castle with nothing, because the count's boy, Geoffrey, had left her with the steward, who couldn't be bothered to find her 'suitable' work. What *was* suitable? she fumed, reaching Westgate and turning towards Market Street. What did the man expect her to do?

'Henri, you are growing so fast, I swear, you are heavier than one of Gytha's grain sacks.' Setting her son on his feet, she took his hand and swept on.

'Suitable work? Hah!' What was suitable for someone of her station? Neither lady nor peasant due to her—she glanced at the top of her son's head—supposed mistake. A mistake, Emma gritted her teeth, that she would never regret as long as she lived.

At the corner of Staple Street a woman with eggs in a basket caught her eye. Eggs. Emma's mouth watered; she had not eaten an egg in an age. But, of course, the days were growing longer and with the longer days, the hens would be coming into lay. In her other life, when she had been a thane's daughter at Fulford, Emma had loved hunting out the first eggs of the season. A wave of longing took her and she missed a step.

'Fresh eggs, mistress?'

She cleared her throat. 'Later, perhaps.'

The Staple lay in front of her, a wattle-and-daub building that was almost as large as her father's mead-hall. Its thatch was dark with age, and smoke gusted from louvres in the roof ridge. The Staple was the most popular tavern in the town, and this morning the door and shutters had been flung wide to admit the air, the spring sunlight and, of course, the customers. Emma had friends inside. Not powerful ones, but friends none the less. Perhaps they could help her.

Emma stepped over the threshold, holding fast to Henri.

A huddle of merchants were haggling over the finer points of a deal around the central fire, a band of off-duty troopers were drinking at one of the trestles. Other than the tavern girls, there were few women present. Hélène and Marie were in the shadows at the far end of the room, filling clay jugs with wine from a barrel. Behind the women stood the wooden screen that concealed the doorway to the adjacent cookhouse. To one side, against the further wall, a stairway led to the communal bedchamber that—following a design brought in by the Norman invaders—had been built under the eaves.

Several heads turned as Emma made her way towards Hélène and Marie. There certainly were plenty of pests from the garrison here today. Emma found herself swishing her skirts out of the way of more than one grasping hand. Reaching the trestle under the loft-chamber, Emma took a place on a bench and let out a sigh of relief.

'How goes it, Hélène?'

Hélène stuck a stopper in one of the jugs and smiled. 'Fine.'

'I have a couple of favours to ask,' Emma said.

'I'll be with you in a moment.'

Henri tugged his hand free and skipped behind the wooden screen, lured by a mouthwatering smell of fresh bread.

'Hello, Henri.' Hearing the voice of Inga, the tavern cook, Emma relaxed. Inga would keep Henri safe. 'Are you hungry?'

'Yes!'

Leaning her head against the whitewashed daub, Emma closed her eyes. She had been humiliated, Sir Rich—ha!—had humiliated her.

Telling that boy of his to make sure she had 'fitting' work, when he must have known that the steward would give her short shrift. The steward's lips had curled as he had said, no, he did not think there was any work in Winchester Castle for a lady like her. And his tone…

'All right, love?' The bench creaked as Hélène came to sit next to her.

Emma opened her eyes while Marie drifted into the main body of the tavern and began flirting with a young archer. 'I confess it, I have been better.'

'Someone call you *nithing* again?'

To be called *nithing* was to say that you did not exist, that you were lower than the low. Which, Emma thought bitterly, she was. An outcast. She had been a lady and she had had a child out of wedlock. Would she ever be able to hold her head high again?

Again she sighed. 'Not this time, although that has been cast in my face in the past.'

Hélène patted Emma's knee. 'Not by anyone I would let through these doors, dear, rest assured. You are no more *nithing* than I am.'

'My thanks.' Emma gazed earnestly at Hélène. 'I would have you know that your friendship means much to me.'

Dark colour washed into Hélène's cheeks. 'You value my friendship? You know what this tavern is…what the girls…' she all but choked '…and yet you value my friendship?'

Henri emerged, smiling, from behind the screen with a slice of bread dripping with honey clutched tight in his fist. Emma laid her hand on Hélène's. 'You must know I do. This is the only place, apart from the mill, where Henri and I are accepted, fully accepted. You and Gytha are dear to me, you let me be…myself. You don't judge me.'

Hélène snorted and her wave took in Marie, now sitting on the lap of the archer, whispering in his ear. 'Judge you? Running this place does not give me the right to step into a preacher's shoes. Not that I would want to….'

'No, of course not. But you understand me.' Emma reached out to wipe a trickle of honey from the corner of her son's mouth. 'You know how life does not turn out quite as one expects it to and unlike some—' a brief image of cold grey eyes flashed into her mind '—you accept me for what I am.'

'Of course I do. Tell me, what was it you wanted to ask?'

'I need work,' she said, bluntly. 'Do you have any?'

Hélène lifted a brow. 'I am sorry, Emma, the girls here take turns in seeing to the laundry.'

Emma's shoulders slumped. 'I was afraid you would say that. Dear Lord, what am I to do?'

'Surely there is more than enough for you at the wash-house?'

'There's not *any* at the wash-house! Bertha—oh, Hélène—it is quite dreadful.' Keeping an eye on Henri who was wandering back behind the screen for more bread, Emma lowered her voice. 'Judhael is back! He has threatened Bertha.'

'Surely not?'

'Yes, yes, he has—there were marks on her wrist. Hélène, Judhael is not a...gentle man.'

'You are saying Judhael hurt Bertha?'

'*Yes!* You don't know him as I do. Why, he beat the Fulford cook once for speaking out of turn.'

A warm hand came to rest on Emma's knee. 'That is why you never returned to Fulford. You were afraid he might find you.'

Emma swallowed. 'Yes, that's it. But it has all been for nothing, he has found me anyway. He has been bullying Bertha and...oh, Hélène, it is worse that that—he knows where I live, as well. He has been to the mill—'

'Judhael has made threats there, too?'

'He set a fire.' While Hélène stared at her, frowning in disbelief, Emma explained about the fire and the threats that Gytha had been given. Finally, she laid bare her deepest fears. 'Judhael does not know about Henri. But if he should learn he has a son…' She clenched her fists. 'He must not get his hands on Henri, I will not let him!'

'So that is another reason why you refused to return to Fulford.'

'Yes. I would never trust Judhael with a child and I always knew that if he should return, it's the first place he would go. I *must* keep Henri from him.'

Hélène's frown deepened. 'Emma, I still don't understand. How did Judhael find you? No one at Fulford would have betrayed your whereabouts.'

'No, of course they would not. I haven't the faintest idea, unless…'

'Unless…?'

'It has to be the gown.' Rubbing her head, Emma took a deep breath. 'A couple of weeks ago I met Cecily in the market. I mentioned Gytha's marriage and Cecily misheard me. She thought I was talking about me, that *I* was considering marriage.' Emma looked at the floor. 'You see, it is what Cecily wishes for me. She is so happily married and she wants me to be happy, too. You will say it was foolish of me, but I didn't correct her. If I were married, it would help expunge the shame of Henri's birth.'

'And…?'

'The next time the Fulford carter came to Winchester for supplies, Cecily had sent me a betrothal gift. It is a gown, the most magnificent pink gown I have ever seen. Of course I shall never wear it—'

'Never wear it! Why on earth not?'

Emma grimaced. 'It is fit for a queen—what would I be doing with a gown like that? But never mind that. It must have been the gown that brought Judhael to me.'

'He followed the carter from Fulford?'

'He must have. With the result that I have no work and must look to find new lodgings, as well. I won't let Gytha and Edwin risk themselves for me.'

'You may lodge here with us, Emma,' Hélène said firmly. 'I may not have work, but I can offer you lodgings.'

Tears pricked behind Emma's eyes. 'That is very kind, but I don't want to cause you any trouble any more than I want to cause Gytha trouble. What if Judhael comes here?'

Hélène waved towards the door where a man was lounging on one of the benches. Emma had seen him hefting barrels about the inn; he was built like a house. 'Tostig will see us safe.'

'Nevertheless, I would not put you at risk.'

'You would be more than welcome.'

'My thanks. Perhaps I will stay here while I think what to do. I wish I had some way of repaying you, but until I do find work…I even tried up at the castle this morning, but there was nothing there, either.'

Hélène was studying her intently. 'Something upset you up at that place, I can see.'

'Mmm.' It was stupid; Emma could not think why she was still upset, it was not as though this kind of thing had never happened before. But she had believed Sir Richard, had really thought he meant to help.

'Tell me.'

Emma opened her mouth with Sir Richard's image in her mind and the words *pompous hypocrite* forming on her tongue when Frida banged through the doorway. Frida was scowling and there were splotches of angry colour on her cheeks. Emma blinked; it was hard to believe she was looking at the same girl who had paraded so confidently across the castle bailey less than half an hour ago.

'That man! Bloody Norman!' Frida spat, flouncing towards them, blatantly ignoring the fact that most of the customers in the Staple were Norman by birth. Her yellow skirts whisked past the fire, perilously close to the flames. She thumped on to their bench with such force, the bench rocked.

'That was quick,' Emma blurted, before she had time to check her words. Her cheeks scorched. 'Forgive me, Frida, but I saw you in the bailey, less than half an hour ago.'

Some of the anger left Frida's expression as her mouth twitched. 'Yes, I was in the stable. But I expect Sir Richard could…' shooting Henri a glance, Frida made a suggestive gesture '—I expect our garrison commander could do it quickly if he had a mind. Only he didn't.'

Hélène leaned forwards, a line between her brows. 'What happened?'

Frida shrugged. Unpinning her veil, she folded

it and held it carefully on her lap. Her yellow gown and veil were too good for everyday wear; they would be put into storage to await a special occasion, a special admirer.

'Sir Richard and I,' Frida spoke with a slow precision that was quite out of character, 'agreed that we should not suit.'

Hélène's mouth fell open. 'Not suit—what nonsense is this? You are my *best* girl. You have a natural curves that make sacking look like silk. You know how to behave—in short, Frida, you have all the virtues a man like Sir Richard could expect in his *maîtresse*. And what is more, you only keep to one lover at a time! Is the man a eunuch?' Huffing, Hélène leaned back against the wall. 'I don't understand it. There must have been something… There were no angry words between you?'

'No, *madame*.'

'You didn't mention Raymond, did you?'

Frida lowered her gaze.

'You did! Oh, you foolish, foolish girl, I *told* you, not a word about Raymond. Most men wouldn't care about such things, but some are more choosy. Some men like to pretend their *belle amie* has only known them. Such a man would not want to hear his lover is pining for another, even if he is paying for her services.'

Frida's eyes glittered, a tear sparkled on one of her lashes. 'I only asked him if he knew how Raymond had died.'

Hélène made a sound of disapproval, but her eyes were kind. 'I suppose you had to. Did he know?'

Shoulders slumped, Frida shook her head. 'I do not think so. Sir Richard said something about the fighting in the north being hard and…and bloody. I don't think he saw Raymond fall. I know it was stupid of me—how can a commander be expected to watch every one of his men at every moment? It was just, I hoped…' Her voice trailed off and she wiped her nose with the back of her hand.

'Frida, you allowed yourself to get too fond of Raymond, I did counsel you against it.'

'I remember. I know I should not have mentioned him to Sir Richard and am sorry for it.' Frida lifted her eyes. 'It was not easy making myself understood, and not easy understanding him, either. That is why he turned me away.'

'Because of his poor English?'

'Because I have no French. That, he said, was why we would not suit. I…I do not think it was because I asked about Raymond.'

It was Emma's turn to direct a look of incredulity at Frida. 'Sir Richard didn't want you because you don't speak Norman French?'

Frida began pleating the veil on her lap. 'He can barely speak a word of English, and my French is just as bad. Apart from one or two…' her lips edged up and she shot a glance at Henri who had returned and was single-mindedly cramming the last of his bread into his mouth '…choice words. But I did manage to gather that Sir Richard's English deserts him completely at times.'

'He wants conversation?' Hélène's expression was all confusion. 'With a woman? Lord, the man has changed. I know he took an arrow to the shoulder near York, but perhaps another part of his anatomy was affected.'

Frida made a negative gesture and a flash of humour lifted the edges of her mouth. 'I did not see that part of him, but the rest looked perfectly hale. Oh, yes.' Rising, she turned for the stairs to the loft room where the girls kept their belongings. At the foot of the stair she looked back. 'I can't say I am sorry, though, he seemed detached to me, very detached. It chilled me. Despite all those muscles, I am not sure I would want him as my…admirer.' Slowly, she continued up the stairs.

The fire crackled. A dog ambled in from the street and flopped down by the hearth.

'Frida, turned down by Sir Richard.' Hélène shook her head. 'I would never have believed it.'

There was more here, Emma sensed. 'Oh?'

'The man has something of a reputation, which is odd when you consider he himself has never actually visited the Staple.'

'Really?'

Seeing Emma's look of disbelief, Hélène laughed. 'No, never. This is the best place for miles. My girls are clean, they are well fed and they know better than to steal—a man likes to know that his silver is safe while he—'

Emma cleared her throat and jerked her head pointedly at Henri, whose round blue eyes were taking in Hélène's every word.

'As I was saying, dear, my girls are honest. And knowing Sir Richard's reputation, I was surprised that he never patronised us. Then this morning his man appeared—'

'His squire, Geoffrey?'

'I think that was the name. You would think Sir Richard would like to pick his own girl, wouldn't you? I would if I were a man. Not him.' She paused, brow puckered. 'Perhaps that is what

Frida meant when she said he was cold. No matter. He refused her, my best girl—I don't understand it. What can he want?'

Emma's heart began to thud. 'Send me.'

'Eh?'

'Send me.' She gave a smile and knew it was twisted. 'I can wear the pink gown.'

'Are you mad? You're not one of us, you can't…'

'Think I don't know what to do?' Emma ruffled her son's hair. 'Here's proof.'

'Don't be ridiculous! Your reputation…'

'What reputation? I am *nithing*, Hélène, I have fallen from grace, and this child, this bas—'

Gasping, Hélène clapped her hands over Henri's ears. 'Emma, have a care!'

Rising abruptly, Emma began pacing up and down in front of the wine barrel. 'Let him hear, Hélène, let him hear, he will hear soon enough, so why not from me? Like most of the girls here, I am a—' conscious of listening ears, Emma lowered her voice '—a fallen woman. *Exactly* as you are.'

'But your birth! Your father was—'

'I am like you, my friend.'

Hélène's lips curved, but she shook her head. 'You are not like us, indeed, Emma, you are not.'

'How so?'

Hélène leaned forwards. 'You are not truly fallen, not in the way me and my girls are.' Emma made an impatient movement, but Hélène rushed on. 'Oh, to be sure you have an illegitimate child, you committed the sin of fornication, but you did it for love.'

'I don't love Ju…him. I *don't*!'

'You don't today, but you did at the time. Whereas we—apart from the occasional aberration like Frida with her Raymond—we do it purely for coin. There's a difference. You, my dear, are not truly fallen. Neither are you *nithing*.'

Emma's eyes prickled. 'Only you, my friend, would see it that way.'

One of Hélène's brows arched upwards. 'Don't forget Gytha, she is your friend, too. There's Aediva too, and Frida, and Marie…'

Emma had to laugh. 'Point conceded, I have many good friends. But most of the townsfolk see me as fallen.'

'Leofwine doesn't. Nor does your sister, for that matter.'

'No. But seriously, Hélène, I need your help.'

'There must be other ways. I won't send you to Sir Richard. You, a thane's daughter, putting yourself forward as a *maîtresse*? Never!'

Emma fiddled with her purse. 'He said his steward would find work for me, but the steward said there was none to be had. Clearly, despite the friendship Richard of Asculf has with Sir Adam, he had no real intention of helping me. So I shall put myself forward for another kind of work.'

'As his bedmate?'

'*Yes*! Frida let him refuse her, but Frida is grieving and she needs time.'

'I know.'

'Besides, I *can* converse with him, my French is as fluent as his.'

'Your mother,' Hélène murmured.

'Exactly—which of your girls can speak his language as well as I?'

'None, but that doesn't mean—'

Emma took Hélène's hand. 'Send me. He won't turn me down. I won't let him.'

A knowing light entered Hélène's eyes. 'You like him.'

Emma dropped Hélène's hand as though it scalded. 'Sir Richard?' His image flashed before her, a vivid image of him as he had been in the stable. That thick brown hair, those grey eyes that surely were more clever than cool, that broad chest, so pleasingly—yes, privately Emma would admit to this—his chest was most pleasingly muscled… 'No. That is, I…I agree with Frida, Sir Richard can be distant, as if his mind is elsewhere.'

'Do not lie, Emma, you are not good at it. You like Sir Richard.'

'I scarcely know him.'

Hélène made a dismissive movement. 'What has that to do with anything? You are attracted to him, that much is plain. When you stormed in, I knew something had happened, and by that I mean something significant, not merely that the castle steward had no employment for you. You find Sir Richard attractive.'

'I do not!'

Hélène lifted an expressive brow and smiled an infuriating smile. 'You are attracted to him and, what is more, I believe you like him also. I know you, Emma of Fulford, and you would not be asking me to send you to him if you did not. You may have a bast…this child here, but you are *not* like us. And if you are considering, even for one moment, becoming that man's concubine, it is because in some quiet corner of your soul you feel more than a passing liking for him.'

'Don't be ridiculous!'

'Have it your own way.' Rising, Hélène shook

out her skirts. 'You must excuse me, I need to ask Inga if she has enough in the way of provisions for the evening meal. We are busier now the garrison's full up again.'

'Hélène, will you help me?'

'You really believe you have it in you to play the part of his whore—because that is what you would be—his whore?'

'Yes. *Why not*?'

Shaking her head, Hélène rested a hand lightly on Emma's son's head. 'Take Mama back to the mill, Henri, and help her pack up your belongings.'

'Why?'

'You are coming to live at the Staple for a time.'

Henri's face brightened; he did a little jig. 'Honey on bread, honey on bread!'

Hélène laughed. 'Yes, sweetheart, every day.'

Emma bit her lip. 'I cannot pay you…'

'We can discuss that later. I don't think that is a situation that is going to last.'

Chapter Four

Later that same night, Emma waited until Hélène was alone sitting at her usual table under the loft overhang. From there Hélène could keep close watch on the wine butts and the measures the girls were handing out. Smoke was swirling up into the blackened roof space along with the drone of many voices. Platters banged on to trestles; knives scraped on pewter plates; torches flared. A serving girl passed with a platter, and the smell of beef braised in rich red wine lingered in the air.

Emma and Henri had already moved into the Staple. They had been allocated space in one of the screened sleeping areas in the loft. Henri was worn out with excitement and had been put to bed, which left Emma free to raise the matter of payment with Hélène.

'About my rent,' Emma said. 'I have worked out how I may be able to pay you.'

'There is no hurry, I really can wait. Wine?'

'Please.' Emma took her place on the bench. 'But I don't want you to wait. And with Judhael so eager to speak out against me, Heaven knows when I will find work. Would you like to look at the gown? I would be prepared to sell it, if you like it.'

'The one your sister sent you?'

'Yes. It is very fine.'

'I am sure that it is, although—' Hélène's lips curved '—knowing your sister, it will be the gown of a lady rather than a…shall we say, a tavern girl.'

'Perhaps.'

'I know your sister. Still, my girls might be able to use it when their wealthier admirers want to play at being great lords. Go and put it on, so I can really see how it looks.'

'Now?'

'Why not?'

Emma nodded agreement and, taking up a candle from the table, headed for the stairs.

The loft chamber was airy and ran fully half the length of the building. It was divided in two by thick wool curtains. One half was used as a sleeping chamber for travellers while the other, divided into sleeping areas by yet more curtains, belonged to Hélène and the girls. Emma and Henri had been given one of these.

Despite the size of the loft, the private spaces were cramped and simply furnished. Like nuns' cells, Emma thought wryly, except that some of these cells were put to uses that would scandalise any nun. What would Mother Aethelflaeda, the Prioress of St Anne's, say if she found her here? No doubt a penitential fast would be the least of it.

Indeed, a few years ago, Emma herself would have been scandalised by what went on at this inn. Yet today… She sighed. So much had changed.

Henri was deeply asleep. Setting the candle safely on a stool, Emma reached under their bed and quietly pulled out the bundle that contained the gown. She began to undress.

Sounds of merriment came muffled through the floorboards. You wouldn't believe it was Lent. Yet more to scandalise Mother Aethelflaeda. Laughter rolled up the stairs; it squeezed through the cracks in the floorboards. One man brayed like a donkey, another responded with a shout that nearly raised the roof.

Smiling, Emma shook her head. To think that the Staple was only a stone's throw from the Cathedral and Nunnaminster....

Setting aside her workday gown, Emma reached into the bundle and drew out Cecily's gift. The sumptuous fabric was heavily encrusted with silver-and-gold threadwork. There was also a filmy silk veil in a paler hue to wear with the gown. Emma's throat ached. These lovely things were fit for Queen Mathilda, and Cecily had remembered that pink was her favourite colour. Emma was touched beyond words. She hated to sell them, but sell them she must. And while they were indeed more suited to a noblewoman than a tavern wench, if Hélène liked them, she would give her a good price, better than she might get elsewhere.

The candle-light flickered as Emma drew the gown over her head. Tugging at the lacings, she tied them off, staring down at herself critically. The gown was cut fairly low at the front and it gaped a little. Frowning, she readjusted the lacings and tugged the bodice into place. She must have lost weight since her measure had been taken at Fulford. As Emma shook out the veil, a small stoppered bottle—glass, it was such a rarity—rolled on to the bed. This was yet another of her sister's gifts; it had been tucked into the fabric the day the carter had brought it.

Removing the stopper, Emma sniffed. Rosewater. It was her favourite scent; Cecily had remembered that, too. It must have been imported. Blinking hard, Emma dabbed some at the wrists and neck, and carefully replaced the stopper. She might have to sell the dress and the veil, but it would not hurt to keep the rosewater. Slipping the bottle into her bundle of everyday clothes, she set about arranging the silk veil.

Curtains brushed her shoulders as she made her way back to the head of the stairs. A piercing whistle cut through the din. By the fire at the middle of the inn, Ben Thatcher, a man with more looks than sense, was giving her the eye.

Cheeks brighter than the flames in the hearth, Emma hurried downstairs and dived into the relative safety of the shadows at the cookhouse end of the room. Another appreciative shout came flying towards the wine-butts. At her table, Hélène scowled at Ben Thatcher and waved Emma over.

'That the new girl, Hélène?' Unrepentant, Ben shouted over the general clamour. 'How much?'

His companion made a coarse gesture and muttered an aside. Ben spluttered into his ale.

'It is the dress that is for sale here, Ben Thatcher, so mind your tongue,' Hélène said, tugging Emma to her. 'Never mind them, dear. They are good lads, but—strong ale and weak minds...' She looked Emma up and down. 'Ooh, yes. I see what you mean, that gown is fit for a queen. You look well in it, Emma, very well. Indeed, I am not sure that you should sell it. I am sure you will find another way of repaying me.'

'If times were better, I would not sell it. I love it, but...' Emma shrugged '...you know how things are.'

'I wonder that you can bear to part with it.' Hélène took the fabric of the skirt between her thumb and forefinger. 'This cloth, shipped in from the east, would you say?'

'I think so.'

'Are you certain about this? What will your sister say?'

Emma grimaced. 'I hope she never finds out. I shall certainly not be telling her.' She spread the skirts to demonstrate their fullness and gave a mocking curtsy. 'See? Every detail is perfect.

The lacing ribbons are silk, and this veil is light as a cobweb.'

'It hangs well. I do like the way the skirts swing. Yes, it is perfect. A little large at the bosom, perhaps.'

Flushing, Emma put a hand to the neckline.

Hélène batted it away with a smile. 'No, let it be. It is quite…alluring like that.'

Emma fussed with the neckline. 'Gudrun made it. She and Rozenn—the Breton seamstress—have been working together and…'

A movement by the door caught Emma's attention. She frowned.

'Emma, what's amiss?'

'I…I…no matter. Except—was that Sir Richard's squire I saw leaving just then?'

'Possibly, he does occasionally favour us with his custom when Sir Richard is in residence. He likes it here, even if his knight does not.'

'Excuse me?' A man's voice cut in behind them. 'Lady Emma?'

Emma whirled and her stomach lurched. *'Azor!'*

The hood of Azor's head was up and he was standing in the deepest shadows, but Emma knew him at once. Judhael's comrade, Azor, was a former housecarl of her father's. He, too, had allied himself with the Saxon resistance. So it *had* been Azor she had seen on Mill Bridge…

Azor looked pointedly at Hélène and jerked his head in the direction of the screen. Hélène backed away. Catching Emma by the arm, Azor drew her into the darkness between two large wine caskets.

'Lady Emma…' Azor's eyes raked her from head to foot; his beard—threaded with grey nowadays—quivered. 'No wonder it took so long for me to find you. When I heard you were…in difficulties…I imagined the worst.'

Emma swallowed. Azor had her fenced in with his body. Her hands began to shake. 'Where is he?' Her voice rose. 'He is not here?'

Azor flung a glance over his shoulder. 'Hush, no names, eh?'

'I am not stupid.'

Azor's lip curled as he looked at her. 'I thought he might have caused you trouble when he visited your friends, but in my worst nightmares I would not have imagined this.' His gaze took in the tavern, while the sneer on his lips spoke of a high disdain for tavern girls. He twitched clumsily at Emma's skirts. 'Bedding with men for coin, are we?'

Emma's heart was fluttering like a netted bird.

Was Judhael in the inn? She had hoped to have at least a couple of days' grace…

Henri! Emma did not care what Judhael or Azor thought of her, the important thing, the most important thing, was that they should not find out that she had a son. Thank God Henri was safe upstairs.

'Well?' Azor gave her a little shake, such as he would never have done when her father had been alive, he would not have dared.

Emma lifted her chin. 'It is none of your business what I am or what I do.' Azor still had her boxed in. Laying a hand on his chest, she gave him a shove. 'Please let me pass. I was having a private conversation with Hélène, and you interrupted us.'

Azor snorted, but in the flare of the torches it seemed his expression had softened. 'The Lady Emma I used to know would have died rather than consort with the likes of Hélène.'

Conscious of Hélène hovering like a guardian angel behind Azor, Emma bit her lip. 'Hélène is a friend, a true and loyal friend when many have deserted me.'

'The woman's a whore! Hell, my lady, Ju—he will kill you when he finds you.' Again, the harsh features appeared to soften; his voice became gentle. 'He wants you back, my lady. It has become an obsession with him.'

'Let me pass.' Emma's mouth was dry, for she feared Azor spoke the truth. Judhael might well kill her. It was a struggle to keep her expression calm, when every nerve was shrieking at her to pick up her skirts and dash upstairs to check on Henri. She must know that that he was safe. *Azor might have found me, but please, God, let him not learn about Henri.*

'My lady, there is no need to look at me like that. You must not fear me, I came to warn you—'

'Excuse me, sir,' Hélène broke in. She had found a wooden cup and was filling it with wine from one of the barrels. As she approached, trying—bless her—to draw Azor's attention, Emma willed her friend not to mention Henri. 'You are new to the Staple, are you not? Please accept a cup of our best red. It is come in a recent shipment from Aquitaine in the land of the Franks.' She lowered her voice. 'King Harold himself never drank better.'

Azor looked doubtfully at the wine and more narrowly at Hélène. 'He drank Frankish wine?'

Hélène smiled. 'Indeed he did.'

'But I didn't order it.'

'Take it, sir, with my compliments, as a welcome to the Staple.'

'Waes hael.' Mouthing the traditional Saxon toast, Azor grudgingly nodded his thanks, but his eyes never left Emma's and she knew he had not finished with her.

Nevertheless, she made to push past him, not trusting him an inch. 'Excuse me, if you please.'

Someone threw a log on to the fire and sent up a shower of sparks as the door opened to admit two men. The fire flared.

Silence gripped the room. Squinting past Azor's shoulder, Emma tried to see what everyone was looking at, but Marie was moving between the tables, blocking her vision.

Emma was not the only person to notice the silence; Azor turned to look, too. 'Swithun save us!' Thrusting the cup at her, he ducked deeper into his hood.

Sir Richard of Asculf, garrison commander, paused in the doorway as a trio of troopers jumped to their feet and saluted sheepishly.

Richard had heard of this place—what man in the garrison had not? The prettiest girls in Wessex worked here. Richard was not averse to the idea of using their services—he would hardly have sent for Frida if that had been the case, but this was the first time he had stepped inside the Staple himself. His subordinates needed somewhere where they could be at ease, somewhere where they were not under the eye of their commander. By unwritten law, this was their territory, not his.

If the women here nursed a hatred for Norman soldiers they hid it well, or so he had been told. Saxon tavern wenches who had learned to smile at Norman soldiers.

A swift glance around found Richard surprised. Many of his men were there, of course, sprawled across benches, leaning on tables, sitting with girls on their laps. But overall, the Staple was more orderly than he had expected. The tables, though busy with cups and plates and half-eaten suppers, had a clean, scrubbed look to them; the fire was well built and spare logs and kindling were stacked safely to one side. A mouth-watering smell of beef stew reminded Richard that not only was he hungry, but that the Staple's reputation did not rest entirely on the beauty of the servings girls. The *madame* apparently ran a kitchen fit for a king.

Irritably, Richard addressed the room in

general. 'At ease. *Mon Dieu*, you're all off duty!' As conversation resumed, he turned to Geoffrey. 'You are certain you saw Emma of Fulford in here? I thought I told you to help her find work at the castle.'

Geoffrey bit his lip. 'Yes, sir. I left her with the steward, as you said.'

Richard frowned. 'Left her? You are saying you didn't make certain she was given work?'

'N-not exactly, sir.' Geoffrey shuffled from foot to foot. 'I told the steward what you had said and…and—'

'You went away.'

Geoffrey stared at the floor. 'I…I am sorry, sir.'

'That was ill done, Geoffrey, very ill done. Do you even know if she was given work?'

'No, sir. I am sorry.'

Sighing, Richard dragged off his gloves and held his hands towards the fire. Behind them, the door slammed, candle flames bent in the draught.

Richard acknowledged one of his soldiers with a smile. Belatedly realising who had joined them, a lanky sergeant hastily pushed a girl from his lap. 'At ease, soldier, you've earned a little relaxation,' Richard repeated. He scowled at his squire. 'You had better be right.'

'I am, sir. Look, there at the far end.'

Merde. The lad was right, though Richard could hardly believe what he was seeing. There was Lady Emma of Fulford, flanked on the one side by a huge wine keg, and on the other by Hélène, the *madame* of the Staple. Emma had been talking to a Saxon giant of a man. Negotiating a price for her favours? Lord.

Oblivious of everyone but Lady Emma—this was Cecily's *sister*, her *sister* and Cecily and Adam would never forgive him if he let her continue on this course—Richard marched towards her. The Saxon giant vanished behind an oak post. Richard paid him no heed. 'Lady Emma.'

She gave him a hasty curtsy. 'Sir Richard!'

Taking in her finery, particularly the way the front of her pink gown gaped to reveal far more than it should, Richard's gaze sharpened. 'What in hell are you doing?' *Diable*, it was obvious what she was doing. In that gown, a gown which set off her curves in a discreet yet, oddly, far more tantalising way than the vulgar yellow gown had set off Frida's charms, Emma of Fulford could only have been doing one thing. The woman had been selling herself. With difficulty, Richard lifted his gaze from the alluring dip in the neckline, from the gentle curve of her breasts. The smudges of fatigue under her eyes were not visible in the torchlight. A translucent veil failed to hide her hair, which gleamed like dark gold beneath it.

Hidden treasure, he found himself thinking. Here in the Staple, in that gown, Emma of Fulford had the loveliness and the hauteur of a princess of the Norse.

Her brows snapped together. 'What business is it of yours, sir?'

Richard shook his head. 'Just look at you. Is this the first time you have…done this, or is it something you make a habit of?'

Her blue eyes were cloudy, perplexed. It came to him that she was not connecting properly with what he was saying, that her mind was elsewhere.

'My lady, are you drunk?' He leaned closer, intending to discover if she had the smell of wine or mead about her. Instead, he caught the sweet scent of roses, freshness and roses. Hastily, he drew back.

'Drunk? Certainly not!'

Her eyes, dark in the uncertain light of the torches, were scouring the tavern behind him. Searching for her lost customer? Richard clenched his fists. 'You are a thane's daughter,' he said through gritted teeth. 'What would your sister say? Lord, have you no shame?'

'He's gone.' Those dark eyes were full of shadows. She put a hand to her head. 'Saint Swithun, help me.'

Whatever was the matter with the woman? How could the loss of one customer mean so much to her? Was she so desperate?

Firm action was clearly going to be called for.

Pink skirts rustled as she made to move past him. 'Sir, you must excuse me, I need to go upstairs.'

Richard had her by the arm before he had time to think. 'A moment.'

'Sir,' the *madame*, Hélène, cut in. She clicked her fingers and another Saxon, all muscle, appeared at her side. Not a threat exactly, but close. Geoffrey's hand crept to the hilt of his dagger.

Richard gave the woman a direct look. 'Madame Hélène, I presume?'

'Sir?'

'Lady Emma and I have matters to discuss, private matters. She will accompany me back to the castle.' By Saint Denis, that sounded as though he intended buying Emma of Fulford's favours, which he most certainly did not. At least…Richard was opening his mouth to clarify himself, but Madame Hélène got in first.

'Emma, are you all right?'

'Yes, yes, I am fine.' Emma smiled, but her smile made a liar of her—it was vague and abstracted. 'Sir Richard, please, I *must* go up to the loft.' She laid a hand on his arm, white teeth worrying her lower lip.

'No, you are coming with me.'

'I am?' Emma gave him one of those distracted looks and a quick nod before returning her attention to the other woman. 'I am fine, truly, Hélène. I think Sir Richard may even help me.'

At her words, the muscle-bound Saxon effaced himself. Geoffrey let out a breath and his hand fell from his hilt.

Damn right I am going to help you, Richard thought. *But not perhaps in the way that you are expecting*. Grasping her hand, he led her past the tables, past outstretched legs, past the dogs lazing at the hearth and out into the night. He could not let her continue on this course; his friend Adam would never forgive him.

'No cloak,' he muttered as the inn door snapped shut behind Geoffrey and the chill March air rushed into his lungs. 'We have left your cloak behind.'

'My cloak?' She gave a wild laugh and jerked against his hand. She was trying to break free and she would no doubt have succeeded if Richard had not maintained the firmest of holds. The moon was up, the stars were visible behind the roofs of the houses, and her pink veil glowed palely through the dark. Something—a stray?—brushed past Richard's leg.

'Please, my lord.'

She tried to shake him off, but he would have none of it. 'You are coming back with me.' Swiftly, he removed his cloak and wrapped it around her shoulders. When he set off at a brisk pace for the castle, she began to struggle in earnest.

'No, no!' Slim fingers twisted and wriggled within his. 'Please…' Her voice cracked. 'I must go back. You don't understand.'

'Don't cry, I am not going to hurt you. I just want to get you away from…that place.' He stopped dead at the crossroads where what was left of Golde Street met Market Street. Her breath was agitated; her veil lifted as she peered over her shoulder towards the darkness surrounding the market cross.

What, or who, was she looking for? Richard could see little. Here, a few cracks of light crept round the edge of a shutter; there, a slash of yellow escaped through a slit in some planking, but as to the rest—black night.

'Please, oh, please.'

As she pulled at him, the moonlight fell directly on her cheek where a single tear gleamed like a pearl. *Hell*.

'He will find him, I know he will. He will find him and—'

Richard lost patience. Either Adam's sister-in-law was a madwoman or she was in desperate trouble. In their interview that morning, she had not struck him as mad. He swept her up in his arms, a struggling armful of woman who smelt charmingly of roses. Closing his mind to the twinge in his shoulder, to the stab of awareness of her as a desirable woman, he made for the castle drawbridge.

'Calm down, my lady. Emma, *calm down*. I know you are not an innocent, but really, you cannot be allowed to continue on this course. You were lucky with that Saxon rebel.'

'Lucky? What do you mean?'

'You were lucky not to have had a child. How

would it be if you had to suffer the shame of having a rebel brat clinging to your skirts?'

Silence. Perhaps he was getting through to her. 'You may not be so lucky the next time. We are going somewhere warm where we may talk, and you are going to explain what you think you are doing.'

As they waited for the guard to lower the drawbridge, she kept her face averted. Her fists were clenched under her chin. Quiescent in his arms, but resisting him with every fibre of her being.

While the chains rattled and the drawbridge lowered, Richard exchanged glances with his squire.

'Your shoulder, sir?' Geoffrey said.

'It is fine.'

She was quivering, not from fear, Richard hoped. 'Geoffrey?'

'Sir?'

'Help arrange my cloak over her properly. She's cold.'

Emma's mind seemed to have frozen and she barely saw where he was taking her. Judhael, Henri, Azor, Sir Richard…it was too much. She was also digesting the fact that Sir Richard didn't realise she already had a child, a bastard child. If only she could be certain that Judhael didn't know, too.

Dimly, she recognised she was being carried across the torchlit bailey. Excited barks skirled through the air, and several dogs raced out of the stables—Sir Richard's wolfhounds, the white mongrel.

Sir Richard ducked into a doorway at the base of one of the towers and started up a curling stairway.

Emma would not demean herself by struggling. The man was over six foot tall and his build, well…since she was pressed close to that muscular chest, she could not help but notice that Sir Richard was a powerfully built man. As one would expect of one of King William's officers, a knight and a commander.

It might be disturbing to be held so close, closer in fact than she had been to any man since Judhael, but Emma's mind was fixated on her son.

Did Azor know about Henri? Did he know that Henri was asleep upstairs at the inn? Had Azor perhaps followed them when they had brought their things from the mill to the Staple? Was Azor even at this moment snatching Henri from his bed?

But Emma did not struggle. If she were to engage in a physical fight with Sir Richard, she could only be the loser. He took the stairs in brisk strides, a small entourage trotting at his heels—his squire, the three dogs. No, a physical struggle with this man could only result in ignominious defeat; he had the build of a champion.

She did not speak, either. For this man, this friend of her sister's husband, Sir Adam, did not know the full extent of her fall from grace. He had not heard about her illegitimate son. *How would it be if you had to suffer the shame of having a rebel brat clinging to your skirts?*

Perhaps—Emma slanted him a swift look through her lashes—perhaps other tactics might work here….

Saints, but this Norman was handsome in a strong-jawed masculine way. His hair was thick and brown. A torch in a wall-sconce cast a shadow from his straight nose across one lean cheek. A cheek that this close Emma could see was dark with stubble. His lips—she bit the inside of her cheek; she would not look at his lips—but surely they were too well-shaped for a man?

He paused to draw breath on a landing, or so Emma thought, until his squire pushed past him to open the door.

'That is all, Geoffrey.' Sir Richard gave a curt headshake as the boy made to follow them into the room. 'I will call you if I need you.' The white mongrel almost tripped him. 'And take the damn dogs with you.'

Chapter Five

'Yes, Sir Richard.'

Emma found she was holding her breath as the squire called the dogs to heel and the door closed behind him. Sir Richard's cloak fell away and she was set, none too gently, on her feet. His breathing was uneven. So, too, was hers.

What did he want with her? She could not be long, not with Azor and Judhael at large and Henri stuck at the inn. *Sir Richard does not know about Henri; it is bad enough that he thinks of me as a fallen woman, but if he should find out about Henri—'the rebel's brat clinging to my skirts'?*

She lifted her chin. 'Sir?'

He tossed his cloak over a chest that stood at the foot of a bed. A large bed, Emma noticed, an indecently large bed. She also noticed that it was oddly quiet up here. If she were to scream to be released, would anyone hear? Where had that squire gone? Would he come if she called?

Willing herself not to give in to hysteria, Emma studied him, resplendent in a green tunic edged with silver braid. He was very tall and that handsome face wore an expression in which amusement looked to be mixed with irritation in equal measure. And his eyes, how odd... In this light, in this room, they did not look in the least bit cold.

The sheer physical strength of the man was impressive, the wide shoulders, the muscled thighs, which she had felt for herself as he had carried her up those stairs. But, there was more than mere strength here. She sensed enormous vitality, limitless reserves, an indomitable will. Yes, it was most odd, it was there in his eyes... This evening Emma would swear she could put her life in his hands and rest easy.

But he is a Norman!

Sir Richard might have the strength of the devil, he might be Norman—but Emma had never heard of him being violent or cruel to women. She would not have gone to him for help that morning if she had.

Pointedly, she made a show of looking about

his bedchamber. It was furnished with royal extravagance. The candles in the wall prickets were, by their scent, beeswax. Their light fell softly on to walls patterned with swirls and chevrons in ochres, blues and reds. Tapestries gleamed with gold thread. There was a single shuttered window slit. One of the walls was curved; it must follow the outer wall of the tower. The door was almost within her reach, casually, she edged closer.

There were two braziers, comforting glimmers of heat. Adding more coals to one of them, Sir Richard waved her towards it. 'Warm yourself, my lady.'

My lady. Tears pricked at the back of her eyes. How long had it been since anyone had done her the courtesy of addressing her by her title? *This man had, in the castle stables that morning*. But he would soon stop doing so, once he learned about Henri….

Emma made a grab for the door latch, but he got there before her. She caught the gleam of white teeth as the key grated in the lock.

'There's no escape that way, my lady.'

She bit her lip and stared up at him. The garrison commander had locked her in his tower room and she felt no fear—how strange. Yes, she wanted to get past him to go and check on her son, but she was not afraid. And, yes, she had read him aright; those grey eyes were indeed gleaming with amusement. Richard of Asculf was laughing at her.

'I am so glad I entertain you, sir. But why did you interfere? It would have been better, much better, if you had let me alone.'

Tossing the key on to a bedside chest, he leaned against the wall and crossed his arms. 'I have angered you?'

'Yes!'

'How so?'

'Not only did you shame me before half the town, dragging me out of the Staple before your entire garrison, but you tossed me over your shoulder like a sack of—'

His lips curved. 'I didn't toss you over my shoulder, I carried you. Quite carefully, as a matter of fact.' Pushing away from the wall, he rolled those broad shoulders and grimaced. 'To my own detriment, I might add.'

His shoulder, of course! Emma thrust aside the memory of the wound she had noticed in the stable and snorted. 'I hope it does hurt. Perhaps it will make you think twice before abducting women.'

'Abducting? I rather thought I was saving you.'

Crossing to the curved outer wall, he lifted a glazed jug from a tray. 'Wine?'

'No, thank you. I should like you to unlock this door, I want to go home.'

'Home?' Taking no heed of her refusal, he poured some wine into a glass—*more* glass? Sir Rich indeed—and held it out to her. He grinned. 'Go on, I am not about to poison you, not yet at any rate.'

When Emma took the glass, she could not help but stare at it. He must think her a peasant, but she had never drunk wine from such a goblet. It was smooth to the touch, and had a cloudy yellow tinge to it. Tiny bubbles were trapped in the glass, minor imperfections revealed by the candle-light shining through it.

'It came from France,' he said, observing her reaction.

'It is lighter than I imagined.'

'And fragile.' He lifted a brow. 'Aren't you going to try the wine?'

Nodding, Emma took a sip. It was then that she realised there had only been one glass on the tray and he was waiting for her to finish before he could have some. She took another hurried sip and, blushing, passed the glass back. It felt embarrassing, oddly intimate, to be sharing a wineglass with him. Another surprise. She would have thought, given his reputation, Sir Richard would have two glasses in his bedchamber.

Taking the glass with him, he sank onto the bed. 'Warmer now?'

'Yes, thank you.'

'So where is home? I gather you do not live at Fulford with Cecily and Adam?'

'Heavens, no!'

He rested an elbow on his knee, eyes watchful. He had long sooty eyelashes. And his nose, it was very straight. 'Your sister never struck me as being inhospitable.'

'No, of course she is not, but…' Emma floundered to a halt. She could not fathom quite why Sir Richard had brought her here. This was his bedchamber. An uncommon bedchamber that he did not share with his squire, a private bedchamber such as she had never seen in her life. She had thought only King William would have a chamber to himself like this.

'Emma, where do you live?'

Emma was not sure she should tell him anything. This man claimed he wanted to help her, but in view of him passing her over to that singularly unhelpful steward this morning, she was not certain. However, she could not sense any malevolence in him. Perhaps he was indeed trying to help her. Was it safe to tell him where she lived? *And I am going to have to tell him about Henri. Oh, Lord.*

Sir Richard's loyalty to King William was unquestionable. Whatever she told him, she must make no mention of Judhael and Azor by name, Saxon outlaws whose every breath these past years had been devoted to overthrowing the regime he served. No, she could not tell him about them. She might not want to renew her connections with Judhael and Azor, but they had been her father's housecarls and she did not have it in her to betray them.

'Where do you live?' he prompted. 'Is that so difficult to answer?'

She swallowed. 'I…I have recently taken lodgings at the Staple.'

He made an exasperated sound. 'I thought as much. You fool! And what does your sister have to say about it?'

Emma squirmed. She had done nothing wrong, yet his tone made her want to hide her face in shame. Sir Richard was not going to like it when he learned about Henri. 'Cecily does not know.'

'I should think not. It would break her heart.' His nostrils flared. 'How long have you been there? I don't expect Adam knows about this, either?'

'I only moved in today.' Her chin came up. 'I had no work, no means of paying for our...*my* lodgings.' *Oh, Lord.* Hoping he had not noticed her slip, conscious of an irrational desire to delay the moment when scorn would enter his expression, she rushed on. 'Your steward turned me away.'

But his gaze had sharpened; he hadn't missed it. '*Our* lodgings?'

'Yes.' Setting her jaw, Emma met his gaze straight-on. And why should she not? It wasn't her fault she had been in love and had lain with her man, the times had been against them. And now, with Judhael so changed...

Don't mention Judhael, whatever you say, don't mention Judhael.

'Yes.' Her throat seized up, and she had to swallow twice before she could continue. 'I...I have a son.'

'You have a son?'

'Yes.' His expression was well schooled; it had hardly changed. There was no trace of the scorn Emma had expected, unless he was keeping it well hidden. Hope flared in her breast, and she nodded at the key on the bedside chest. 'And I need to go back to the inn—now—to see that Henri is all right.'

'Your son will be asleep, I should imagine.' Thoughtfully, he tapped the rim of his wineglass. 'He is that blond boy? The one playing by the Itchen, the one who came with you to the stables?'

'Yes.'

'I had assumed he belonged to that other woman.'

'No, Henri is my son, and I should like you to release me so that I may see him.'

'In good time, in good time.' The dark brows drew together. 'I sense there is more you are not telling me. You may confide in me, my lady. Your sister is married to a trusted friend. You must know that I would honour your confidence.'

My lady. There it was again, and again his use of her title had tears stinging at the back of her eyes. Richard of Asculf was an extraordinary man. Far from turning his back on her on learning about Henri, he still seemed disposed to help.

Good, Emma thought, *with Judhael and Azor back in Winchester, I am desperate.*

Even if it is a Norman who is offering help?

Yes, even then.

Emma drew closer, so close she noticed details about him that were new to her. His eyes had small black flecks in them. His pupils were large as he gazed up at her, and his eyelashes were very long. His eyes, she realised with something of a shock, were almost too beautiful for a man. She could see the dark stubble on his chin and smell the wine in his glass and more, a musky male scent that must belong to the man himself. 'I cannot explain. I need to get home. Please, my lord, let me go.'

His gaze ran searchingly over her face, resting for the briefest of moments on her mouth. 'There's more, I would swear, but you will not confide in me.'

Tentatively, Emma reached for his shoulder before recalling his wound and snatching her hand back. 'Please, sir.'

'It doesn't sit well on my conscience to let you go.'

'How so?'

He leaned back, eyes hooded, and gave her a slow smile, a smile that made her catch her breath. 'Let us say I escort you back to the inn. How long before you are back to your tricks?'

'Tricks? *Tricks?*'

In a swift movement he was on his feet and the glass was on the wooden chest. Saint Swithun, the man was tall. With something of a jolt, Emma saw a flash of anger in his eyes. It was gone in a moment and then he was looking down at her with every appearance of sympathy. He smiled, and against her better judgement she found herself responding. She was beginning to see why Cecily and Adam liked this man.

His mouth was most finely shaped, especially when he smiled. It drew her gaze, it drew all of her attention, so much so that when a large finger ran down her cheek, she almost leaped out of her skin. Her stomach clenched.

His smile deepened. 'Emma, Emma of Fulford, what am I to do with you?'

'All you have to do is release me.' Her heart was beating like a frantic drum. He stood too close. This man disordered her thoughts and she did not think that she liked it. No one, not even Judhael in the early days, in the days when she had loved him, had had so…so physical an effect on her. Realising that her attention had been drawn back to his mouth, to that full lower lip, that attractive dip in his top one… Saints.

Deliberately she focused on a chevron on the wall.

Strong fingers found her cheek and he brought her head back so she had no choice but to look into those grey eyes. Her insides tightened. Why was it she had the feeling that he was enjoying this? Her confusion amused him; *she* amused him. It was as though—a wave of anger took her—was Sir Richard toying with her? Had she become a game to him?

'You need saving from yourself, *ma petite*. Cecily would never forgive me if I permitted you to continue your arrangements with the Staple.'

The penny dropped. If Emma had not been thrown by Azor's appearance and worried about Henri, it would have dropped long before now. 'I am not one of Hélène's girls.'

When Emma had been a thane's daughter, she would not have hesitated to have spoken most disparagingly about whores. Women who made money by selling their bodies. But those disparaging remarks would have been made out of ignorance—that and pig-headed stupidity.

Life had been swift to put her right; it had shown her some of the things that might drive a woman to earn her living that way. Hunger and cold, desperation and fear, hopelessness. Of course, Hélène and Frida and the other girls were none of them saints—who was?—but they were among the few, the very few, whom Emma could call friend.

Anger and confusion made knots in her belly. She reached for calm. 'I had hoped to repay Hélène for my new lodgings by washing linens for her.'

His smile grew maddeningly large. His fingers moved slowly over her cheekbone and came to rest on her mouth. 'Of course you were.'

Damn him, he was playing with her. She twisted away. 'It is true.'

Slowly he shook his head and a lock of brown hair fell over his eyes, brown hair that glinted chestnut where the candle-light caught it. His green tunic was intricately embroidered at the neck and the ties were undone. Beneath a cream shirt, she could see the beat of his pulse, a sprinkling of dark hairs.

Her face warmed. 'It is *true.*'

'What about this?' He lifted the delicately hemmed edge of her veil. 'And this?' His hand slid gently down her arm, past her hip to the fullness of the pink skirts. 'This is hardly attire I would associate with a laundry maid in search of work.'

She could feel the heat of his hand through the fabric of her gown.

'This gown...' He cleared his throat and Emma's gaze shot to his face. 'This gown seems made more for seduction. I swear, you might tempt a hermit to break his vows in this.'

Snatching her skirts out of his grasp, Emma scowled. 'Hélène did not need my services as a laundry maid, so I was trying to sell it—the gown, that is.'

The grey eyes gleamed, he gave a bark of laughter. 'Selling the *gown*?'

'*Yes!* Hélène has need of gowns like this, good gowns her girls...' Emma's voice trailed off. Sir Richard would never believe her; it was clear his mind was set.

Mouth amused, he reached for the wine. Adam's friend would not hurt her; indeed, Emma was beginning to see that he had come to the Staple that night with a particular desire to save her—but his proximity was unnerving, there was an unsettling stirring in her insides that she could not identify. She moved away, as it was easier to breathe with a few yards between them.

'Sir?'

Eyes still dancing, he refilled the glass. 'Hmm?'

'I *was* selling the gown. Or trying to.'

'As you say.' He gave her one of his disbelieving smiles.

'Sir Richard, how did you know I was at the Staple tonight?'

'Geoffrey.'

His squire, of course. 'Yes, I thought I saw him.' She tipped her head to one side. 'Did you come to save me?'

'I wanted you to have honest work, which is why I sent you to the castle steward. I had not realised he turned you away, and I would have you know I deeply regret it.'

'The steward mislikes me, because of… because…I…I am not married and I have a son.'

'Geoffrey should have stayed to make certain you were found suitable work. Work—' closing the gap she had so carefully put between them, he took her hand and grimaced at her roughened palms '—work that is fitting for a lady of your station.'

Emma made a startling discovery. She *liked* standing with one of her hands in his. Pulling free, she gave him a straight look. 'I *was* selling the gown.'

Those expressive lips twitched. 'As you say.'

Emma's mind raced. It was infuriating not to

be believed, but there was no time to convince him. *Henri*! How long would it be before Azor discovered she had a son, assuming he did not already know? And after that, how long would it take Azor to make the connection between Henri and Judhael? How long did she have?

She stared up at Richard of Asculf. He might be commander of the Norman garrison in Winchester, but he was Adam's friend and he truly did seem minded to help. Would Sir Richard be prepared to let them stay at the castle for a time? She must find out. The last place Judhael would think of looking for her would be in Winchester Castle. Even he would think twice about crossing that drawbridge....

Different tactics, she told herself, *different tactics…*

'Sir, I…I thank you for your concern. But I must beg you…' To Emma's horror, her voice broke. 'Let me go to my son.'

His expression sobered. He reached for her hand, a simple touch, a gentle touch that had tears spill over and run down her cheeks. She dashed them away, but in truth she did not care if this man saw her tears; Henri's well-being was far more important. 'My son, sir, please.'

A frown as the glass was set aside. 'Tell me, tell me *everything*.'

She shook her head. 'Let me go.'

'Very well, I shall tease you no more.' Formally, Richard offered her his arm. 'My lady, permit me to escort you back to the inn.'

Richard watched, entranced despite himself, as a smile transformed her face. Sunshine after rain, he thought. Rainbows.

'Thank you, sir!'

She whirled, the silken veil drifting out behind her as she dived for the key. The key rattled in the lock, then she flung back the door and gestured imperiously. 'Hurry, sir, please hurry.'

Her smile, her anxiety, her unashamed pleasure at his agreement touched Richard as no one had touched him in years. There was some dark mystery here. *Mon Dieu*, but Emma of Fulford was diverting.

Richard did not have the first idea what was troubling her, but he was finding—somewhat to his surprise—that his desire to help her was genuine and not solely because Emma of Fulford was Adam Wymark's sister-in-law. She was concerned about her son, and it seemed to him that her concern was rather more than the usual concern a mother would feel for her child. The boy's rebel father had to be tangled up in this business, but how?

For some unfathomable reason, Richard felt a connection with her. She attracted him, but it was more than animal lust that could flare up between almost any man and woman, sometimes even when they disliked each other. Lust was there, certainly, for he had felt its pull when he had seen her in the tavern, and again later when he had carried her across the bailey. But, setting aside animal attraction, Emma of Fulford pushed the bad memories from his mind.

This was the first time this evening that Richard had given his nightmare a thought. This woman might not know it, but she was doing so well at distracting him that he was not dreading the oncoming night. And since York, that was cause for celebration. Ever since he had been unable to prevent the cruel death of that poor Saxon child, Richard's nights had been troubled.

With a rustle of skirts, she started down the stairs. Richard followed, but she had not gone more than two turns when she stopped abruptly.

'What now?'

Her eyes were huge in the flare of the torches,

and full of worry. 'I…I cannot go.' She began chewing a finger.

Gently, he removed her hand from her mouth. Rather alarmingly, he had to remind himself to release it.

'Az…th-there is someone…that is…I have just realised, I might be seen.'

Her chest rose and fell. Standing a step above her, the slashed neckline of the pink gown drew his gaze. Richard managed—just—to avert his eyes from the fascinating shadow between her breasts and focus on her face, on what she was saying.

'Would…would you help me, sir?'

'Haven't I said so?'

'I cannot explain fully, but my son and I are in desperate need of a refuge.' She touched his sleeve. 'Would you send someone to the Staple to bring him back here?'

Richard stared. 'You want me to have your son brought to the castle?'

'If you would. I know I shouldn't be asking this of you, but I can't go myself because…'

'You might be seen.'

'Exactly.'

This was becoming more mysterious by the

minute. Richard glanced down at the hand on his arm as he struggled in vain to recall the name of her former lover. It was a small hand, with slender fingers and a slim wrist. If it weren't for the broken nails and lye-chapped skin, it might be a lady's hand. It would help if he knew who or what Emma of Fulford was battling against. She might even, given the allegiances of her one-time lover, be involved in a plot against the King.

Irritated with himself, Richard frowned. That should have occurred to him before.

As he looked down at her, he had to drag his eyes from her breasts again. The faint scent of roses swirled in his consciousness. The woman was bewitching him. Still, she certainly pushed his other problems to the back of his mind— Martin's death and all that entailed, his night-mares…

'Please, will you have Henri brought here?'

'Yes. And I shall go myself. He will recognise me from our conversation this morning.' If Lady Emma's former lover had dragged her into some scheme, it occurred to Richard that it might be best to keep her where he could watch her.

'You won't frighten him? He is only two.'

Richard brought his brows together, and fought

to keep the image of that poor child near York at bay. 'I would never deliberately frighten a child.'

Back in the bedchamber, Emma hovered by the door while Sir Richard went to rouse his squire. She should not have asked him this favour, indeed she wondered that she had dared.

He was a Norman knight with the ear of King William, and she had asked him to fetch her son and give them refuge. *What desperation drives us to do*, she thought. Thank God, he hadn't taken offence.

The low murmur of voices floated up from the floor below. A dog whined. Footsteps retreated down the stairs. She heard the hollow bang of a distant door. Then nothing, not a single bark, not a whisper.

Latching the door, Emma wrapped her arms about her waist and began walking up and down. Her boots brushed across the matting, it was the only sound. A couple of paces brought her to the wall and the warm glow of a brazier. She turned. Up and down, up and down.

The quiet in this bedchamber was most unnerving. Fulford Hall had never been this silent. And City Mill, even in the dead of night, was never so silent, either. Wood creaked, thatch rustled, water hushed under the mill. And beside her, for the past two years, there had always been the soft sigh of Henri's breathing. But here, high in Richard of Asculf's lofty stone tower, with only an empty room below, the silence was total. Stone did not creak. You couldn't hear the mutterings of others as they slept. It felt unnatural.

Emma paused by the bed. She had never been in a chamber like this. The bed, so vast, and that fat mattress, the richly embroidered coverlet…

This was refinement of a sort she had never seen, not even at Fulford. Even in the days before King William had taken King Harold's crown, even when she had been a thane's daughter, she had never known such splendour. The rush matting—it kept the chill from the floor—was woven matting, not simple strewn rushes. The tapestries were as fine as any that had hung in the old Saxon palace—delicately wrought, with split threads for the detailing. Costly gold and silk yarns were artfully intermingled with woollen ones. And the painted walls were simply extraordinary, with swirls and chevrons covering every surface. It was almost like being in the cathedral.

Apart from the bed.

Emma and Judhael, because of the illicit nature

of their relationship, had never shared a bed. *What would it be like*, she wondered, *to wake up in a bed like this, beside the man that you loved?*

Tentatively, she reached out to test the softness of a pillow. Yes, as she suspected, he slept on goose-down. And there, furs and a silken coverlet… Did he sprawl across the middle? On his back or on his front? An unsettling image of Sir Richard asleep sprang into her mind. That large, well-muscled body would be relaxed, that dark hair would be tousled…

As she turned abruptly from the bed, her gaze fell on a shield leaning against the wall, and an object that could only be a sword, wrapped in sacking.

Emma frowned. A travelling chest stood next to them, along with a hauberk. Something about their placing told her that Sir Richard's squire was in the middle of packing. Was Sir Richard leaving Wessex? Was he going to Normandy to see those lands he had inherited?

Lord, that would not suit her at all. With Judhael threatening everyone she knew, she needed Sir Richard's help. She caught the edge of her veil and twisted it round her fingers, thinking furiously.

Was he leaving? Saints, a few days of his protection was not going to be enough, not nearly enough! If he was leaving, what on earth could she do?

Chapter Six

Henri had to be kept safe from Judhael, that was Emma's first concern.

Earlier that morning, when Emma had appealed to Sir Richard for help and had been sent away by his steward, she had dismissed Adam's friend as a source of assistance. But clearly, that assessment had been too hasty. If Sir Richard was to be believed, he had not known how the steward had treated her. Also, he had come to the Staple, solely to help her, or so it seemed. Sir Richard wanted to help her! One of the most powerful men in Wessex, and he wanted to help her.

This was her chance to escape from Judhael once and for all. She might not get another.

Sir Richard's travelling chest was banded with iron and studded. It even had a lock. But if, as she suspected, he was returning to Normandy? That changed everything. She might need his protection, but if he was leaving England… She grimaced.

Different tactics, she thought, *I shall need* very *different tactics*….

There lay his helmet and his sword. For all the room's adornments, he had made it a warrior's chamber. Another helmet lay against the wall, the metal dull with age. There was his shield. Incongruously, a lute lay on its side next to it. The lute was dusty and two of its strings were missing, but it gave credence to the stories of a Norman knight serenading the miller's daughter back at Fulford.

A knight's pennon had been tossed down alongside one of the hauberks. Emma picked it up; it was red and silver. Yesterday by the river, she had seen this pennon, the colours of Sir Richard of Asculf. The lute was the oddity in this gilded armoury, and it reminded Emma of what her sister had told her shortly after Hastings.

'Be wary of Sir Richard, he is a sensual pleasure-seeker,' Cecily had said. 'He plays the lute and serenades my maid, and encourages her to make eyes at him. Adam says that Sir Richard is a man of honour, but I think that women might be his weakness.'

A pleasure-seeker, Emma thought, carefully folding the pennon and setting it aside. If Adam's friend had been a sensualist in 1066, he was likely to remain one at heart. Another memory came back to her. At the wash-house, before Judhael had turned Bertha against her, Bertha had mentioned a rumour that was going the rounds. According to this gossip, some years back the garrison commander had given a gold cross to Adam's adopted sister, Rozenn. Worse than that, Rozenn, a seamstress, had come all the way from Brittany in the hopes of marrying him, only to be rejected when she had arrived.

Could that be true? Could a knight have really planned to marry a seamstress? And if he had promised Rozenn marriage, why wait till the poor woman got to England before turning her down?

Whatever the truth of the stories, they seemed to prove that Sir Richard was indeed a self-indulgent sensualist, a taker rather than a giver. It also appeared that he had a weakness for women. It was therefore most odd that he was not in the habit of visiting the Staple. Perhaps, since Frida had been summoned to the castle, his liaisons were usually conducted in private—here in this chamber.

Yes, that must be it. Emma glanced at the half empty wineglass on the chest. *One* wineglass, just one? Never mind, perhaps there had been two glasses, the other must have been broken; he had warned her they were fragile. Her brow cleared.

Sir Richard of Asculf was a sensualist. But was he rushing back to Normandy? Emma needed to know because if he was, then her best course might be to work on his weakness for women and use it to her advantage.

Absentmindedly, she sank on to the bed. It should not take him long to fetch Henri from the inn. It would be a relief to have her son here, well out of the reach of Azor and Judhael who, with prices on their heads, would not dare enter Winchester Castle itself. The Castle was surely the last place that Judhael would think of looking for her. It could be their safe haven, provided, of course, that Sir Richard truly meant it when he said he would help her.

Emma smothered a yawn. Saint Swithun, but she was tired. She eyed the pillow, which was fat and soft. Another yawn. She had been tired for months; pounding linen day in, day out was back-breaking work and, since leaving Fulford, she had been a light sleeper. Sir Richard would be at least half an hour; she should use the time to rest.

Usually, Emma had to keep half an ear out for Henri, in case he wandered. A mill was a dangerous place. Also, she had lived with her fears concerning Judhael for some years. They too had kept her on the margins of sleep. But here, in this lonely room high above the city...

Reaching up, Emma removed her veil and laid it at the foot of the bed. She loosened her plait and kicked off her boots, sturdy working boots in need of new soles, and somewhat out of keeping with her pink gown.

Sighing, she sank into the generous pillows. The linen smelt of him, of Sir Richard, commander of all in this castle unless King William was in residence. Emma was lying at the centre of Norman power in Wessex and, in her whole life, she had never felt so safe.

She was awakened in the small hours by the dull slam of a door. Whatever time was it? She was in Sir Richard's bed with her son and the length of a candle on a wall pricket told her it had been an hour at most since he had brought Henri to her. She and Henri had the bedchamber—and the bed—to themselves. Having passed Henri to her, Sir Richard had briskly informed her he would be joining his squire for the night.

True to his word, a heartbeat later he had gone.

Voices, male ones, could be heard in the room below. What could be important enough to waken the garrison commander in the dead of night?

Rebellion? Fire? Flood? Or a command from the King? Emma shot upright, heart pounding. Yes, it could be a message from the King!

Pausing only to smooth Henri's hair from his face for, unlike her, he slept like a log, she crept out of bed and dragged a fur about her shoulders. It wouldn't do to be seen wandering the corridors of Winchester Castle in her undershift, but something was happening below and there was no time to dress. Besides, she wasn't intending that anyone should discover her…

Hair flowing down her back, she padded across the matting.

On the half-landing below, the small white mongrel was lying across the door, his wiry coat gleaming in the torchlight. He was an ugly animal, and she prayed he was not ill-tempered.

Thankfully, when he saw her, his stumpy tail

tapped the floor. Smiling, Emma held out her hand and allowed the dog to take her scent before squatting down beside him. Good. This was a dog who liked to be petted. He would not betray her as long as she kept him happy. Stroking him, she put her ear to the door.

'And the King's despatch?' The deep tones of Sir Richard's voice, though muffled by an inch of oak, were unmistakable.

'Here, my lord.' A voice she did not know. The messenger.

'My thanks.' As Emma strained to hear, she imagined that dark head bent over a scroll, breaking open the seal, unrolling it. There came a pause; she pictured him reading. 'Thank God.' Sir Richard's voice again. 'It has arrived. Geoffrey, we will be leaving in the morning.'

Emma's heart sank. *In the morning? They would be leaving in the morning! How on earth was she to secure his help in such a short time?*

'*Tomorrow* morning, my lord?'

That was the squire again. But…*my lord*?

'Certainly, why wait? The King has promoted Sir Guy here. He will command the Winchester garrison, and as far as I am concerned he may take over at once.'

'Thank you, my lord.'

My lord?

'My duty in England is done.' Even through the door, Emma could hear the lightness in Sir Richard's tone. 'I must confess to a longing to see the Duchy again.'

'Yes, my lord. Beaumont is beautiful in the spring.'

Beaumont? What was going on? She pressed her ear to the oak.

'It is indeed, and it is far too long since I have seen the orchards in the valley pink and white with apple blossom.' Sir Richard cleared his throat. 'My congratulations to you, Sir Guy, on your appointment. I apologise for not staying to see you settled, but you will appreciate that since affairs in Normandy are so…uncertain, my presence there is urgently required. Sir Adam Wymark may be called upon to assist if you have any difficulties regarding the men and Nigel Steward knows everything worth knowing about the management of the castle. Both may be relied upon. Before I leave, I will make certain they know to brief you fully.'

'Thank you, Lord Richard.'

The mongrel wriggled on to his back, presenting his tummy for Emma's attention. Absently, Emma obliged him.

'As you are aware, Sir Guy, the commander occupies chambers here in the tower, this one, as well as another on the upper floor. There will also be quarters reserved for you in the garrison hall. I shall be gone shortly after first light tomorrow and until then I shall require these tower rooms. If you wouldn't mind bedding down in the hall until then?'

'Of course, and again, my thanks, I hadn't hoped for private chambers.'

'It is the King's wish. You are doubtless aware that the office of garrison commander would not ordinarily fall on one of his nobles, but Winchester is important to King William. He offers the use of private chambers by way of recompense.'

Footsteps had Emma scrambling to her feet. When the latch rattled, she lunged for the stairs. As she scurried up, the mongrel at her heels, she heard Geoffrey asking whether he should finish packing immediately.

'What's to pack? You've sorted most of it. I have what—a few weapons, some clothes? It shouldn't take long. In any case, Cecily's sister and her son are up there. Get your sleep, Geoffrey, you can finish in the morning….'

Sir Richard's voice faded. The mongrel whined.

'Hush!' Emma stroked the wiry white fur for all she was worth. *'Hush.'*

'Prince, is that you? Where are you, boy?'

Prince—he had named this ugly animal Prince? Emma attempted to push the dog back down the stairs, but the wretched creature stayed put, one ear up, one ear down, eyes shiny as black beads in the torchlight. Cocking his head to one side, he let out another whine.

'Hush, for pity's sake,' she hissed.

Another whine.

The light strengthened. 'Prince?' A warm hand landed on her arm. *'Mon Dieu,* Lady Emma! Did you need something?'

'I…I, yes…that is…no.'

A knowing expression came over Count Richard's face. His lips twitched, almost into a smile. He turned back briefly with a, 'Get some sleep, Geoffrey. We will finish our arrangements in the morning.' Grey eyes raked her from top to toe, taking in the wolf-pelt, her underskirt, her bare feet and—Lord—her unbound hair. Emma's cheeks took fire.

'Come, my lady,' he said, taking her firmly by the elbow. 'You seem to have missed your way.'

She was marched back to the upper chamber and thrust unceremoniously through the door. Like her, Adam's friend was half-dressed, wearing only some unremarkable brown chausses and a linen shirt. He remained an imposing figure. Henri, she was glad to see, was still sleeping like a baby.

Sir Richard closed the door and looked across at the bed, lips relaxing as the mongrel jumped on to it, and curled up beside Henri. The stumpy tail waved.

'He likes dogs?' he asked.

'I beg your pardon?'

'Your son—I take it he likes dogs?'

Emma nodded, and pulled the wolf-pelt more tightly about her shoulders. 'I think he will like that one, though he is wary of large dogs.'

'With reason. My hounds are little better than wolves, but Prince…' smiling, he shook his head '…all he catches are titbits from the table.' His expression sobered. 'Tell me, my lady, what were you doing on the stairs?'

'N-nothing, sir. I heard voices and—'

'You were listening.'

'I sleep but poorly, and when I heard talking, I was concerned.'

'You were afraid?'

Emma saw no reason to lie. 'Yes.' She edged closer. *Thank heavens Henri is a sound sleeper*, she thought, heartbeat speeding up as she prepared to leap in a bold and totally unladylike manner into the dark.

If Sir Richard was leaving for Normandy after first light tomorrow, Emma only had tonight to bend him to her will. In light of what she had just heard, she had questions. *My lord? Beaumont?* But they must wait. She must act now, or lose the chance for ever....

A second, longer step took her right up to him, close enough to feel his body heat. It was a step no lady would have made. Surprise flared in his grey eyes. Cold eyes? Never. Bright eyes, rather, intelligent, interested eyes. They were wholly focused on her; it was somewhat un-nerving.

Taking a deep breath, Emma placed the palm of her hand on his chest. More heat, coming at her through the cream linen shirt. Muscle—this knight was solid muscle and his body was warmer than the brazier behind him. She was half-afraid his touch might burn.

'Sir?' She was conscious of her hair flowing about her shoulders, making her look like the wanton he thought her to be. She was conscious of her thin shift, of her bare feet.

'Hmm?'

His gaze had fastened on her mouth. Good. She leaned even closer as a puzzling thought flashed through her mind. She felt no revulsion at this unseemly proximity only, shockingly, a desire to move closer. Well, she had chosen Sir Richard to be her protector, and her need was powerful. She had her son to think of, and that was apparently enough to overcome any natural reticence. Swallowing, Emma let the need take her and she leaned fractionally closer.

This shouldn't be too shaming. Sir Richard had already mistaken her for a woman who was prepared to sell herself, and a certain…expectancy about his stance, an almost imperceptible tension, told her that he was aware of her, *very* aware in a purely carnal sense. How she knew that was a mystery, because her experience of men had been limited to Judhael. Be that as it may, Richard of Asculf was hardly moving a muscle, but she was certain he found her attractive.

'Sir, I was wondering…that is…you had dealings with Frida this morning.'

His gaze met hers. 'So?'

Emma put her other hand on that broad chest. It trembled only slightly. 'I heard that you turned her away because she does not speak Norman French?'

His mouth edged up at the corner. 'That was one reason. Word certainly travels fast at the Staple, eh?'

'Yes, yes, it does.' A draught hit a candle, and their shadows danced across the painted walls. Mouth dry, Emma licked her lips. His eyes followed the gesture before locking with hers. She stumbled on. 'And…and while I would stress that I am *not* one of Hélène's girls, it has occurred to me that you…' Her cheeks scorched, her tongue stuck to the roof of her mouth. The words stuck, too.

'Yes?' His hands cupped her elbows; he gave the smallest of tugs and then she was leaning fully against him, breast to thigh. Her breasts tightened. 'Please go on. This is—' another quick glance at her mouth '—most diverting.' He reached up to tuck a strand of hair behind her ears, fingers lingering in a soft caress as he tested the texture.

'I speak Norman French, my lord.'

'Quite freely, it seems.' His voice was dry. His fingers were exploring her ear.

His touch did indeed burn, but oddly, it made her shiver. 'My mother was Norman.'

'I remember. And…?'

Wretch! He knew what she was fumbling towards, she was certain. He was relishing her discomfiture, laughing at her shame while she groped her way towards making the most indelicate proposition of her life. Anger was but a breath away. Clenching her hands into fists, she shoved at him, but he had her fast.

'Come on, *Lady* Emma.' His voice was both sensual and teasing. 'Against my better judgement, I find myself curious. What are you trying to say?'

Briefly she closed her eyes then, thanking God that Henri was asleep and could not hear his mama's wanton words, she blurted, 'Sir, I heard you want a woman, one who is fluent in your tongue—I…I ask you to consider me.'

He cleared his throat, eyes flickering over her son before returning to her. 'You want to be my…*belle amie*?'

Eyes widening at his careful turn of phrase, Emma nodded.

'A thane's daughter, offering herself as

a…*maîtresse*?' His gaze returned to the bed and he fell silent.

Thank Heaven the man had the delicacy not to utter a worse word in front of her child… *putain*, whore.

He shifted and stroked her cheek before sliding his fingers through her hair, combing its length. His hand curled round the back of her neck and his thumb moved up and down on her nape, loosing tiny curls of awareness down her back. His scent, the scent Emma recognised from the pillows, filled her nostrils.

His head lowered and his lips took hers. Soft. His fingers curled more firmly round her neck. Secure. Emma was surrounded by warmth. Warmth from the strong body pressed so closely to hers; warmth from the thumb that was moving up and down on her nape; but most of the warmth was flowing from his kiss, from his lips to hers.

Well, good, she needed a protector. And with Richard of Asculf's lips on hers Emma had no doubt that she had found him. If she could only persuade him to take her with him to Normandy, she and Henri would be safe.

When her limbs began to buckle, she stiffened them. Was this delight that was running like fire through her veins? It was not possible. She must remember why she was doing this. She was doing this for Henri; she was doing this so they could both be safe. It wasn't because…delight, it felt very like delight, but it must be relief.

The kiss drew out. His tongue found hers, stroked up and down its length. Emma responded with more confidence than she felt, and instantly the little curls—lust, they were caused by lust—moved deep in her belly. She was—her mind was seriously disordered—she was kissing Richard of Asculf because, because…

Delight? Relief? She moaned. Her motives were getting confused; *she* was confused. It wasn't that she could not break free—rather, she did not want to break free. His kiss burned. But surely it was the unaccustomed heat of the braziers that was melting her limbs, turning them to water? It was not him, it could not be him. She had only chosen Sir Richard because he was powerful and he could protect her. This was the first time she had kissed a man since the winter the Normans had come and she had forgotten how devastating it could be.

Emma wanted to cling, to grip those wide shoulders and push herself against him and never move away. But she could not cling. This was meant to be a seduction, and women who set about seducing men— Saints, why was it so hard to think? She did not know much about seduction, but she did not think that women who were bent on seduction clung. Even when trying to attract a protector.

She must be bold, she must seduce, not be seduced.

Forcing strength into her legs, Emma slipped a hand under the fine linen of his shirt, and brazenly ran it up and down his back. He moved immediately to grant her access. Warm skin. His body was both soft and hard, the skin smooth and silky over the muscles. She could feel the indentation of his spine. His body was toned, the body of a warrior. Her hand continued to explore. She felt ribs and the slight abrasion of chest hair. His breath was flurried in her ear, uneven. Hot. Her toes curled into the matting. Emma *liked* caressing Sir Richard's body and he, if the uneven breathing was anything to go by, liked it in equal measure. Good, this was meant to be a seduction, he was meant to like it.

He let out a toe-curling groan, subtly altering the angle of the kiss, before drawing back and covering her cheek with kisses. Another groan, he was definitely not averse to her. Good. Shamelessly, she pressed her breasts against him.

Lightly, he nibbled her ear. His hold tightened, and he brought his lips back to hers.

Emma opened her mouth. She was dissolving, and with every second that passed she could feel more and more of those curls of awareness in her belly. It must be lust; it was certainly desire. No one could deny that Sir Richard of Asculf was handsome. And resting against her belly, she caught her breath, she could feel…him, hard and hot against her. Ready. He desired her. Urgently.

Seduce, seduce, she reminded herself. *This is likely your one chance to seduce him*. But in truth this seduction, if that was what this was, was too easy. It felt inevitable, it was as though it were happening without thought or will. Her fingers were running up and down his spine, they were pulling at the ties of his hose. They were sliding round the back, lingering over the fascinating curve of his buttocks, they were holding him to her. And she certainly wasn't trying. It took no effort, this seduction business, Emma thought, when it was Sir Richard you were seducing.

Inhaling, she pulled his scent deep into her

nostrils, a scent that spoke of safety, of coming home, though she knew that last was false. Home? With Sir Richard of Asculf? Wasn't it bad enough that she was making a wanton of herself, did she have to be ridiculous, too?

Again she told herself she was seducing him.

But it was hard to remember that with that musky male scent befuddling her. It dizzied her, when she could not afford to be dizzied. As his tongue played with hers, she heard another moan. Shamefully it was hers.

If Richard of Asculf took her body tonight, would he want her with him on the morrow? Would he take her with him when he went to Normandy? She could only pray. This must be good, this seduction must be *perfect*, as Emma could not be left behind. Judhael's arrival back in Wessex had put Winchester out of bounds. It was no longer safe for her here.

Dear Lord, please do not let Henri wake.

Hooking her fingers into his chausses, she began easing them down.

A hand clamped over hers, his head jerked away. 'Enough.'

Cold, there's a cold draught, Emma thought, blinking up at him. 'Mmm?'

'That's enough.' He moved back.

His hair…well, it looked as though he had been sparring with one of the other knights. The opening of his shirt was quite undone—had she done that?—and his breathing, Emma noted with satisfaction, was as ragged as hers. He watched her with an odd expression that she could not read. For a moment his eyes looked almost black, then he blinked and she realised she must have imagined it. They were once again cool and watchful—the eyes of one of King William's most trusted men.

'Be careful, my lady…' he cleared his throat '…you know nothing about me.' He bent to retrieve the wolf-pelt which had fallen to the floor unheeded. With a slight smile he handed it back to her. 'And I think that is enough kissing for tonight.'

'Sir?' *Now or never.* Emma knew her cheeks must be as red as his pennon. She took a deep breath. 'Will you not take me as…as your *maîtresse*?'

Chapter Seven

He had been moved by their kisses. She knew that he desired her body. Which was why, when she looked at him and saw the measuring way in which he regarded her, her heart sank. Those dark-lashed eyes were grey as a January sky and just as cold. Merciful heavens, what was she to do?

'I am tempted, but—' he thrust his hand through his hair '—never mind where I found you, you are my friend's sister-in-law and I am minded to treat you with respect. I do not wish to demean you.'

'Sir?' Blinking, she hugged the wolf-pelt to her.

'*Mon Dieu*, woman, have you thought this through? What about your reputation?'

Her jaw dropped. 'My reputation? Ever since my son was born,' hastily, she lowered her voice, 'I have been a fallen woman.'

He shook his head, frowning. 'You are a thane's daughter, Lady Emma of Fulford. As the elder, by rights it is you who should have married Adam.'

'But I did not marry Adam! How could I when I was carrying…another man's child?'

'It would have saved a great deal of trouble if we had known that at the time.'

Emma set her jaw. 'Would it have made any difference? Anyway, I do not recall being given a choice. Your King ordered me to marry Adam and I could not obey, which is why I ran away.'

He was watching her thoughtfully. 'Adam would never have forced you. It is not in his nature.'

'How was I to know that when you rode in as conquerors?'

'We were conquerors, not monsters. In any case, your Saxon Harold had broken his oath to my liege lord. The Pope himself did endorse William's claim to England.'

'You Franks believe that because it suits you, because you want our land. That is what it comes down to, a battle for land.'

'These are tired arguments. Isn't it time to let the past go?'

She glanced significantly at her son. 'I cannot—the past is with me every day. And in my mind thoughts of how things might have been rear up to taunt me.'

'Emma, if you had stayed in Fulford a little longer, you would have discovered Adam's nature for yourself. I have known him for years and I have never known him to be cruel. He would have helped you.'

Emma lifted her chin. If he was looking for an apology, he would have a long wait. This was some seduction, she thought. A minute ago it had seemed to be going so well, but somehow it had gone badly awry. With a sigh, she resigned herself to failure. She would just have to find another way to secure safety for her son.

Biting her lip, she braced herself for rejection. What a fool she had been to think she could influence this man! He was a knight; he had commanded the Winchester garrison *for years*. Some misplaced sense of honour, solely due to his friendship with Adam, must have made him drag her out of the Staple earlier. He had brought her to his chamber, but that did not mean that he wanted her or that she could influence him. Clearly, Sir Richard of Asculf liked to choose his own women.

Was that her mistake? By seeking to influence him had she offended his sense of pride? Or was it because of her connections with known rebels, with Judhael and Azor?

He was speaking to her, shaking his head. 'You are a thane's daughter; the position of...*belle amie* is not one I would have chosen for you. Do you really want it for yourself?'

Pinning a smile to her lips—perhaps all was not lost—Emma stepped towards him. 'The life of a thane's daughter is behind me,' she murmured. 'My future lies in another direction.'

'As my lover?'

'Yes.' Confidence was pouring out of her like water from a sieve, yet she kept that smile in place, going so far as to curl her fingers into the front of his shirt. 'Your language is also mine, though why that should matter to you is a mystery. I have heard you speak English and it is quite acceptable.'

He rubbed his forehead, and it came to Emma that Sir Richard was weary. The campaign in the North must have used up much of his energy, yet because of some crisis he was returning to Normandy to resolve yet more conflicts. Did the King ever grant him rest?

'My mastery of English is not entirely reliable, there are times when it deserts me completely.

But your facility with French is not the issue.' He put his hands on her arms and slid them down to her fingers. 'Listen well. Your past liaisons—'

'You mean, liaisons with men?'

'Yes. I cannot change them, but I for one would not have made a whore of you.'

Richard felt her flinch and heard the swift intake of breath. She thought he was rejecting her. Her eyes were dark in the candle-light, confused and wounded. She had felt his lust for her while they had been kissing, she knew he wanted her. She tugged at her hands, but he held fast. 'Listen. The King has released me from command here, I return to France.'

'Yes, so I heard.'

'So you *were* listening!'

Her cheeks darkened as she ducked her head to look at her toes. Bare toes. She had been in bed with her son when Sir Guy's arrival had awoken her. They were pretty toes, especially when not blue with cold as they had been by the wash-house. And her legs… Richard was calling to mind the alluring shape of her calves when the implications of what she had said sank in. 'You knew I was leaving tomorrow.'

'Yes.'

'And yet you were prepared to lie with me?'

'Sir Richard, I…we need to leave Winchester.' She tipped her head back and looked up at him from under her lashes. It was a winsome expression such as she must have learned from the other girls at the Staple. 'It is a matter of some urgency. I confess to hoping that you might learn to like me enough to take me—us—with you.'

She smiled. There was, Richard thought, a touch of *tristesse* to her smile. And, extraordinarily, such innocence in the woman, to think that a man might lie with her for one night and take her with him! Something was driving her to make this proposition, and undoubtedly it concerned her old lover. If only the man's name… *Judhael!*…that was his name, Judhael. Clearly he terrified her. This woman was desperate and Richard was to leave Wessex in the morning. Lord, what a coil.

He could walk away, of course. Yes, he could send a message to Adam, informing him what Emma was up to. He could let Adam unravel this mess. Adam had, after all, married into Emma's family.

But why had she not returned to Fulford already? She was afraid, afraid to return to Fulford.

Whatever was threatening her in Winchester, must be just as much a threat in Fulford….

What might she be driven to do if he simply walked away?

While Richard's mind worked, his thumb was running absently over her fingers. 'You want to go to Normandy, my lady?'

'We need to leave Winchester. And you recall that my mother was Norman. If…if you do not choose to…to keep me for long, it might be possible for us to find our Norman relatives and make a fresh start with them.'

There was more she might tell him, Richard sensed, waiting. What was so urgent that she must suddenly be leaving Winchester? One moment she was petitioning him for work at the castle, and the next she was in a lather to leave. The outlaw Judhael had to be at the bottom of this.

He let the silence stretch out. He had often served as a negotiator, so he knew the value of silence. It unnerved some people and they rushed to fill it with speech; perhaps Emma would reveal her fears to him.

While he waited he looked at her. It was no hardship. Her hair gleamed like a curtain of gold in the soft light of the candles. Those huge blue eyes looked out at him past long dark lashes. He even liked her nose. She had a pink mouth with a slight pout to it, and when she was smiling—perfection. She was pretty, was Emma of Fulford. With her gaze turned beseechingly on him, Richard found time to wish that she could like him for himself, not for what he could do for her.

After a few moments, Richard realised he was staring at a woman who would not easily reveal her secrets. He was also beginning to realise that he could not in all conscience leave her behind when he left Wessex. In her present state of mind, she would fling herself at the first man who came along. And that thought…it did not please him, it did not please him in the least. Besides which, Adam would geld him if he allowed that to happen.

The next step would be tricky, though. Despite everything that had happened to her, she had her pride. He would have to tread carefully, lest he offend her.

'My lady, I might yet take you as my woman—'

Her fingers tightened on his; her face transfigured. 'You will take me with you to France?'

His gut clenched. *Mon Dieu*, she was more than pretty. Face lit like this, Emma of Fulford was beautiful. 'As I was saying, I might take you as my woman.' He grinned. 'We have proved there is a strong…attraction between us, but we must come to terms first.'

Her expression lost some of its shine. 'T-terms?'

Lord, at times the woman appeared a complete innocent. 'We must understand what to expect from each other.'

Richard would play along with her request, he would take her and her son to Normandy, where she could be his 'mistress'. In name only, naturally, so her pride would not suffer. But he would not tell her that, not yet, because she might refuse to accompany him. And she *must* accompany him, for if ever anyone needed saving from herself, it was Lady Emma of Fulford.

Further, he would take a chance with her and trust her with news of his altered status. She wouldn't be able to spread it about if he kept her close; her old friends were not likely to visit the castle. Yes, if he kept her close till the morrow, there would be little time for her to make use of the information and after that, God willing, they would be in Normandy when it would no longer matter.

Limpid blue eyes were staring up at him. 'Yes…yes, of course.'

'Ours will be a simple…monetary arrangement.' Leading her to the bed, careful not to disturb her child, Richard sat on the edge and pulled her down beside him. Toying with her fingers, he caught the faint scent of roses. 'If you are in agreement you must be prepared to leave in the morning.'

'Yes, sir, I am.' She bit her lip, her gaze earnest. 'But I will have to send a letter to Cecily. I shall have to say something that will put her mind at ease. If Henri and I vanish, she will worry and—'

'Yes, yes, of course you must send your sister a message, I shall be sending one myself. But listen to what I have to say. There are matters you must understand before you agree.'

'Yes, sir.'

'The County of Beaumont was, until a week ago, in the keeping of my cousin Martin. Martin had an accident, his horse threw him and he dislocated his shoulder, or so it was thought.'

'I believe it is a common injury among those of the knightly class.' Pulling her hand free, she turned to adjust the bedcovers over her son.

Richard's lips twisted. 'The most common. Dislocated my own once when Roland— But that is of no account. Suffice it to say that Martin died.'

'He died?' A light hand touched his. 'I am sorry.'

'That is not the whole.' He lifted an eyebrow. 'How much could you hear from the other side of that door?'

Flushing, she lowered her gaze. 'Not much. Only that you were leaving. I did catch the name Beaumont and heard your squire and the messenger call you "my lord".'

'There is good reason for that, I have inherited my cousin's county.'

She went white. 'You are a *count*?'

'Yes.'

She sucked in a breath. 'You are made count and you let me proposition you like that? *My lord*—' she put heavy emphasis on his title '—I see it amuses you to make fun of me.'

She made to rise, but, catching her arm, he held her back. 'I do no such thing, I assure you.'

Hesitating, her eyes searched his.

'Truly, Emma, I do not mock you.' Lifting her hand to his lips, he kissed it.

Slowly, she subsided. 'You are Count of Beaumont?'

'Yes.'

When she folded her hands on her lap and frowned, he heaved a sigh of relief.

'You said your cousin died of a dislocated shoulder? That hardly seems likely.'

'We suspect Martin had other, hidden, injuries.'

'Internal ones?'

'There is no other explanation. At any rate poor Martin is dead and the King—you realise he is our Duke in Normandy?'

'Of course.'

'The King has tonight endorsed my inheritance. That is the news Sir Guy brought. King William has released me from my obligations here and I leave for Normandy in the morning. I am telling you this because I want you to know everything when you make your decision.' He reached once more for her hand. 'I would be honoured if you would accompany me to Beaumont. I desire you as my mistress, Emma, but I need you to be clear about exactly what I am offering you.'

'You want me to be your mistress.'

Her smile lit her whole face, and it warmed Richard's heart. *Saint Denis*, he thought, *that smile is lethal, it pierces to the core*. 'Mind that I can never offer you marriage. Ours will be a temporary liaison, and should you have a child as a result, I will, of course, give that child my protection.' That was an easy promise to make, since

Richard did not actually intend bedding her. *In name only*, he reminded himself, *in name only*.

She bit her lip. 'I am to be your Herleva.'

'I beg your pardon?'

'King William's mother was called Herleva. She was Duke Robert's lover and they never married. Like me, she was a washerwoman and—'

'Ah, yes, I recall. Her legs must have lured him,' Richard said, keeping a straight face. 'As yours lured me.'

'My lord?'

'When I returned from the north, I saw you by the river. You had been resting by the riverside and your legs were bare.'

Her toes curled into the matting and until that moment Richard had not realised how expressive toes might be; it was most endearing.

Her cheeks went pink. 'I hoped you hadn't noticed.'

'I noticed.' He shrugged. 'Be that as it may, Duke Robert cared for Herleva when their liaison was ended, and you need have no fears on that score. I shall see to your care too.'

'Duke Robert found Herleva a nobleman for a husband when he….when they were no longer lovers.' She swallowed. 'Will you find one for me?'

'If that is your wish, though I cannot promise you a viscount.'

She gave a jerky nod. 'Your terms are acceptable, my lord. I will accompany you to France.'

'I thank you, but it is an important decision and now you know the whole, you should sleep on it.' He kissed her hand. 'I should warn you, though, there will be some need for discretion.'

'Oh?'

'Martin had a fiancée, Aude de Crèvecoeur. They were betrothed some years ago, and their wedding was to have taken place this summer. It was…is…a matter of politics.'

She nodded her understanding. 'A dynastic alliance.'

'Exactly. Lady Aude took up residence at Castle Beaumont some time ago, and I find myself in an awkward position. There are those who feel strongly that I myself should fulfil my cousin's obligations with regard to Lady Aude.'

She tipped her head to one side as she looked at him and a long strand of hair fell forward, gilded by candle-light. A tiny line formed between her brows. 'Lady Aude will expect to marry you, is that what you are saying?'

'In a nutshell, yes. Once a suitable period of

mourning is over, of course. The reasons for a marriage between the Comte de Beaumont and Aude de Crèvecoeur have not changed, even though there is to be a different count. Lady Aude is a well-respected lady and her brother, Lord Edouard, is reputed to be something of a stickler for protocol. For myself, I don't have the slightest desire to marry her.'

'Assuming you want heirs, you will have to marry at some point,' she said. 'Why not marry Lady Aude if it is politically expedient?'

Richard was hard put not to grimace. 'Lady Aude was beautiful in Martin's eyes, not mine. I do not find her attractive.'

Her eyes went wide. 'You mislike her because of her looks?'

'In my youth I used to tease Martin about her. Ugly Aude, I called her. Drove him mad like nothing else.'

'I can imagine.'

He pressed a kiss to the back of her hand. He let his lips linger, taking in the warmth of her hand, letting the scent of roses fill his mind. He was conscious that in striving to reassure her, he might have come over as somewhat dispassionate. A small show of ardour would redress that.

Until he had her safely away from here, she mustn't suspect that he no intention of bedding her. Turning her hand over, he pressed a number of kisses to her work-roughened palm. Her fingers quivered in his.

'Emma, I do not find you in the slightest bit ugly and I do most certainly desire you for my lover. Accompany me to Beaumont. As long as you understand the need for discretion, all will be well.'

'We must be discreet because of Ugly Aude?'

He winced. 'Forget that name for her, please, I should not have mentioned it. Think about my proposal, Emma. You have my word that I will treat you with as much honour as I may.'

'I will come with you, my lord.'

'Sleep on it, I would not have you say I forced you.'

She coloured. 'You are not forcing me, my lord.'

'And another thing—when we are in private, do you think you might call me Richard?'

'Richard, yes, I think I can manage that.'

'As I said, I do not wish to marry Lady Aude, but it may be expedient for me to do so. I will be glad to have you with me.' *For the journey to Beaumont, at any rate.*

'Because you do not like Ugly Aude.' Large eyes held his. 'I will be your compensation.'

'Yes, but only for as long as you wish. Afterwards you will be free to find your relatives.'

'Or to marry the husband you say you will provide me with.'

Richard frowned. 'Yes, yes, if that is your wish. You will find me generous. You may have money, clothes, jewels, whatever you desire within reason. And…' he reached behind him to touch the small bump beneath the bedcovers '…when the time comes for us to end our liaison, I will ensure your son is fostered in a noble house if he so wishes. Should he develop a yearning for knighthood, I might even foster him myself.'

'Henri might become a knight? An illegitimate Saxon?'

'He is part Norman, is he not?'

'Yes, oh, my lord…' Her eyes became glassy with tears.

Reaching out, Richard tucked a golden strand of hair behind her ear and pushed himself to his feet.

'Think about it. It can't be worse than the life you are living, but think quickly, my lady. I shall need your decision by first light.'

She jumped to her feet and a small hand took his. 'My lord—'

'Richard, remember?'

'Richard...' she cleared her throat '...I have given you my answer, I do not need more time. Provided you swear to see to the welfare of any child we may have...'

'I swear it, though if there is a child, I may reconsider *your* future. The complications...your reputation in Normandy...' He shook his head. 'Emma, these are weighty matters. Take tonight to consider them.'

Small fingers reached out, and came to rest against his shirt. Richard liked the way she touched him with those worn but capable hands. Bold and unafraid. As if it were her right. Their gazes met and he saw in her eyes that she really would agree. His mood lifted as though the thought of her running those hands over more of his body was something to look forward to. Indeed, already his pulse was quickening....

In name only, he reminded himself. *She is coming with me so that I may protect her, from herself and whatever terror it is that drives her. She will not really become my mistress. I shall not touch her.*

Her hand slid up, hooked round his neck and

brought his head down to hers. Her kiss was brief and surprisingly cool, but it fired his blood. His loins throbbed. *In name only.* Richard held down a groan, and before he realised what he was doing, he had taken her by the hips and pulled her close. His body seemed to be having a hard time remembering his good intentions.

'I trust you,' she murmured. 'I trust that you, Adam's friend, will honour your word. Thank you for honouring me with your confidence, and thank you for giving me this chance to leave Winchester. And for Henri, too—a knight…' her nostrils flared and she swallowed '…I thank you and I accept. I will accompany you as your *maîtresse*, for as long as you may require.'

Richard smiled and reached for her hair. As he caressed it—so long, so silky—the scent of roses filled the room. 'Then we have an agreement.'

Pretty lips angled towards his. 'When do you wish our contract to start, my lo…Richard?'

He lowered his lips. *Just a kiss, just one small kiss.* 'Mama? *Mama?*'

She wrenched herself out of his arms. '*Henri*! I am sorry, did we wake you, sweetheart?'

'Mama…' the child's voice was slurred with sleep. 'Mama, kissie, kissie.'

The child had seen them!

Richard waited for her swift denial, but Emma surprised him. Smoothing down the coverlet, she sank on to the bed and stroked her son's head. 'Yes, darling…' she lowered her voice, but he caught the words '…I was kissing Sir Rich.'

The boy murmured. Then, seeing Prince curled up next to him on the bed, he smiled and wound his arms about the dog's neck. His eyes closed.

Smiling himself, Richard turned for the door. The boy was safe with that ugly dog, it was as soft as they came. His heart felt lighter than it had for weeks. Richard would always regret not being able to save that Saxon child near York. In helping Emma and her Henri, perhaps he was doing something to set the balance straight.

'Richard?' She padded after him.

'Hmm?'

Great eyes stared up at him, anxious eyes. 'You…you do not wish to…to…' Her cheeks were crimson.

'Not here, not tonight. There will be time enough later. I trust you will honour our contract when we get to Normandy.'

'As I trust you, my lord.'

Raising her hand to his lips, Richard let himself

out. His smile faded as he made his way to the chamber below. It was not going to be as easy as he had first thought, keeping her at arm's length.

The attraction was there on both sides, certainly. But that was not the reason she had set out to seduce him for that, Richard realised, was what she had been about, trying to seduce him. Unless he was very much mistaken, Lady Emma was running from Judhael of Fulford; she was protecting her son. But what father would drive the mother of his child into living the life of a washerwoman rather than return home to those who loved her at Fulford?

When Richard caught himself wishing that soon Emma would prove she did indeed trust him by unburdening herself to him, he dismissed the thought as ridiculous.

Chapter Eight

Honfleur! Their ship, with its chunky curved prow and striped sails, was entering the port and as the swell began to slacken, Richard could barely master his impatience. Normandy! Home at last. On his left, the mouth of the Seine was falling away behind them, a broad expanse of water that narrowed fast as it wound its way inland, Jumièges, Rouen, Paris…

The ship's design mirrored the longboats of the Norsemen and the creature carved on the prow was a demon, a demon with red glaring eyes. Many Norsemen had settled in Normandy; it was part of Richard's heritage. Norsemen, Northmen, Norman. Viking blood flowed in his veins.

He gripped the ship's handrail and ran his gaze over the approaching harbourside. Clouds scudded across the sky and sea-foam filled his nostrils. At his back, a sailor shouted, a rope creaked, a sea-bird shrieked. The wooden houses and storage barns that hugged the harbour's edge were coming into view—single-storey buildings roofed in the main with shingles and reeds. Beyond the houses and barns, a thickly wooded hill sloped steeply up. Already the trees were beginning to green. Oak, ash, beech.

He grinned and inhaled deeply. Home.

'Count Rich! Count Rich!'

Richard was not the only one in his element. Emma's boy was skipping across the deck towards him, heedless of the dangers of snaking ropes and sailors scrambling to bring down the sails. He was a quick-witted child; witness the speed with which he had altered his name for Richard on hearing the way the men addressed him. Once more it came to him that Henri bore an uncanny resemblance to the Saxon boy he had seen butchered near York. The white mongrel was trotting after him, close as a shadow. The wolfhounds, less tractable, had been put on leashes and were tethered near the horses.

'Clear the deck!' the helmsman bellowed.

Stepping forward, Richard reached for the lad, blanked out the twinge in his shoulder and hoisted him clear. He clicked his fingers. 'Prince, sit!' The dog obeyed, tongue lolling.

Richard glanced towards the covered awning beneath the prow platform. As a shelter it was crude, but Emma and the maidservant that Geoffrey had managed to find her had been swift to take refuge inside. The flap was down and there was no sign of movement, not that Richard expected it. The ship had barely left Bosham before both women had turned green. *Mal de mer*. It was not something Richard had ever suffered from.

Since Geoffrey was amidships with the horses and the wolfhounds, Richard sighed and settled Henri on his hip. He didn't know the first thing about looking after little boys and wasn't in the least inclined to learn, but for the time being, he was stuck with Henri. Unlike his mother, Henri was the best of sailors. Richard shot another glance towards the awning. Perhaps *mal de mer* was not the only reason Emma was keeping out of sight. Had his 'arrangement' with her made her uncomfortable? Was she perhaps finding it difficult to face the others in his entourage?

What on earth was he going to do with her? Lord. In truth, Richard's offer to take Emma with him had been made on impulse, to prevent her from hurling herself at the first man who came along. He had had to act quickly. Despite her child and the fact that Richard had found her in the Staple, she still had an intriguing air of innocence about her.

One thing was certain, Adam and Cecily would kill him if he didn't do his best by her. He grimaced as he pondered their reactions to the messages he and Emma had sent to Fulford before their departure.

And as for Emma herself, she had asked him to find her a husband when their 'liaison' was ended. Sighing, Richard smiled at her son. He could take his time over picking Emma a suitable husband. He would think about that later, after he had dealt with the unrest in Beaumont and when he had learned more about Emma herself. 'Your mama is something of a mystery, Henri,' he said.

'Count Rich?'

'Mmm?' The child had inherited his mother's eyes, large, blue...

'I had a boat.'

'Did you, lad?'

'It was lost.'

'Was it? What happened?'

'The river ate it. But look…' All smiles, Henri waved a fist towards the bristling quays. 'More boats. Lots.'

'Yes, lad, more boats. And that—' Richard waved at the woods, at the land beyond them '—that is Normandy.'

'Normandy.'

Eagerly, Henri absorbed it all. He looked as excited as Richard felt, only unlike Richard, Henri was able to display his excitement. A count could not make a parade of his feelings. Though it had been over three years since he had seen his homeland, Count Richard of Beaumont must conceal his emotions. The tears might be pricking at the back of his eyes, but they would never fall.

Richard ruffled Henri's hair. He was not used to children, but perhaps he might like this one. It was fortunate that Emma had seen to it that her boy understood French, as well as English. Indeed, Richard thought ruefully, the child's English was better than his. Witness the way Henri had already managed to twist the two Saxon mercenaries round his little finger. Not to mention the new maid, Asa.

'My lord?' Emma was picking her way across the deck, holding her skirts clear of ropes and tackle. She looked pale after her bout of seasickness, but her veil was back in place, its hem lifted gently in the breeze. 'I'm sorry. Let me have him.'

'He is fine,' Richard said. Thank God, her manner towards him seemed fairly natural; she was managing to conceal any unease she might be feeling at their supposed relationship. The only sign of it that Richard could see was a slight tension about her eyes. 'I was showing him the land of his forebears.'

She nodded, and gave the harbour and approaching hillside an appraising glance. 'It looks very much like England.'

'It is in many respects. It is arguably more beautiful, especially with the trees coming into leaf. Wait until you see the orchards in Beaumont, the trees weighed down with blossom, the doves roosting in— I will show you.' He stopped abruptly and hoped he had not revealed too much. 'You are recovered?'

Pulling a face, she put a hand to her stomach. 'Not entirely, but the worst must be over. I am sure that once we are on dry land this queasiness will pass.'

'The swell is already easing.'

'Thank Heavens. Now, my lord, you must pay that shoulder of yours some respect.' Brushing aside his protestations, Emma lifted Henri from him and settled him on her own hip. 'Please tell me what is happening in your county. I ought to know something about it. I would have asked earlier, but there was no time before we boarded and then I was sick and had no heart for questions.'

'Very well.' They had a few minutes before the ship docked. Richard shifted a couple of feet. 'Here, my lady.' He indicated a spot where they could sit and lean against the ship's side and not be under the crew's feet.

'Your cousin, Count Martin—you said his horse threw him?'

'Yes, he died over a week since from some unknown internal injury.'

'Were you close?'

'Close?' Richard found the question disturbing—he and Martin *had* been close, but what business was it of hers? 'I do not see the relevance of that question.'

'You think I am impertinent.'

A gull screeched past them, a flash of white. Emma of Fulford had something about her, something that made Richard think that perhaps he could share his most private confidences with her. Before this, there had only been Geoffrey and it simply was not done for a man to bare his soul to his squire. 'We knew each other as boys,' he said, finally. 'We were fostered in the same household for a time, but later our ways parted.' He shrugged. 'Martin was destined to be Count, while I, as his cousin, son of a younger son...'

'You had manors of your own, though, before your cousin died?'

'Yes, they are not far from Falaise, but they are nothing to compare to Beaumont itself.'

On her lap, the boy stirred. He stuck his thumb in his mouth and leaned his head against her breast. He had worn himself out dashing about the deck. Envying the boy the comfort of his mother's arms, Richard looked away, focusing instead on the canvas stalls rigged up in the stern of the ship. Roland's head was visible over the top of one, his white mane streaming out like a banner. The hills behind Honfleur were drifting closer and the mouth of the Seine was lost to sight behind a spit of land.

'Your voice tells me that you love Beaumont, my lord. Describe it to me.'

'Beaumont is, to my mind, quite simply the

most beautiful place in the Duchy. The Castle is set on a plateau overlooking a curve of the river.'

'Which river it that?'

'The Orne.'

'So your castle is strategically placed?'

'Yes, Beaumont is a buffer county.'

Richard paused, uncertain how much he should tell her. He had only been granted leave to return to Normandy because it was in King William's interests to have Beaumont in the hands of a man whose loyalty could be relied upon. Martin had been such a man; he was such a man. King William of England, also Duke of Normandy, did not give his trust lightly.

'It is complicated,' he said. Two powerful Counts, Argentan and Alençon, had holdings nearby. Both of them had from time to time made threats against the Duke and a large part of Richard's role as Count of Beaumont would be to continue to keep watch on behalf of his liege lord.

Richard felt awkward, unused to political discussions in which women took part. His mother had never taken much interest in his father's affairs; indeed, his mother had never taken much interest in anything apart from the Church. Richard glanced at Emma, surprised and not a little shocked at himself for even considering further confidences. Her lover had been a Saxon rebel.

And then a distant memory rushed back. Lucie, his father's *maîtresse*.

Lucie had been small and plump and dark, and his father had valued her for the comfort she had given him when Richard's mother, having done her duty and provided him with three sons, had walked away from him straight into the arms of the Church. Lucie had also, Richard recalled, liked to sit talking with his father long into the night. Had his father been discussing matters of politics with her? He sighed. He would never know the answer, for his father and Lucie were both long dead. 'Lucie,' he murmured. He was not really intending to make Emma of Fulford his mistress, but should he ever do so in truth…

'Lucie, my lord?'

Richard looked at her, at the sleeping boy in her arms. He should keep his discussions with Emma of Fulford as brief as possible and tell her nothing that she could not work out for herself. Her lover had been a known rebel and while his instincts were telling him that he might trust her, she was little more than a stranger.

'Beaumont has many faces,' he said, temporising. 'It is a rich and fertile country and that alone makes it covetable, but its chief attraction is the position of Castle Beaumont itself, high on the hillside overlooking the river.'

Emma's veil blew over Henri's face; she tucked it out of the way. Candid eyes met Richard's, straightforward eyes, eyes he wanted to trust. He was conscious of the impulse to confess that he had no intention of making her his mistress. He wanted to watch those lines of strain ease. *Wait until we reach Beaumont*, he told himself. *When I have her safely there, then I shall tell her*.

'Your castle is a watchtower,' she said.

'Exactly. Duke William—here in Normandy he is Duke—Duke William has endorsed my claim to the county because he knows I am his man.'

'What are the names of the neighbouring counts that Duke William is so concerned about?'

Richard shot her a sharp look. He had surmised that Emma of Fulford was intelligent despite her past mistakes, but this was too nice a matter to be discussed in full hearing of a deckful of sailors, some knights whose loyalty was yet to be tested, and a couple of Saxon mercenaries who had only joined his company at York. 'Later,' he murmured.

Nodding her understanding, she stroked her son's head, lulling him, he supposed.

Richard leaned back against the side of the ship, while Emma turned her face to the sun and closed her eyes. For all her beauty, she was an easy woman to sit with, he realised, surprised. Companionable. She didn't make a man feel he had to speak unless he wanted to. He studied her profile, the high brow, the upturned nose that was so like her sister's, the full lips. She was wearing the limp green gown she had worn when she had come to the castle, begging for work.

That sumptuous pink gown was much more pleasing, shamefully pleasing. Richard could not say why that was, because the pink gown was not in itself indecent, but something about it made him want to tease it from her so that he could discover if what lay beneath was as promising as he imagined.

Did she have other gowns like it? He doubted it. Emma would need more clothes while he decided what to do with her. Richard frowned. But they must be sensible ones; it wouldn't do for her to distract his knights from their duties.

Oh, Lord. Richard's frown deepened. At Beaumont, Emma would most certainly meet Lady Aude. Yes, Emma must get some good clothing. And as soon as they arrived at the Castle, he would explain that he was going to find her a husband.

But she definitely needed more gowns. Perhaps he should have thought of it before, but he had been so eager to reach Normandy that he had hustled them out of Wessex with scarcely time for thought.

'What's the matter, my lord?' She had caught him staring at her.

'Nothing.'

Blue eyes narrowed. 'I can see *something* is wrong…'

'I was thinking about my cousin's fiancée.'

'Ugly Aude?' Her lips twitched.

Diable, she had remembered. 'I wish you would forget I said that, I have the feeling it will be held against me. But, yes, I was thinking of Lady Aude. She will be waiting for my arrival at Castle Beaumont.'

'How will she react when she sees me?'

Richard's jaw tensed. 'She will accept you.'

'She may not be so compliant, my lord.'

'She will if I order her.'

Emma lifted a brow and said nothing.

'But your attire does leave something to be desired.'

'I have the pink gown—'

'That,' Richard said firmly, 'is too rich a gown for every day. I would not wish you to wear that about the Castle.'

Her eyes went wide. 'It is a perfectly decent gown, Cecily chose it!'

'Nevertheless, that is my wish.'

She bowed her head, giving every indication of obedience. 'Very good, my lord.' Her veil fluttered.

Richard had the niggling feeling that far from indicating her agreement, she was in fact hiding her eyes from him. With an exasperated sound, he flicked at her skirt. 'Emma, this simply will not do.'

She sent him a wry look. 'I dress like a washerwoman, you mean.'

'I didn't say that.'

That nose lifted. 'Well, until a couple of days ago that is what I was, a washerwoman.'

'Is that truly all you were, a washerwoman?'

'What do you mean?'

'Emma, I found you in the Staple—'

'I was selling the pink gown!' Henri murmured a sleepy protest and she lowered her voice. 'Why will you not believe me? You are the most stubborn of men.'

'Be that as it may, we have made our agreement and if time had not been so pressing this should have occurred to me sooner.' He smiled. 'You will need respectable clothes, more gown and veils and…and silk girdles and suchlike. And shoes that look as though they were made for a noblewoman rather than a ploughboy.'

She bit her lip and yanked her skirts over boots that even the most partial of admirers would not call elegant. 'At least I can ride in these. But I…I expect you are in the right.' Unexpectedly, she smiled. 'We can't have Lady Aude thinking you have chosen a beggar for your concubine.'

Impulsively, Richard took her hand and kissed her slender, work-reddened fingers. He was conscious of his two Saxon mercenaries, watching them, but what harm? They were men of the world; he had hired them after a particularly brutal skirmish near York. 'You always look charming, even when you are wearing a dress that is the colour of pond slime.'

'Pond slime? Why, do be careful, my lord, my head will be turned by such flattery.'

The ship juddered and a sailor tossed a hawser to the dockside.

Richard was grinning as he pushed himself to his feet. Taking the child from her, helped her up. Across the deck, Geoffrey and the knights were steadying the horses ready to lead them off as soon as the gangplank was lowered. Animals were usually unloaded before cargo.

She touched his arm. 'Do we go to Beaumont this evening, my lord?'

For himself, Richard would have Roland off the ship and be in the saddle in no time. He still might, Roland would need exercising after the stress of the sea-crossing, horses never took them well. The hounds could come, too. He glanced at the child, at the child's mother. 'No, my lady, not tonight. Henri is tired.'

'Yes, he is. I...I thank you, my lord.'

'Tonight we will lodge in an inn. We shall leave for Beaumont in the morning. Perhaps you may use what is left of the day to see to your wardrobe.'

Her gaze was steady. 'Yes, I must not let you down. Nor must I alienate Lady Aude.' Her mouth edged up at the corner. 'It is a thin line you would have me tread, my lord.'

Richard nodded. The wind had teased a long strand of hair out from under her veil. He had to curl his fingers into his fists to stop himself reaching forwards to tuck it back in place. *In name only*, he reminded himself. *This pretence will not be for long.*

Far too aware of Emma's thigh pressing against his, Richard broke off a piece of bread and dipped it into his soup, a mouthwatering broth, rich with mussels and fish and flavoured with wine. Geoffrey had chosen the inn well. They kept a fine table at the Mermaid, and Richard was ravenous, having spent the evening exercising his animals. He had also hired a mare for Emma to use the next day, since the horse she had ridden from Winchester to Bosham harbour had been returned to the garrison stables. Asa, however, could not ride. Sir Jean had volunteered to have her up behind him, pillion, as they had done on the ride to Bosham.

Richard turned to Geoffrey, seated on his other side. 'God willing, the beds here are as good as the soup. After last night's interruptions, I could do with a full night's sleep.'

'I tested the mattresses, my lord. They are not feather ones, but they didn't seem too bad.'

'Not too many lumps?'

'No, my lord,' Geoffrey said. 'They don't smell musty, either. But we will be sleeping in common.'

'That is only to be expected. It is rare indeed is the tavern that can offer its customers private accommodation. We may count ourselves lucky that there is a curtain to screen us off from the living area.'

'Yes, my lord, I know, but I was thinking of your quarters at Winchester Castle and...'

Richard caught the flash of concern, albeit quickly masked, in his squire's eyes and turned quickly back to Emma. Geoffrey knew he was having trouble sleeping. Hell. Richard had never had trouble sleeping, not until York.

Emma's thigh was warm where it rested against his. After they had disembarked from the ship, he had pressed a purse into Emma's hand and sent her off in search of new attire with the maid and Sir Jean as her escort. Her skirts were heather coloured this evening rather than the muddy green; she had clearly had some success at the Honfleur market. This gown had a much finer weave; it was good cloth, practical but attractive. The purplish hues made her eyes seem bluer than ever.

'I like this soup.' Emma sent him one of those irresistible smiles. It made him long to forget his resolution not to make her his mistress. Beside her, Henri was eating with as much relish as his mother. In between mouthfuls, he was slipping pieces of bread under the table to Prince. Richard pretended not to notice.

'You are no longer feeling ill, I see.'

'No, thank goodness. At the time I never thought I would eat again.'

'I am glad you are recovered.' He glanced at her gown. 'I see you found the market.'

'Yes, my lord.' She reached for her wine.

Delicately shaped hands, Richard noticed, not for the first time. *Hands that surely had not been made for pounding linen from dawn to dusk.* Hands that Richard wanted to feel on his skin again, as soon as possible. *In name only.* Hastily, he called his thoughts to order. But Emma's mouth was moist from her drink. He wanted to kiss her, to take the taste of Emma mixed with wine onto his tongue. In his dreams perhaps, if he won a little sleep. Richard shook himself and tried to listen to what she was saying.

'We were in luck, my lord, we found two gowns that had been made up for someone who had failed to collect them, and the length was perfect.'

'Two? You will need more than two.'

'We bought fabric also. Enough to make two *more* gowns and…a cloak. Surely that will be enough?'

'Shoes?'

'No, my lord. I…I…' She looked away, colour rising.

He touched her arm. 'What?'

She ducked her head, whispering under her breath, 'I felt uneasy spending your money. I wanted to give you some back.'

'Emma, listen to me. We have an agreement.' *Until Beaumont, that is. And it is all pretence.* But as those blue eyes raised to meet his, Richard realised he was finding it increasingly difficult to remember that. He wanted Emma of Fulford, and every time he looked at her his good intentions seemed to fly out of his head.

It was a pity he had not found Frida appealing; it had evidently been far too long since he had had a woman. Every time he looked at Emma he wanted her. And she, she was Cecily's sister… Lord. 'You must have suitable clothing. Two gowns are not enough.'

'I have the pink one, too, don't forget that.'

An image of Emma wearing the pink gown in the tower room at Winchester leaped into his mind. She had been flushed then, with his kisses. 'How could I forget it?'

'My lord?'

Richard tore his eyes from her lips. 'We shall make do with what you have for the moment. We will be passing through Falaise on our way to Beaumont. Perhaps you may find more there. And shoes. The market at Falaise has more to offer than the one here.'

She set her cup down and fingered her skirts. 'You don't like this?'

'It is fine, for travelling. The colour suits you better than—'

'Pond slime?' She lifted an eyebrow. Her eyes gleamed in the torchlight, and Richard found himself on the receiving end of another of those lethal smiles. *Saint Denis, save him.*

The talk drifted on to other matters, from the length of the ride from Honfleur to Falaise to a discussion on the merits of the mare Richard had hired for her. Finally, she noticed Henri drooping over his bowl. 'My lord, if you will excuse us?'

'Of course.'

Pallets had been set out on the other side of the fire. Richard remained at table while Emma and Asa led Henri past the looped-back curtain.

Emma twisted back her veil as she bent over her son, and Richard allowed his gaze to linger on her shape. It was a fine shape, with a narrow waist and a gentle outwards flare at the hips, all woman. Lady Emma of Fulford could tempt a saint whatever she wore. Uncomfortable, he shifted on the bench. 'Geoffrey?'

'My lord?'

'I know you said we are sleeping in common, but are there any screens behind that curtain?'

Geoffrey frowned. 'No, my lord. It is set up as a single sleeping chamber.'

'There is not even a division for male and female?'

'I am afraid not, my lord. I am sorry if you do not approve, but I was told the Mermaid provided the best suppers in Honfleur. And despite the bed-chamber being open to the rest of the inn, thieves are not thought to work here.'

'It is fine, Geoffrey. Better, perhaps.' At the far end, the women had found blankets. Emma was tugging off Henri's shoes and unbuckling his belt. 'It is reassuring to know they will be within hail.'

Having to keep awake to watch out for Emma and Henri was in fact the last thing Richard needed, but he probably wouldn't be doing much sleeping in any case. *Merde*. What with his recurring nightmare, this newfound lust for Emma of Fulford would be hard to bear if he could not satisfy it.

'Geoffrey?'

'My lord?'

'Keep an eye on them for me.'

Geoffrey's jaw dropped. 'That is to take precedence over my duties to you?'

'No, of course not, just watch over them whenever you can. Particularly if I am not close to hand.'

'Yes, my lord.'

'If I have to go out tonight and you need me, it is likely you would find me in the stables.'

'Yes, my lord, I know.'

Chapter Nine

It had been some time since Count Richard's entourage had taken to the pallets behind the sleeping curtain, but Emma lay wide-eyed and restless. The inn blankets were scratchy and she really was not comfortable in a room full of strangers.

The mattress rustled with her slightest movement. Of course, this was not the first time Emma had slept in common, but the Mermaid was a world away from her father's mead hall. Emma had grown up at Fulford Hall and she knew everyone. More recently, she had slept in the mill with Gytha and her husband, Edwin, but they were certainly not strangers.

Even last night in Count Richard's bedchamber Emma had managed to sleep after she had grown used to the unnerving silence. It had been so peaceful in that lofty tower. Further, she had known without a shadow of doubt that, even if Judhael discovered where she was hiding, there would be no way he would follow her into Winchester Castle bailey, never mind the private chambers of the garrison commander. She had been safe.

As she was tonight, for Count Richard occupied the pallet next to her. He was asleep. She had seen him put his sword close to hand before covering it with his blanket.

Emma sighed. Yesterday night she had been in Winchester, in *England*. Today she had travelled further than most people travelled in their entire lives; she had crossed the Narrow Sea. This was foreign land, this was *Normandy*. Of course, her mother had been born here. Emma had imagined that she would feel pleasure to see the Duchy, but one thought dominated.

Judhael. Count Richard's departure from Winchester—his *conroi*, the horses, the dogs—could hardly be called covert. Half the town must have witnessed her riding out in his company. Had anyone told Judhael? And Count Richard's destination was no longer a secret. Might Judhael take it into his head to follow her to Beaumont?

Saints. She chewed on a fingernail. Would Judhael be haunting her for the rest of her days?

Tears pricked at the back of her eyes. Impatiently, she blinked them away. One could feel very alone in a roomful of people—how strange.

Henri was snug in the pallet on her right, her son, whom she adored. This journey was for him, Emma reminded herself, to keep him safe. And she did have friends in Winchester; perhaps no one would tell Judhael where she had gone. And even if he did follow her, the pursuit must take him some time. Yes, surely she could dismiss him from her mind, for a while...

A horn lantern hung on a wall hook over her bed. Others were dotted about the sleeping area, warm glowings in the gloom. In the dim light Prince the mongrel was just visible, curled up at Henri's feet. And beyond Henri, a bump on the pallet beyond. Asa.

Asa was Saxon. Emma had already begun to like her, and if Count Richard was to be believed, Asa was to be her personal maid, at least for the duration of Emma's arrangement with him.

Neither Henri nor Asa were having difficulty sleeping. Logically there was no need for Emma to be worrying, since Richard had ordered that his party occupy the entire corner of the room. Doubtless, he had grouped them together for safety. And, judging by the heavy snoring coming from one of the Saxon mercenaries and one of the knights, their escort did not feel threatened here.

In short, everyone was perfectly content except her. At that moment, the person on Emma's left hand flung back his blanket and mumbled in his sleep.

Well, perhaps not quite everyone….

Emma did not want to look his way, lest anyone should see. Yes, she felt safe with Richard at her side, but she also felt shame. She was to become his mistress and she did not know how to behave, feeling awkward about the arrangement. He had said nothing to any of their companions about her status, nothing that might embarrass her; nevertheless, it seemed that the role of mistress would take some getting used to. And, while no disparaging remarks had come her way, Emma was continually bracing herself to receive them.

Count Richard had been the last of their party to take to his bed. Emma had feigned sleep when he had appeared, though she had to admit to being glad it was he who was sleeping next to her and not one of the knights. Hearing another indistinct mutter—was he having a nightmare?—Emma held her breath and listened.

Movement. It sounded as though he was fighting with his blankets. He groaned and then clearly, some words came to her.

'Hold! *Hold*, I say!'

More muttering, a sharp intake of breath, a muted groan. Silence.

'Merde.'

The bed ropes groaned; he must be sitting up. Turning her head a fraction, Emma peeped out. Yes, Richard was awake, he was pulling on his boots, putting on his cloak. He was moving away; first came soft footsteps, then a gentle rattle of curtain rings and a rush of cold air.

Emma bolted upright. What hour was it? Midnight must be long past. Earlier, she had been embarrassed and not a little shamed to find the man who had bought her for his mistress publicly settling down next to her, but with Richard gone, any hope of sleep had apparently fled. She had to admit, she did feel safer with him close by.

What was he doing?

Pushing back the itchy blanket, Emma grabbed her boots and cloak and slipped through the curtain in time to see the tail of Richard's cloak whisk through the door. The latch clicked shut behind him.

Embers glowed on the hearth. A couple of sailors were slumped over an upturned wine jug, another cast a bleary look in her direction. Taking one of the horn lanterns from its hook, Emma walked briskly to the door.

The stables—Richard would be looking in on his beloved war-horse.

Following his broad-shouldered figure across the yard, she saw him lean heavily on the stable door post as he went in. Likely he was still half-asleep.

Gathering up her skirts to keep them clear of the straw, she followed. Dark. Quiet. The soft harrumph of a horse.

'Lord Richard?' She lifted the lantern.

He was standing with his back to her, arms braced against an empty manger. His head was bowed, his dark hair was tousled and he gave no sign that he had heard her. He must have been looking into Roland's stall; she could see the pale gleam of the big grey's coat as he shifted from one foot to the other.

'Richard?'

He raised his head, but he did not seem to see

her. His hand was clenched, the knuckles bone-white. Emma's blood went cold. His eyes were silver in the lamplight, unearthly, and there was no recognition in them, none whatsoever. The two wolfhounds sat motionless at his feet, like stone sentinels.

She drew closer, skirts catching in the hay. 'My lord, it is Emma.'

'Emma?' There was a blankness in his voice, too, as if he had never even met her, let alone chosen her to be his mistress.

The hairs rose at the back of her neck. Richard's brow was gleaming with sweat. How odd. To be sure, the animals warmed the stable, but it was nowhere near as warm as it had been in the inn. Something was wrong here, very wrong. Tentatively she reached out, touched that clenched fist. 'Can you not sleep either? Richard, what is it?' Remembering the way he had called out, she added, 'Did you have a nightmare?'

He blinked, shook his head and stared for a moment at her hand, before slowly uncurling his fingers and linking them with hers. His grip was like iron, grinding her bones, and she had to brace herself not to flinch. She sensed, rather than saw, the moment he came back to himself.

'Yes, since York I... Never mind, it was just a dream.' The dazed look had gone, he was fully awake. 'Just a bad dream.'

Recalling that isolated bedchamber in the tower of Winchester Castle, Emma looked up at him and wished she could see into his mind. She wriggled her fingers and his grip eased. It could not be easy bearing his heavy responsibilities. As a commander, so many looked to him for decisions from dawn to dusk. He deserved some peace. And, yes, he had long been in the habit of coming to the stables for snatches of it, she realised. He did not like people to know about his nightmares and the animals would not mind if he shouted in his sleep.

Hadn't she found him in the stables with his animals when she had come in search of work at the castle? Animals do not pester you with questions or, as she had done that day, with petitions for help. They accept you as you are, just another man. The powerful man she had chosen as her protector was, it seemed, not completely invulnerable. But he had his pride; he would not want to discuss it.

She made to pull away. 'My lord, you are tired. I shall leave you in peace.'

He laughed and, releasing her, flexed his

shoulder. 'Tired? You might say that, but I doubt that I shall sleep.'

'Your shoulder disturbs your rest also, I think.'

His head tilted to one side as he reached out and took the lantern from her. 'Emma, why did you follow me?'

'I could not sleep, either. I thought perhaps we might talk, but I see you need rest.'

'Talk? I would be more than happy to talk.' Richard found a hook for the lantern and turned back with a grin. The strange mood brought about by his dream had lifted—helped by Emma's appearance in the stable. He stared down at her. She looked lovely. Beneath the hood of her cloak her hair gleamed like gold. She had removed her veil and loosened her braid when she had gone to bed, but she was still wearing the heather-coloured gown.

'I am not the only one to find sleep elusive. You are nervous of sleeping among strangers,' he said.

'Yes.'

Her smile was shy and very beguiling. And it was astonishingly powerful, reaching deep inside him. Emma of Fulford looked beautiful tonight. But then she always did, whether standing by the Itchen in rough work clothes or standing in his bedchamber in Winchester in that pink gown. 'It would not matter what you wear,' he muttered.

'My lord?'

'Richard, remember?'

She gave him another of those exquisite smiles, shy yet flirtatious—the combination was lethal— and Richard felt his thoughts beginning to scramble. Did she know what she was doing?

He had dragged her out of the Staple, concerned that already Emma of Fulford had become one of Hélène's girls. But all day he had been studying her and he had come to the conclusion that he might have misjudged her. It was obvious she had needed money; perhaps she *had* been selling the gown. Just the gown.

It would be good to know for sure. Perhaps, if he tested her, he might learn the truth. He would not go too far, Adam would never forgive him if he took advantage of her, but a test, a small test. And she was amenable, she had asked to become his mistress…

The brooch at her cloak winked in the light. Beneath the cloak her breast rose and fell. *Yes*, Richard thought, *a little test*…

Gently, he touched her cheek. 'Perhaps, as I do, you think it is time.'

'Time?' Emma's heart began to race, her stomach tightened. Richard's pupils had darkened, they looked almost black, save for a rim of silver. Did he mean what she thought he meant?

'Our agreement. It is time you fulfilled your…obligations.'

She bit her lip. He was standing with the lantern beside him and while she stared up at him, he shifted so his broad shoulders blocked out the light. She could no longer see his eyes. His fingers had found her ear; they were busily tracing the shape of it, gentle but determined. 'I…I…so soon?'

'Soon? It does not seem too soon to me, *ma petite*. Today has dragged as though it were an eternity.' A strong arm reached for her and Emma found herself pulled against that broad chest. 'I can wait no longer. You had a reprieve last night because of Henri, but I have need of you tonight, and since you have so fortuitously sought me out…'

Heart beginning to pound, she lifted a brow, and tried for a lofty tone. 'Here in the hay, my lord?'

'Yes, Emma, here in the hay.'

'With the animals?'

'I promise you they are very discreet.'

'But, Richard, I—'

His mouth came down on hers and her objections were left unspoken. He gave her no chance to protest. Indeed, her legs went swoony in an instant; he scattered her protests to the four winds. Pushing her cloak aside, his hands were on her hips, pulling her securely against him. But objections remained, swirling in the back of her mind. It was unexpected, it was too soon, she hardly knew the man—mind you, she had known Judhael her whole life, she had *loved* Judhael, and what good had that done her?

Emma liked the feel of Richard of Beaumont; his certainty dizzied her. He was so tall, so strong and—she could feel him, hard against her belly— leaving her in no doubt that he wanted her.

Thank God, this was her safe time.

Emma's friendship with Hélène had made her privy to many women's secrets, and chief of these was the knowledge that certain times of the month were safer for the indulging of carnal appetites. She had been woefully ignorant when she and Judhael had become lovers, but since then she had taken the trouble to learn. That was why she knew that this was her safe time. Henri was a great blessing in her life, but a second child out of wedlock? No! Of course, last night in Winchester Castle Richard had promised to take care of any child they might have, and she believed she could trust him in that regard, nevertheless…

'Love me, Emma.' His voice was dark with desire.

'Someone might come in, and the…the dogs,' she protested, weakly.

Sighing, he looked at the hounds and clicked his fingers. Immediately they left the stall, passing out of her line of sight.

'They will sit by the door and act as our guard. Better?'

'Yes…no…that is…'

'Kiss me, Emma. This time you must kiss me, I want you to woo me.'

'You want *me* to woo *you*?'

His smile was crooked. She had the strangest feeling he was observing her most intently. 'Yes, that is what you do, is it not? Seduce me, show me what you learned at the Staple.'

She swallowed, paralysed by shyness. 'Now?'

'Yes, Emma, now. I want your hands on me.'

There was no point repeating that she was not used to this—he did not seem to believe her.

Besides, it was too late, she had accepted his protection, the passage to Normandy, his coin. She was bound to him.

Reaching up, Emma pushed her hands into his hair. It was easier than she might have expected, though her hands had begun to tremble. His hair was thick and silky and as she ran her fingers through it, he leaned into her caress, grey eyes watchful. That slight smile lingered on his lips, and when she stroked the back of his neck, his eyes half-closed, like a cat's. There was not a trace of the vulnerability she had glimpsed when she had followed him into the stables.

'You like touching me, Emma, don't pretend otherwise.'

Murmuring agreement, Emma was fast discovering she did like touching him; her hands caressed his ears, his cheekbones. Tentatively she found his mouth, tracing the shape of his lips, a shape that had attracted her from the first. Turning his head, he drew her finger inside, teased it with his tongue. Tingles started up in her stomach, her breath was becoming uneven. And always he was watching her through those half-closed eyes, observing her reaction.

His request for her to woo him was hardly surprising, given the agreement they had made. But Emma did not feel ready for this. Surely one should know a man before…before…

However, Richard of Beaumont was not an easy man to gainsay. He had pushed her hood back and his hands were playing in her hair, loosing it, spreading it over her shoulders like a second cloak. And, for all that he was such a powerful man, taller and stronger than Judhael, his movements were gentle and unhurried. The way his eyes, dark and almost black at this moment, were looking at her…the word *reverent* came to mind. But underneath the gentleness she glimpsed ruthless determination. He would not be crossed in this. They had made their agreement, he had bought her, and he would have her.

Going up on her toes, Emma pressed her lips to his cheek. She could feel stubble on his chin, she could smell him, that purely male scent that was Richard. She recognised it from his pillow last night and from the kisses they had shared in the tower room.

'You are elf-fair,' he whispered in her ear as he nipped at her ear-lobe, her neck. 'Hair like moonbeams.'

It was hard to breathe here in the stables. And,

as Emma sank down with Richard on to sweet, clean straw, she wondered if he expected her to protest. Shame on her, but she wasn't going to. Apparently, it wasn't simply her body that was conspiring with him in this seduction, her mind was too. The shame of it....

Her cheeks were burning. He was covering them with kisses even as he lay her in the prickly straw. He was muttering incoherently in French. She caught the words, *ma belle*, *chérie*, as he stroked her breasts through the heather-coloured gown. Her breasts swelled. She wished he was touching her naked skin, she wished she was touching his naked skin. Yet more shame. Richard made her feel wanton; with him she *was* wanton. Lust, this was lust. How dreadful. Emma did not love this man, but his touch was firing her blood. Saints.

'Roses,' he muttered.

'Hmm?'

Smiling, Richard drew back to look at her even as his hand swept her body from breast to thigh and she shuddered with pleasure. Straw shifted. 'You smell of roses, exotic roses.'

'Cecily gave me some scent.' Why was it so hard to speak? 'I...I do not think it was made in England.'

'Mmm.'

He had lost interest in the rose scent, he was tugging at the hem of her skirts, eager fingers were sliding up her calves, over her thighs…

Richard was desperate, desperate to have her. It was becoming increasingly hard to remember that he was only testing her, that he must not bed her in truth. His thoughts had never been so tangled. *Mistress in name only. Adam. Must not take advantage.* As he dragged up her skirts, he pressed his face into the fragrant warmth of Emma's neck, kissing every inch of skin that he could get at. Which was not much. The neckline of her gown was ridiculously high.

Pulling back for a moment, he scowled at it. She had chosen a remarkably modest gown. Had she chosen it deliberately to keep him at bay? Oddly, it was having the opposite effect on him. He burned for her, he burned.

Richard dipped his head again, cupping a breast through the heather-coloured fabric while he fumbled with increasing impatience for side-lacings. He did not want to shame her by taking her naked in a stable, not when a stable-boy might walk in on them, but he ached to touch more of her skin. *Must not take advantage…*

'Damn.'

'What's the matter?'

'No lacings.'

She bit her lip and the flush on her cheeks went a couple of shades darker. 'They are at the back, my l—Richard.'

'Safely out of reach, eh?'

'Y-yes.'

Her bashfulness was adorable, it had him utterly disarmed. Was it calculated? He did not think so. Somehow Emma of Fulford had kept her innocence, which was extraordinary in a woman who had born a child out of wedlock. Still he had to be sure, he did not want the test to end quite yet….

'It's a good trick, the innocence,' he said.

'Innocence?'

'Never mind.'

Richard found her shy seduction of him completely enthralling. When she had gone up on her toes like that and had kissed him so tentatively, she had shifted his mood abruptly from that of a man who needed a woman but who could control his needs, to a man who needed a particular woman: her. As for control…his mind clouded, he was all need.

Worse, she was making him feel that there might be a real connection between them, that the physical act with Emma of Fulford might be more that the mere spilling of his seed. Richard could not recall anyone else making him feel like that.

His mind was no longer under his command. He was only testing her, and he was guiltily aware he ought to stop, but even his hand had developed a mind of its own, moving without him willing it. 'It must be a knack,' he muttered, watching as his hand traced the fascinating warmth of her inner thigh.

'Hmm?'

Confused, Richard looked into her eyes and the sense that this was not simply a roll in the hay intensified. Those blue eyes were focused entirely on him, her pupils had dilated in the lamplight and, for a second or two, he knew—he *knew*— that if he were the only man in her world, his life would be so much richer. 'Madness.'

'Hmm?'

'You are a clever woman, Emma of Fulford.'

Her fingers had crept to the ties of his hose and as they trailed tentatively over his stomach he shuddered. 'Lord!'

She snatched her fingers back. 'No?'

Taking her hand in his, he returned it to his body, to that part of him that was straining for her touch. 'Yes,' he managed. The promptings of his conscience were by now mere whispers in the back of his mind, he could hardly hear them. 'More firmly, sweetheart, more firmly.'

Hot, he was too hot. Wrenching off his cloak, Richard tossed it behind him and only then noticed that Emma was still wearing hers. Perhaps if it was unfastened, it would seem as though he could get at more of her. He tore at her brooch and shoved the cloak aside.

'Richard.' She stroked his cheek, and a small, work-worn finger touched his upper lip. But all the while her other hand, her other hand….

'Mon Dieu!'

He hiked her skirts up to her hips and she bit her lip. It made him want to kiss her and he followed his instincts, losing his tongue in her mouth, playing with hers, pressing his body against her. Her beautiful hair was spread out over the straw; her eyes held him in thrall. He was panting, she was panting.

It was most unsatisfactory. Richard couldn't get at her properly, and he wanted to get at her.

She couldn't get at him—he suppressed another gasp—except for a certain part of his anatomy. He continued exploring the tantalising shadows between her legs. Straw shifted. Heated sighs. She moaned, and his insides tightened. Her body told him it wanted his, and he pushed towards her.

And yet, he was not entirely happy. He longed to free her body from her clothing, but he couldn't. They were in a stable; because anyone might walk in on them, this coupling would have to be one of the quickest and most basic of his life. That damn gown, Richard thought, as he moved over her, kissing the tiny part of her throat that was accessible, there was simply too much of it; a nun's habit wouldn't be more chaste.

But those fingers of hers, they were clever, they knew what they were doing, Emma was helping him, easing him into position, as if she sensed how impatient he was to be in her.

He lifted his head, his conscience forgotten. She *liked* his touch. Her eyes were closed, her cheeks were dark with colour, and her head moved from side to side with each panting breath. Shorter and shorter, her breaths were getting shorter and shorter…

Opening those eyes, she raised her other hand

and brought his head down for a searing kiss. She kissed a lot once she forgot to be shy. Richard rather liked it. Nudging her legs apart, he allowed her to put him where he most wanted to be.

He gave a swift thrust. She gasped as though he had surprised her. Startled by that gasp, not entirely lost to reason, Richard held back, but one of her arms wound round his waist and he forgot everything except that he was inside her.

'Richard.' Acceptance, even satisfaction in her tone.

Richard still longed to be out of his tunic and for her to be out of that damn gown, but that no longer seemed so important. They were one. Her body was fully clothed, but it was firm and it had welcomed him. He drew away and pushed back. Her other hand fisted in his hair, keeping his head next to hers, not that he was in a mind to move away. She was kissing his cheek, his neck. Breathy little moans warmed his ears, moans which came and went in time with his movements.

Moans which would, if he were not careful, have this finished in a moment. *Think, man, think. Make this last.*

Richard managed to snatch at a stray thought, moving faster despite himself. Her apparent innocence…her shyness…it must be genuine. Confusion clouded his mind and he pulled back, smiling at her moan of protest.

Her hair was beautifully disordered, silver skeins trailing about her. Bits of straw everywhere. He found the rhythm again while her fingers clung, urging, helping. No, not innocent. There was Henri, of course, but…

Blue eyes smiled into his and Richard felt his control slipping. There it was again, that peculiar sense of connection. It was in his mind; such things only existed in the old ballads.

'Richard,' she murmured.

Richard was finding it increasingly hard to think, never mind speak. There was an ache in his chest and the tension was building to an irreversible peak. He framed her head with his hands and kissed her into silence.

No more words, no more thought, just this blind animal movement, back and forth, back and forth, yes, *yes*. And she…no, not innocent, not in the least bit shy. Not when her moans and breaths matched his so precisely. Not when her body gripped his so tightly.

They were one: one animal, one being. Here in the straw, they…

With a final push, a shout that was both satis-faction and frustration filled the stall.

And then, after a few soft kisses, a few gentle murmurings, quiet returned.

Holding the guilt at the back of his mind, Richard fell headlong into sleep.

Chapter Ten

Something warm and soft was nuzzling Richard awake.

'Emma.' Richard's lips curved, he reached out….and got an armful of hound and a wet tongue in his eyes.

With a grunt, he sat up and rubbed his face. No Emma, not a trace. The dawn light fell on his cloak. It looked as though the entire garrison had trampled it into the hay. There was Roland, his grey ears twitching over the top of his stall. There was no lantern on the hook; she must have taken it with her.

'Run off, did she, boy?' It was only to be expected. That shyness, Richard was certain, was genuine.

206 Runaway Lady, Conquering Lord

Guilt rushed at him, sobering as a pail of cold water.

What had he done? He had bedded Lady Emma of Fulford as though... Lord, this had not been his intention. He had suspected she found their arrangement awkward, embarrassing, but he had decided that a little temporary embarrassment on her part was a small price to pay if it got her out of Winchester and clear of whatever was haunting her. Once they reached Beaumont, Richard had fully intended releasing her from their supposed arrangement. But now...

This wasn't supposed to happen.

Rising, he shook out his cloak with a frown. He had treated her badly and must somehow make amends. Although...his lips formed a smile, she had not seemed to object. Quite the contrary....

His brow cleared. And he had slept last night— how he had slept! He glanced at the indentation their bodies had left in the straw. Lying with Emma of Fulford had given him the soundest night's sleep in months. If only he could keep her...surely the nightmares would leave him? No, he must be realistic. The reality was that he could not keep her. There was his cousin's obligation to Lady Aude, which he might have to honour, whatever he might say. Hell. He wanted to keep Emma, he wanted her to be his mistress in truth.

Richard nodded as he caught the eye of a sleepy stable-boy as they crossed on the threshold. *'Bonjour.'*

The boy flattened himself against the door frame. *'Bonjour, M'sieur Le Comte.'*

The yard was lost behind grey swirls—a sea fret. The air was damp with it.

Yes, the best cure for his nightmares would surely be to go on sleeping with Emma of Fulford. Somehow he must arrange it.

And Adam and Cecily? How will you explain it to them?

He would find a way. He had to keep Emma of Fulford. Only the next time they slept together, he would make sure they were in a proper bed. He wanted that rare thing in this world, privacy with a woman. Asa could look after the boy while he and Emma… What did she look like naked? His loins ached.

Lord. Grimacing, Richard adjusted his chausses. The sooner he found a decent bed, the better. She wouldn't be running away from him so quickly next time, if he had to tie her down to keep her in place.

Emma was in the habit of running away, it seemed. She had run away from marriage with Adam Wymark in 1066. Richard was under no illusions about her desperate need to accompany him to Normandy. It was only because she was in effect running away again. From that former lover of hers, from Judhael of Fulford. At the end of that first year in England, that man's name had, Richard now recalled, been on everyone's lips. Back then he was known to be ruthless, dedicated to the lost Saxon cause. Time would not have altered that. Richard grimaced, as an unpleasant thought hit him like a blow to the gut. Emma was running away from Judhael—would the time come when she would run away from him?

Thrusting the thought to one side, Richard strode through the mist towards the inn. So what if she ran away again? His heart was not engaged and it never would be. The woman did not live who could capture him mind and soul. His mind was fixed on his county, and his service to Duke William. And after his duties were done? There was little room for anything else.

He squinted skywards. Everything was grey, it was impossible to see past the sea fret. His nostrils twitched—bacon, someone was frying bacon. His stomach growled.

But even though Richard knew it should be an easy matter to replace Emma of Fulford in his life, when he pushed open the door of the Mermaid and saw her at table next to Henri, his spirits lifted.

Their party had broken their fast and Emma and Asa were packing their belongings for the journey, though truth be told, Emma's mind was not on the task—it was back in the stable reliving her moments with Richard. Her previous experiences had left her apprehensive about what she might expect when he bedded her, particularly as she and Richard hardly knew each other. She need not have worried. She was unable to keep a reminiscent smile from playing about her lips as she folded one of Henri's tunics and put it in a saddlebag. Her reticence had been no match for Richard's eagerness. The attraction that she felt for him had undoubtedly weighed in his favour, but one moment above all lived in her mind, the moment when they had become one. He had hesitated, only briefly to be sure, but there had been that heart-warming vulnerability in his eyes when he had looked at her, making certain that she had been content. She sighed. It might be wishful thinking on her part, but she was beginning to think she had found a rare man indeed. Not only was he strong and powerful, but it seemed that he was also a man who at the very moment of their joining took care to see that she was content.

Noticing an unnatural quiet, Emma looked up. Henri was no longer with them. Frowning, she dropped the saddlebag on to the bed. 'Asa, where's Henri?'

Asa glanced across to the space in front of the tables where only moments ago Henri had been playing with Prince. 'I am not sure, he was by the fire with that white dog, he must have wandered off. I am sorry, my lady, I didn't notice. Shall I go and find him?'

'No, I'll go. Asa, take our things to the stables, if you please, the Count is anxious to leave. I won't be long.'

'Yes, my lady.'

Grabbing her cloak, Emma hurried to the door, struck by the irony that since she had agreed to become Richard's mistress, she had in some measure regained her former status. Other people were following his lead in addressing her as 'my lady'.

Outside, a fine drizzle was washing the mist away and the wooden walls of the houses were dark with damp. Emma shrank into her hood and looked to right and left. There were plenty of townsfolk, cloaked like her against the rain, hurrying about their business. A man pulling a handcart; a baker with a tray of loaves shrouded in sacking; a handful of people around a fish stall. But no Henri. Heavens. A cold hand clutched her heart. This was a port and there were dangers in a busy port for a small boy, particularly when that small boy was dangerously fascinated by boats….

By the time Emma reached the harbour she was out of breath. Rain gleamed on the quays. Masts pointed skywards, sails were tightly furled. Ribbons of mist trailed over the sea, but the breeze was strengthening; soon it would blow them away.

The ship they had come in on remained at its mooring, next to another, which Emma had not noticed the previous day. There was no sign of Henri here, either.

On another quay, a group of fishermen, faces

darkened with sun and wind, were sitting on packing crates under an awning, mending their nets. Further off, at the end of one of the jetties, men in one of the fishing boats were getting ready to sail, apparently confident the sea fret would not last.

Wheels rumbled over the planks. Another handcart, a boy taking a load of fish baskets to market—proving that at least one of the fishing boats had been out early, braving the mists. In the cart's wake, a couple of seagulls fought over fallen scraps.

A dog barked. A man shouted.

Prince! The white mongrel was loping along one of the jetties, a fish fast in his mouth and Henri—*Henri*!—was skipping alongside him, grinning from ear to ear.

His path was taking him dangerously near the jetty's edge.

Grabbing her skirts, Emma hurtled towards them. 'Henri, come here!'

'Mama!' Henri, still grinning, waved and turned towards her.

Her son had drawn level with a dockside tavern when the door opened and two men emerged, one with a bucket. The man with the bucket tossed the contents—a stream of fishguts and innards—into the water. Seagulls appeared out of nowhere, screaming, wings flashing.

Henri slipped on the mess and went hurtling towards the edge.

'*Henri!*'

The other man broke step and glanced idly towards Henri.

Emma's heart stopped.

Azor! Azor was in Honfleur? The nightmare was back.

Time seemed to freeze. There was movement, though; the man with the bucket got to Henri first, Emma reached him a moment later, and while she gathered him to her, she was dimly aware of Azor's gaze on her.

When she lifted her head from Henri, Azor was at her side, staring down at her. 'My lady?'

The man with the bucket retreated.

'Azor.' Emma knew her smile must be as frozen as her wits. Azor, here? She had not been granted the reprieve she had prayed for. Her heart began to thump.

Azor's gaze was intent as he took in Henri's features. 'This is your *son*?'

Emma swallowed and wished for a miracle.

'How old is he?'

She hugged Henri to her, tears stinging at the back of her eyes. No words. What could she say? Despite being one of her father's housecarls, Azor had always been Judhael's creature.

Azor caught her arm. 'My lady...this boy... your son...how old is he?'

'Two. I am two and—'

Emma clapped a hand over Henri's mouth. Too late.

Azor's gaze met hers. 'Judhael has a son,' he murmured. His grip tightened and he began pulling her towards a gap between the tavern and the next building. 'Take care, my lady, lest Judhael see you.'

Dread was a wave of nausea that weakened her knees. 'Judhael is in Honfleur as well?' Of course he was, she had known it the moment she had seen Azor.

'Aye. Judhael...as I tried to tell you at the inn, my lady, Judhael is determined to have you back.'

'Someone saw me leave Winchester.' Emma's heart was banging like a drum, her mouth was dry with dread. If she called out, would anyone hear? 'I feared as much.'

'Yes.' Azor's expression softened. 'But do not

fear me, my lady. I know your time with Judhael is over.'

'You do?'

Azor nodded. 'I came to the Staple to speak to you. It is true that Judhael wants you back, but I wanted you to know that I am doing my utmost to persuade him on to another path.'

She stared. 'Truly?'

'Aye, it is no longer safe for us in England.' Azor lowered his voice, a great, shaggy bear of a Saxon with a gentle voice. Why had she only now remembered that? Azor had always had a gentle voice. 'That is what I was trying to tell you. I wanted to warn you to stay out of sight for a few more days. England has nothing to offer us and Judhael…Judhael is a man who needs an occupation.'

'Yes, he always has.' *Azor was trying to help her!*

'So I thought, if we were to become mercenaries, Judhael would have something to fight for, to get involved in. The life of an outlaw has twisted him, but if he found a leader willing to trust him, perhaps he would no longer dwell on the past, on what might have been….'

Emma nodded. Azor was making sense.

Richard employed Saxon mercenaries; indeed, lords in many corners of Christendom were beginning to do the same. And it was beyond question that Judhael's febrile energy had always needed a harness.

'There is much demand for Saxon warriors in other lands,' Azor continued. 'I hope to persuade Judhael to come with me to Apulia.'

'Apulia? Isn't that part of the old Roman Empire, far across the Alps?'

'Not any longer it isn't, not since Robert Guiscard… Never mind, my lady, that is where I hope to take him, Apulia.'

'It must be weeks away.'

'Aye.'

Emma was so startled at what she was hearing that she made no protest when Azor drew her deeper into the alleyway. Dimly she recognised that he was indeed trying to protect her, trying to keep her out of Judhael's sight. As well as the white strands in his beard, there were lines on Azor's face, lines that had not been there when she had known him in Fulford.

'My lady, the Normans in Apulia are carving out kingdoms for themselves. The Eastern Emperor has a fight on his hands.'

'Apulia?' It wasn't easy absorbing the full import of this. Saint Swithun help them, Azor was hoping to take Judhael with him to Apulia....

Azor jerked his head in the direction of the harbour and released her. 'Get away from the port as quickly as you can, my lady. Judhael wants to see you, but I am working on him, trying to make him see that the life of a mercenary is the only thing left for a pair of housecarls who have lost their lord.' He grimaced. 'It is a long road persuading him.'

Emma glanced towards the port and the screaming gulls. 'But surely he knows where to find me? It is no longer a secret where we are going.'

'You go to Beaumont.' Azor's eyes filled with regret. 'Is it true that you have become Beaumont's whore?'

Emma lifted her chin. 'Richard has offered me his protection.'

Azor sighed. 'So it is true. I did not want to believe it, but I can see how such a life might have its appeal.'

Emma drew her head back. 'You are not shocked? Not going to throw names at me?'

A smile of understanding lightened his expression. 'Shocked? When I have put my sword up for hire, the sword that I swore would serve only a Saxon king? No, my lady, you do not shock me. And you have your son to think of. In any case, I hear that Count Richard is not a bad sort—for a Norman.'

'He has hired Saxon mercenaries himself. Two have come with us from Winchester.'

'They could do worse. They say your Count is a good commander, a fair man.'

'Yes.'

'I am hoping Judhael and I shall meet more of his kind in Apulia, men who are ready to give seasoned Saxon warriors a chance. Such men deserve loyalty. I pray he appreciates his good fortune in you.'

Emma blinked away a rush of tears, Azor's matter-of-fact acceptance of her altered, immoral status moved her. 'You won't tell Judhael about Henri?'

'Not I. I was trying to warn you back in Winchester, so that you might stay out of sight until we had gone. Judhael can be like a terrier the way he gets hold of things, and should he learn about the boy…' he shook his head '…I will never convince him to go to Apulia, never. He is still trying to chase after you. His reactions were never temperate.'

'No.' Her smile was sad. 'At the time I thought him moved by great passion. But you are in the right, Azor, Judhael is not a temperate man. You do swear not to mention Henri to him?'

'You have my word.' Azor gave her a gentle shake. 'Get you gone, my lady, and quickly. I will win him round to my way of thinking in the end.'

Emma did not need telling again. The dark bruises on Bertha's wrists and the smoke writhing about the yard at City Mill flashed into her mind. She looked up the alley. 'I can get to the Mermaid that way?'

'The Mermaid? Ah, yes, I saw it last eve. It was too dear for us. Yes, continue down here, turn left, then left again at the end, the Mermaid should be ahead of you. God be with you, my lady.'

'And with you.' Emma started down the alley, Henri tight in her arms.

When she turned, Azor was watching her, a giant bear of a Saxon with premature lines on his face. 'Take care of him, will you, Azor?'

'Don't I always?' He made a shooing motion with his hands. 'Go, and quickly. He could return at any moment.'

Judhael was in Honfleur! The very thought made Emma trip over her skirts as she flew into the stable yard with Henri. Richard was standing at the stirrup of the Saxon mercenary named Godric, deep in conversation. Relief flooded her entire being when she saw him.

He was frowning, but as he looked across his frown cleared. 'My lady, you have kept us waiting.' His words were for his men, but the touch on her arm and the searching look he gave her were for her and her alone.

'I am sorry, my lord, Henri was looking at the boats.' It was a struggle not to look over her shoulder. Judhael—in Honfleur! The saints had surely been watching over her when they let her bump into Azor and not Judhael.

Richard lifted an eyebrow at Henri. 'Would you like another ride this morning, young man?'

Henri held out his arms. 'Please! Henri be squire!'

Richard lifted Henri from Emma, and the part of her mind that was not occupied felt relief that Henri went so easily to him. 'A squire is it today?' Richard grinned. 'I thought you wanted to be a sailor.'

'Squire! Squire!'

'Well, you have some growing to do before

that might happen. But if you sit up with Godric here and do everything he says, we shall see. One day, perhaps.'

Emma hovered at Richard's elbow while Henri was settled before Godric. Godric's mount must be a Saxon packhorse—it was shorter than Roland by several hands—but there was still a long way for a boy to fall.

'Not too high for you, Henri?' she asked.

Henri grinned and clung to the front of Godric's saddle, looking, Emma had to admit, as happy as a lark.

'He's fine,' Richard said, leading her away. 'Which is more than can be said for you, *ma petite*. What's amiss?'

Emma focused on a leaky water trough, on the moss growing beneath it. 'Amiss? Nothing, I was concerned that we had been keeping you waiting, that is all.'

Catching her chin, Richard made her meet his gaze. 'No, that's not it, something has…flustered you. What happened?' His mouth became grim. 'Someone accosted you?'

'No, my lord. It…it was Henri, he got too near the edge of the quay and he slipped. For a moment I thought…' She trailed off. Those grey eyes were very searching at times. 'It is the truth, don't look at me like that!'

Fortunately at that moment, Geoffrey emerged from the stables, leading a mare. Eagerly, Emma turned towards it and made her voice light. 'Is this the horse you have hired for me, my lord? Isn't she pretty?'

With an effort, Emma wrenched her mind out of the obsessive channel it had fallen into. They had been riding for a couple of hours now and for almost every moment of it she had been thinking about the past. About Fulford and Judhael. About Judhael and Henri.

Was it cruel to deny a father sight of his son? No, it was not cruel, her mind answered back. Think about Bertha's wrists and the fire at the mill. Judhael was lucky to have Azor, a loyal friend who was trying to help him. But, friend though he was, Azor had not claimed that Judhael had reformed. And he would have to reform for Emma to want to see him.

After the Saxon defeat in the Great Battle, Judhael had taken to lashing out at her; indeed, he had gone so far as to beat other women, including taking his anger out on the Fulford cook,

Lufu. The Norman invasion had turned the hot-headed Judhael into a dangerous stranger—a bully given to browbeating his fellow rebels, a man who hit women, herself included. What might he not do to a little boy?

Miles had passed unnoticed on the pretty brown mare, Emma realised, while her mind had been looping round and round like a Celtic knot pattern. Round and round and no escape. She forced her gaze outwards.

The road was following the course of a stream and the land hereabouts was thickly wooded. There were no familiar landmarks. This was Normandy, and that was the sum of her knowledge. The last shreds of mist were twisting through the trees—had the sea breezes blown it from Honfleur? Had the fishermen set out to sea? As far as she could tell they had got away from Honfleur without being seen, but was Judhael already on their trail?

Emma ought to feel safe. She was at the centre of a cavalcade currently headed by Richard and a couple of his Norman knights. They were bearing full arms—the shiny helmets, the leaf-shaped shields, the heavy swords. Geoffrey must have been swift to have Richard's shield repainted, for the silver pale running through the crimson field had been replaced by a gold one. Similar pennants fluttered at either end of their troop. And why not? This venture had Duke William's blessing.

This purposeful parade through Normandy was, she supposed, like the trumpeting of a herald, Richard announcing his altered status to any with eyes to see. But Emma could no longer delude herself that she was safe. Judhael knew her destination, and if Azor failed to convince him to set off for Apulia…

The horses' hoofs thudded over last year's dead leaves and beech mast. In the thickets, wood pigeons cooed.

Godric rode beside her with Henri on his lap while the other Saxon mercenary, Theo, followed immediately behind with Sir Jean and Asa. Geoffrey and the other squires brought up the rear.

At the outset, Henri had been wide-eyed and alert, but his eyelids were beginning to droop and the way he was slumping against the mercenary's front warned Emma he was entirely reliant on Godric to hold him in place.

'Are you all right, Godric? Henri is half-asleep.'

Godric smiled. 'Do not worry, my lady. I have him.'

Richard's helmet caught the light as he turned and drew rein to fall in beside her. The way was narrow; he waved Godric ahead.

'Tired, my lady? You have been very quiet.'

'I am fine, thank you.'

'You ride with confidence.' Richard pulled off his gloves and tucked them into his belt. 'You must have ridden much at one time.'

'We had ponies at Fulford. I have missed it.' She shot him a sharp look. It was easier than she had imagined to meet the grey eyes behind that noseguard. Last night when Emma had crept out of the stables, she had been filled with a complex mixture of shame, guilt and delight. Shame at what she had done, at what she had become, and guilt and delight because this man's touch had given her such pleasure. She might have entered into this relationship for protection, but his body delighted her. Saints.

Her mother, Philippa, would turn in her grave if she knew, just as she would have done if she had ever learned about her illegitimate grandson. And if her father had been alive? Thane Edgar would have beaten her, no question.

But, disconcerting though it had been to meet Azor at Honfleur, Azor's ready acceptance of her current status—Count Richard's woman— somehow made it easier for her to come to terms with it, too. How strange. These were difficult and dangerous times.

Four years ago, Emma would have died rather than consider selling herself.

Four years ago, she had been a complete innocent. Four years ago, England had been Saxon.

'Will we reach Beaumont today, my lord?' she asked, careful since they were in company to use his title.

Removing his helmet and looping the strap round the pommel, Richard shook his head. His face was stern; he remained very much the commander, but she could see behind the commander's mask and his grey eyes sent her a look of such warmth that a pang of longing shot through her. It was so powerful it pained her. Would he look at her like that if he knew that Judhael was chasing after her? She did not like keeping secrets from him and longed to confide in him. Foolish girl. Confide in a Norman count?

He ran his hand through his hair. 'Today? No, Beaumont is two or three days' solid riding and maybe longer with your son and the maid.' He grimaced at Asa sitting behind Sir Jean, clinging to the knight's swordbelt as though her life depended on it. Asa was not a natural horse-woman. 'Tonight we will be lodging at Crèvecoeur.'

'Crèvecoeur? The home of your cousin's fiancée?' A hard lump formed just below her breastbone.

'Yes, Lady Aude was indeed born at Crèvecoeur. Her brother Edouard, Count of Corbeil, has held it since their father's death.'

'You go to discuss your cousin's obligations to Lady Aude,' Emma said. Even to her own ears, her voice sounded small. The news discomfited her, badly. But this should not affect her…when they had made their agreement, Richard had told her about Lady Aude, making it plain that he was in some way obligated to the woman. Politically and morally. Back in Winchester, she had thought nothing of it. But that had been before…before…

The grey eyes were fixed on Sir Stephen, the knight at the head of their *conroi*. Richard had much to think about and his mind had left her again.

Emma watched him covertly. He needed allies and it made sense that the Count of Corbeil's sister should marry him. Count Richard of Beaumont would think nothing of taking a wife he could not warm to if it would bring him prestige and advantage. Emma found herself contemplating the line of Richard's nose—so straight—and the thickness of his hair, hair that had felt soft and springy under her fingers. And his hand on the reins, that casual strength, his easy stance on the big grey. All of it attracted her.

Heavens, what was she doing, making an inventory of the man's physical attributes! His political ambitions were far more pertinent.

'Do you need Count Edouard's support, my lord?'

A broad shoulder lifted. 'It could be useful, but he needs mine more. His grandfather was disgraced for a time and his lands declared forfeit.'

'Forfeit?'

'Yes, even today, many of Count Edouard's holdings remain in dispute. His title—Count of Corbeil—is merely a courtesy title.'

'I see,' Emma said, though she didn't see at all. Surely Count Edouard's support must be questionable, if his family had been disgraced?

'However, Lord Edouard will be able to brief me on the latest developments in Normandy.

Some news does, of course, cross the Narrow Sea, but more may be gleaned from someone who is making Crèvecoeur his home.'

Emma nodded. 'I expect Lady Aude will be useful to you in that regard also.'

'She will. Despite their ancestors' dark past, some prestige still attaches to the family. Emma…' he smiled '…I think we should discuss your position in my household. I would have you understand, I will honour my obligations towards you, but I will not flaunt you at Crèvecoeur.'

The hard lump in her chest began to burn, as though she were jealous. Of Ugly Aude? Of a woman Richard did not really want?

'As you will, my lord,' she said, bowing her head. It was then that she was taken by the urge to lash out. It had the force of a tidal wave. Why, she could not imagine, for Richard's words had not hurt her—how could they when he was nothing to her? He was simply a man with whom she had made an agreement, for their mutual benefit. She looked up, narrowing her eyes. 'Crèvecoeur—it is an oddly apt name that Lady Aude bears.'

'Hmm?'

'Crèvecoeur means heartbreak, does it not?'

'You know it does, your French is as fluent as mine. What of it?'

She tipped her head to one side. 'It may not have struck you, my lord, because you have always known her by that name, but it is a cruelly ironic name for a lady who has lost the love of her life.'

That beautifully carved mouth twisted into a bleak smile, but he did not reply. Silence, save for the plodding of the horses' hoofs and the creak of leather.

Already Emma was regretting the urge to wound him. For one thing, she sensed she had not truly hurt him, and she must bear in mind at all times that it was in her interests to keep him sweet, not to alienate him. Whatever had come over her?

'Why that name, though, my lord? Your cousin died only recently, and I take it their family have long been known by it.'

'The name could in some way be connected with the forfeiture of their land…but, no, it cannot be that. The family bore that name before the land was lost. I do not know its origins. I have yet to meet Lord Edouard personally.'

'Oh.'

The pain in Emma's chest was beginning to ease. She sucked in a breath. Good. Because that proved she was not beginning to like him more than she ought to. Her position in his life was uncertain, and, despite his promises about looking after her, he could set her side at whim. She must ever be charming, she must ever entertain. With Judhael at her back she—and Henri—needed Richard de Beaumont more than ever. She was his mistress and only if she remembered that—must charm, must entertain, not wound—would he honour her and keep her safe in his castle at Beaumont.

The land they were riding through was thickly covered with trees. Tall oaks with wide trunks stretched their branches across the road. There was a stream to one side with ash trees marching along its banks. Ahead of them, the forest looked as dark and deep as any in Wessex.

'Where are we, my lord?'

'A few miles outside Pont-l'Evêque.'

A prickling sensation at the back of Emma's neck accompanied the return of that most unwelcome of thoughts—had Judhael seen her running away from the port, was he following them? Gritting her teeth, she fastened her eyes on Sir Stephen at the head of their column and willed herself not to look back. *Don't look back. Remember Lot's wife.*

'Emma, what are you thinking about?'

Sweet Mother, this man's perceptions were subtle indeed for a soldier—he noticed her slightest shift of mood. She snatched at a likely answer, one he might accept. 'I think I will miss England, my lord.'

Leaning across the gap, he briefly ran a finger down her cheek. 'You may return any time you wish.' He smiled. 'Though, naturally, I hope you will choose to stay.'

His shield bumped her thigh. Emma held his gaze, conscious that even the lightest of his touches melted her every defence. His hair was ruffled by the breeze, beautiful thick hair with a chestnut glint to it, and as a lock fell into his eye, she squashed the impulse to smooth it back. He was dangerous, was Count Richard de Beaumont. He fascinated her, and that disarmingly subtle intelligence seemed to invite confidences. Not to mention that his person was attractive enough to undermine the will of a saint. Emma bit her lip. And she was definitely more sinner than saint, as last night had so conclusively proved.

Richard distracted her so much, she was in danger of losing sight of her motives in accompanying him to Normandy. Henri must be kept safe, and to that end she must start a new life which might or might not—her heart contracted—involve remaining with this man.

He touched her nose, the gentlest of touches.

More defences melted inside.

His hand fell away, his shield nudged her hip. 'In any case…' he stared over Roland's ears and cleared his throat '…you have become my mistress in truth.'

She frowned, conscious of a sinking sensation. 'Was that not what you intended from the first?'

'Not exactly. I…' the lean cheeks darkened '…I confess I misunderstood your motives for being in the Staple.'

'You wanted to save me from myself.'

'Yes. I had no intention of making you my mistress in truth. Last night was not meant to happen. I am sorry.'

He was apologising? Did this mean he no longer wanted her? No, *no*, she needed him! Emma gripped the reins. 'You are trying to go back on our agreement?'

But he had abruptly ceased to listen. At a shout from the head of his entourage, he had spurred forwards and the intimate moment was lost.

Chapter Eleven

Later, Richard again fell back to check on her and their conversation could resume.

'Emma, listen to me. I am trying to treat you with the honour your innocence deserves.'

Emma looked meaningfully at Henri. 'My lord, I am not innocent.'

'No, but neither do you belong at the Staple. I was mistaken in you and for that I apologise. Last night I was carried away and I treated you badly. Adam and Cecily would have me pilloried.'

'Adam and Cecily are not here. Please, my lord, do not set me aside.'

The grey eyes seemed to look into her soul. 'You are content for our agreement to stand?'

'More than content.'

His knee nudged her thigh. 'Emma, will you not trust me with what is troubling you?'

She tore her gaze away and stared at an approaching oak. 'No, my lord.'

He sighed. 'We shall discuss this further, my lady. But in the meantime, I would still have you accompany me to Beaumont.'

She sent him a sidelong glance. 'You promised me a knight as a husband.'

'Did I?'

'Yes, you did. But originally—' she kept her voice light '—I thought to seek out my mother's family—'

'Not yet awhile.' Again his lean cheeks darkened. 'I took advantage of you in the stable and I would be certain there is no child as a result. Besides, I enjoy your company.'

'My lord, I enjoy yours also,' Emma said. And that, she realised, was not flattery but the plain truth; she did enjoy his company. 'I am perfectly happy that our arrangement should stand.'

He rubbed the bridge of his nose. 'Emma, I will be honest with you. It is likely that I shall have to marry Lady Aude, but it is you whom I want in my bed. And not just for pleasure, but as my mistress, my chosen mistress. I can talk with you, I am beginning to enjoy your company and I would like it for longer.' He grinned lopsidedly. 'I think you might be an acquired taste, tart as you are at times.'

'Thank you, my lord.' She made her voice dry. Tart? *Tart?*

Reaching across, he took her hand and squeezed it. 'I will provide well for you and Henri, for as long as you are content with our agreement. But please understand this, you would be my honoured mistress.'

'Yes, my lord, I am content.' *Save for the fact of your marriage to Ugly Aude.* That rankled, more than it should. But, none the less, Emma felt her mood lifting. Richard was not about to discard her. And if she wanted his continuing protection—she would *not* look over her shoulder, Judhael was *not* following her—she must go on pleasing him.

His smile lit his face. 'Good, I am glad you wish our agreement to stand, but I want you to understand that tonight, when we reach Crèvecoeur, we will not be together. It is one thing for you to become my mistress, but quite another to flaunt you before my bride's brother.'

'I understand, of course.' *Charm. Entertain.*

Smiling what she hoped was her most beguiling smile, Emma made a show of looking about her. The road was beginning to climb, brambles were twisting along the track, interspersed here and there with the yellow flare of gorse. 'The mist has lifted, my lord. At last I may see some of your country.'

The town of Crèvecoeur was little more than a village, much smaller than Winchester. A few ramshackle streets hugged the road leading to the castle, which was a simple motte and bailey like the ones King William had thrown up in England shortly after the Great Battle. There were no stone buildings that Emma could see, and an air of dilapidation hung over the place. The inhabitants stopped to stare, eyes dark with suspicion.

Strangers in Crèvecoeur.

Women and children dived for cover. Doors and shutters snapped shut as they rode past. A shiver ran down Emma's spine.

Ahead, Crèvecoeur Castle was lit by the evening sun. It sat on a rise above the houses, and like the town it appeared to be built entirely of wood. A moat surrounded the palisade, but it needed dredging; the ducks were swimming through pondweed. And surely those trees at the base of the palisade should be cut back? Emma was no military strategist, but years at her father's knee enabled her to see that the trees offered handhold and foothold to anyone wishing to break in. Why, her Henri could climb them blindfold!

Their party trotted over the moat through the deepening twilight, hoofs beating hollow on the boards. The gates opened into a grassy inner yard, where a herd of goats was grazing at one end. Goats? In the bailey?

Doors were hanging off the stables at crazy angles, the thatch was bald in places and even as Emma looked she could see why. As a thrush landed on the roof of an outbuilding, it twitched a loose straw from the roof and flew off with it.

It would appear that Crèvecoeur had been deliberately run down. Lord Edouard's grandfather might have forfeited his lands, but whoever had been given stewardship of this place—their neglect was criminal. When had Lord Edouard regained possession? Unless he was incompetent in the extreme, it must have been only recently.

Beside her, Richard was eyeing Crèvecoeur in

grim-jawed silence, his face a studied blank, but Emma knew he was as startled as she. They exchanged glances.

Emma received a tight smile and a nod and then Richard dug in his spurs and urged Roland to the head of their *conroi* to meet the Count of Corbeil.

After that silent exchange of glances, Richard was as good as his word. He did not flaunt Emma of Fulford at Crèvecoeur. In truth, he ignored her. That curt nod, that almost insignificant exchange of looks, was to be the last private contact between them for some time.

While Richard sought conference with Lord Edouard, Emma was shown into the hall by a gangling, buck-toothed maidservant and told to make herself at home. It was a relief to find that her presence in Richard's entourage had been tactfully explained with half-truths. She was an Anglo-Saxon noblewoman in search of her mother's family in Normandy. Hearing of Count Richard's journey, she had begged passage with him that he might escort her to her family.

It was no surprise that the lodgings at Crèvecoeur were rudimentary, and after a basic but surprisingly satisfying meal of bread and venison, Emma found herself setting out pallets for Henri and herself. Asa and Geoffrey would be sleeping nearby, thank goodness.

There had been no sign of Richard for over an hour. As Emma stretched out on the mattress, the maidservant pinched out the candles on the table. The fire glowed. A dog yawned.

Emma stared up at the sooty rafters, the charcoal-coloured walls. This hall was very like her father's, except that her mother had had the walls of Fulford Hall freshened with limewash each spring. These were grey and pockmarked with holes that looked to have been made with an arrow. Had someone been using them for target practice? There was no doubt, Emma thought, half-asleep already after the long ride, her father would have put the man who had stewarded this place straight in the stocks.

Henri was sound asleep; playing at squire on Godric's lap had worn him out. Emma allowed her eyelids to drift shut, and while she listened to the rustlings of Asa and the others readying themselves for bed, her tired mind struggled to make sense of the odd scraps of information she had managed to pick up since arriving.

Lord Edouard, holder of the courtesy title of Count of Corbeil, was younger than she had expected, not much more than twenty. While he appeared to be energetic, she gathered he had indeed only recently returned to Crèvecoeur. This went some way to explaining the general air of dereliction.

The Comte de Corbeil had fallen on Richard as though he were a long-lost friend, and had born him off to the chapel—another of the slipshod buildings within the palisade—for their conference.

Perhaps Richard could advise him. Lord Edouard certainly looked as though he would appreciate good counsel. Would Richard's marriage to Lady Aude be part of their discussions? Would Richard honour his cousin's obligations, or might sight of Crèvecoeur have given him pause?

Opening weary eyes, Emma glanced at the door. There was still no sign of him—when would he be back? Would he sleep in here or would he choose the stables? Her lips twitched. There would be no visits to the stables for her tonight.

She must confess, she had enjoyed the way Richard had fallen asleep with his strong arms wrapped around her. The big body of his had done more than make her feel safe. For a time, last night, she had felt…cherished. Which was ridiculous, impossible. Richard had given in to his baser instincts last night, and had fallen asleep with her in his arms because he was tired. It had meant no more than that.

When Emma next closed her eyes, Judhael entered her thoughts. Apulia. Lord. Would Azor really convince Judhael to become a mercenary?

The next thing Emma knew it was morning and Henri was dragging off her blanket.

'Mama, break fast? Break fast?'

Suppressing a groan, she sat up. Every muscle ached, stiff from yesterday's riding.

Others were up before them. Lord Edouard's men and Richard's were at table; it was a wonder she hadn't heard them. Richard was biting into an apple. Emma found herself examining his features with that now familiar ache in her belly. Already Lord Edouard was deferring to him….

'Mama?'

Flushing, Emma wrenched her gaze away. Richard had warned her how they must not draw attention to each other at Crèvecoeur; nevertheless, it rankled when he didn't so much as acknowledge her presence. He did look past her, though, when the doors opened and light tumbled across the threshold.

Two men strode in. 'Lord Edouard!' The dust of the road was still upon them and their faces were taut, their eyes intense.

Brow clearing, Lord Edouard beckoned to them. 'Lord Richard, these are the scouts I mentioned, Rognald and Mark. I expected them back before this.'

Spurs clinking, the men approached the board. Questioning glances were thrown at Richard and his knights. 'My lord?'

'Are you well?' Lord Edouard asked. 'You suffered no…accidents?'

'No, my lord, everything went as planned. But we do bring news. Permission to speak freely?'

'Certainly. Count Richard of Beaumont, allow me to present Rognald and Mark.'

Rognald inclined his head. 'Please accept my condolences with regard to Count Martin, my lord.'

'I thank you.'

Swordbelts were unbuckled; a maid brought water for washing. The scouts were given space on a bench, more food and drink was brought, platters were pushed towards them. Emma strained to hear more.

The man named Rognald glanced at Richard. 'It is doubtless as you suspected, my lord. Argentan and Alençon must have learned of your cousin's death a few days ago as there have been unusual troop movements in both counties and at the borders. And even, I fear, in Beaumont itself. Lady Aude bade me give her brother a message.'

'Yes?'

'Lady Aude wishes us to make plain that unless word comes from you, my lord—' Rognald looked Richard in the eye '—and quickly, she might find herself in the position of having to surrender to the Count of Alençon or his commander.'

Silence fell. Richard rested his chin on his hand and stared frowningly at the scouts. Lord Edouard had lost colour. The Count of Corbeil looked alarmingly young, and while Emma knew that many younger men had dealt with such matters, she wondered if Lord Edouard had the experience.

Seeing Henri was about to speak, she pulled him into her lap and put her hand over his mouth. 'Hush, sweetheart.'

Several seconds passed. Abruptly, Richard pushed himself to his feet. 'Change of plan. We leave at once for Falaise. Edouard, my apologies, we shall have to wait to further our acquaintance.'

Lord Edouard rose. 'I understand.'

'Geoffrey, the horses.'

'Yes, my lord.' Snatching a hunk of bread from the table, Geoffrey ran from the hall, scooping up his pack from his mattress on his way out.

Richard gripped Lord Edouard's arm. 'I thank you for your hospitality and for sharing your intelligence with me. I shall see that you do not regret it. We need each other, I think.'

'Indeed.'

'One thing further. I hope it does not come to this, but should Aude need a refuge, I take it she will be welcome here?'

'Assuredly.'

'My thanks. Sir Jean, Stephen…'

As one, Richard's men were on their feet. Emma's heart began to pound. They were leaving? What about her?

They were halfway to the door when Emma scrambled up. 'My lord?'

Richard turned and for a moment his eyes were

as cold as the stones at the bottom of the Itchen. 'Lady Emma?'

She put her arm round Henri and jerked her head towards Asa. 'What of us?'

'You won't be able to keep up.'

She swallowed. 'Are we to remain here?' She could not remain here. *Judhael!*

A nod. 'It would be safer, if Lord Edouard will…'

'Of course, of course.' Lord Edouard smiled. 'They must stay.'

'My lord, *please*!' Richard's fingers were drumming on his sword hilt. In his mind he was already in Falaise, already hastening to Beaumont. Emma stumbled towards him.

'Lady Emma, we are, as you have no doubt heard, in something of a hurry. You need an escort, I cannot spare one.'

Emma lurched for his sleeve before she could check herself. She could feel the strong arm beneath the cloth, the heat of his body. 'My lord, let us follow as quickly as we may. We do not need a large escort.'

Lord Edouard stirred. 'I could spare some men to escort the lady to Falaise.'

'Oh, thank you!'

Richard drew Emma to one side, away from listening ears. She could not read his expression. Angry? Abstracted?

'Please, my lord, let us follow you.'

Penetrating grey eyes searched hers. Then, 'Since Lord Edouard is prepared to lend his assistance, I suppose I could spare Sir Jean. Jean!'

Sir Jean retraced his steps. 'Lord Richard?'

'You will escort the ladies.'

'Yes, my lord.'

'Take Godric. And, Jean, I aim to reach Falaise shortly after noon. Duke William has pledged me his support, so I will see what I may drum up there in the way of troops. That being done, we shall be continuing to Beaumont immediately.'

'You will have to change horses.'

'Indeed. So when you reach Falaise, make sure Roland and the other mounts are well rested. When they are, you can bring them with you the rest of the way.' He rubbed his forehead. 'Come to think of it, the dogs would be better travelling with you, too.'

'Yes, my lord.'

Richard gave Emma a curt smile. 'I shall command a larger escort for you at Falaise. Rest there a night—the child will need it as much as the animals. With luck I shall see you the day after.'

'Thank you, my lord.'

Turning on his heel, Richard followed his other knights out of the hall.

'So, my lord…' Sir Jean turned to Lord Edouard '…how many men can you spare so that these ladies may reach Falaise in safety?'

Emma was unable to tear her gaze from the empty doorway. This put Richard doubly in Lord Edouard's debt. For his support and assistance in conveying her to Beaumont and also for sharing the scouts' report. She chewed her lip, and though the answer was none of her business, a question jumped into her mind.

Would these events make Richard more, or less, likely to marry Lord Edouard's sister?

A sinking feeling gave her the answer. It also told her that she minded far too much.

The sun had burned the morning mists away. In other circumstances it would have been a pleasant journey, but with her much-diminished escort, Emma grew increasingly uneasy. She found herself torn between the urge to peer over her shoulder—the thought that Judhael was hot on her heels was not to be shaken—and worry about what might be happening at Beaumont.

When would Richard get there? Was a battle likely? If he was hurt...

She took no pleasure in the violets and daisies that starred the wayside; she was blind to the flare of the gorse and deaf to the warbling of birds in the bushes. She wanted to reach Falaise. No, be honest, she wanted to reach Beaumont. She and Henri would be safe with Richard. He would never wed her because she was a fallen woman and no lands or prestige would ever attach to her, but it seemed he felt some guilt about having bedded her in the stables at Honfleur. If she was careful, he really might keep her for his mistress.

And if Judhael arrived in Beaumont? Surely even Judhael must eventually realise that she would never go back to him?

After crossing a featureless plain the road became sunken and full of ruts. The earth was dark red, the colour of a fox's coat.

Emma was tired. Her veil was hot and itchy, she longed to rip it from her head and wash her hair. Richard's dogs on the other hand, were inexhaustible. One of Lord Edouard's men had them on long leashes and they were bouncing along beside his mount with as much spring in their step as when they had set out from Crèvecoeur. Even the little white mongrel had more energy that she did, having no difficulty keeping pace, either.

'Only a mile to go,' Sir Jean said.

Asa was wrapped round Sir Jean, sitting as close as a girl could get to a man when riding pillion behind him. Her cheeks were pressed against his mailcoat, which had to be uncomfortable, but Asa was wearing the dreamiest of smiles. A warning bell rang in Emma's head. Did Asa fancy herself in love with him?

Rolling his shoulders as if to shake off a burr, Sir Jean added, 'Falaise is directly ahead, my lady.'

The road curled as they approached a vast stone keep, and Asa was pushed out of Emma's mind. Great walls seemed to have grown right out of the rocks, casting a long shadow. The rockface was sheer and the castle walls rose up like mountains—they made Emma's party look as significant as a column of ants.

A thriving market was in full swing at the foot of the walls, and there were peasant farmers and soldiers everywhere. A troop marched ahead of them on the road, helmets and leaf-bladed spears catching the sun. There were knights, too; pennons waved, horses whinnied. Children squealed and weaved in and out of the crowd, and the air was heady with the scents of baking bread, of roasted meats and spilled wine.

The river glided placidly past the rugged mass of stone that was Falaise Castle. A willow trailed thin fingers into the water. This was where Duke William's father had first seen Herleva, the beautiful washerwoman who had become his lover, but there were no women washing clothes today, just a pair of swans, drifting serenely with the flow.

Lips twisting, Emma gripped her reins. Herleva had given the young Duke a son, the son who would later go on to conquer England, but he had not married her. Dukes did not marry their mistresses. She clenched her teeth. Had Herleva loved her Duke? Or had she, like Emma, had other reasons for taking a noble lover?

Resolutely, Emma fixed her eyes on the approaching gateway and her mind on the days to come. Count Richard marry the mistress who had once been a washerwoman? Never.

They entered the castle. Never before had Emma seen so many soldiers in one place; it was most disquieting. She was allocated a place in the ladies' bower with Asa and Henri—it was a relief to escape the Great Hall. Sir Jean saw them settled, then marched off to inspect the escort that Richard had found for them and to see to the horses.

They next saw Sir Jean shortly after breakfast as they all climbed into their saddles. Count Edouard's men had vanished and there were several different faces in their escort.

Emma exchanged greetings with Sir Jean. She was so stiff that she could barely move, but she made no complaint. The aching muscles would ease on the journey and besides, she wanted to reach Beaumont, and safety, as quickly as possible.

The mist had come down and was cloaking the landscape when they rode into Richard's new county. Beaumont. Emma recalled Richard mentioning orchards, but these were lost behind a shifting grey veil, along with the peasants' fields and the river valley.

'Beaumont, my lady.' Sir Jean waved at a shiny wet wall rising up on their left. 'The castle is up yonder.'

Asa craned her neck to see. 'The top is lost in the mist,' she murmured, before letting her cheek settle back against Sir Jean.

Richard had mentioned that Beaumont was in effect one of Duke William's watchtowers. 'The castle is not a wooden motte-and-bailey, like the one at Crèvecoeur, Sir Jean?' Emma asked.

'Oh, no, my lady, Beaumont was built to last.'

On their right a stream rushed past, swollen by spring rains. Alders and willows loomed out of the mist. Emma caught the scent of wild mint and her stomach rumbled. She was hungry, doubtless the others were hungry, too—riding certainly sharpened the appetite.

They dug in their spurs as the road went sharply upwards. One of the dogs began to whine. Higher and higher they went, the trees falling back into the mist. Emma saw a village, a village green, a well. Finally, the horses' hoofs clattered across a wooden bridge and they trotted into the bailey. The dogs strained at their leashes, quivering with excitement.

Stone walls surrounded them, gleaming with damp. Up here, the mist was thin enough for Emma to make out that Beaumont Castle had been built in the usual Norman style—a large stone keep in the form of a tower with adjacent outbuildings and stables. And more soldiers, of course. The place was crawling with soldiers. And horses, and archers, and…

Emma's stomach cramped. Where was Richard? And how should she greet Lady Aude if she should meet her? Would Lady Aude even acknowledge her? Perhaps the people here would shun her as some of the townsfolk in Winchester had done. Was she to be *nithing* here in Beaumont?

'My lady, welcome!' Geoffrey had spotted them and was elbowing his way through a knot of troopers. 'You have made good time. My lord did not expect you until tomorrow.'

Dismounting, Emma eased her back with a grimace. 'It has been a hard journey. I am somewhat out of practice, I fear.'

She moved to take Henri down from Godric, but Geoffrey got there first.

'Permit me, my lady. Hello, Henri.'

'Hello, squire.'

Sir Jean came to lead Emma's horse away. Asa watched him go, longing large in her eyes. Oh, dear.

Geoffrey smiled at Emma. 'Please come with me, I will show you to your quarters.'

Thus it was, that moments after her arrival at Beaumont Castle, Emma and Asa were whisked through a great hall with a span large enough to rival the King's Great Hall at Winchester. But this was not quite like the hall at Winchester—there was some sort of fireplace set into the wall. Into the wall? Flames were vanishing into the stonework.

Emma had never seen the like of it before, but since Geoffrey was carrying Henri along at such a pace she had no time to remark on it, nor to notice much else. At the far end of the hall, a door opened on to a stairwell. Geoffrey led the way and, gripping the rope handrail, Emma followed him, dimly aware of Asa at her heels.

After several turns, Geoffrey kneed open a door. 'This way, my lady.'

A sliver of light came from an arrowslit high in the wall, but a sudden chill raised goose bumps on Emma's neck. She shivered and came to an abrupt halt in a shadowy chamber that was less than six feet in length and width. A coffer and a narrow bed took up almost the entire room. A large cobweb stretched across a row of hooks; there was nothing else. When Asa came up behind her and peered over her shoulder, her breath warmed Emma's cheek.

'Henri's bed is underneath that one,' Geoffrey said.

Emma nodded. When Henri's bed was pulled

out, there would be no standing room. Still, it was better than she might have expected. Privacy, for her and Henri.

'There you are, my lad.' Geoffrey set Henri on the main bed.

Privacy, but…Emma's thoughts ran on…not much space. And no refinement. She had not known what to expect, had worried that she might become something of an embarrassment and it would seem she already was an embarrassment. She and Henri were being tucked out of sight. Would she even meet Lady Aude? It had been naïve of her to expect as much. Richard had likely only reassured her to be polite. Nevertheless, it was, frankly, disappointing.

Henri tucked his thumb in his mouth and curled up on the bed.

'I shall see your things are brought up,' Asa said, backing away.

'My thanks.' Emma sank on to the bed.

At the door, Geoffrey turned back. 'And I will send someone with Henri's supper.'

Emma forced a smile. 'That is kind. He is probably too tired to eat at the moment, but he might be hungry later.'

'I am glad you did not linger in Falaise, my

lady,' Geoffrey added, moving towards the stairs. 'Lord Richard has been asking about you.'

He has missed me, has he? Emma thought, as she took off Henri's shoes and shifted him—already lost to the world—into the centre of the mattress. *He has a pretty poor way of demonstrating it, hiding us away in this cramped storeroom.* She frowned. No, she mustn't be ungrateful; Richard's mind was probably entirely fixed on securing the borders of his unexpected inheritance. This room had to be better than being made to bed down in the main hall, where everyone would know when she was...or wasn't...in favour.

Removing her cloak, Emma blew the cobwebs off the hooks and hung it up. She had not known what to expect as Richard's mistress, but she couldn't help wishing for a warmer welcome.

Chapter Twelve

Richard, Comte de Beaumont, was deep in thought. In the spacious bedchamber at the top of the west tower, he was wearing tracks in the matting. He must act and act decisively if he was going to hang on to his county. Matters here were worse than he had feared.

Reaching the bed—a bed with a carved oak bedhead that was even larger than the one he had had in Winchester—he turned on his heel and resumed his pacing.

A narrow window sat high in the wall and the shutter was folded back to admit the last of the day. It would not be long before Geoffrey came to light the candles.

Yes, matters were worse than he had feared. Someone, *likely someone living within these walls*, had broken into the armoury. Half the arrow store was missing and the other half had been destroyed. The swords had been blunted and it would take the armourers a week to right the damage. He could hear the grindstone as he paced. Naturally the knights had their own arms, but what about those of lesser rank? In the event of a sudden attack by Alençon or Argentan, Richard would need every able-bodied man he could lay his hands on. But if there were no arms for them?

Merde. He rubbed his eyes; they felt as though they were filled with grit. Not sleeping did that to a man. He couldn't think straight. Last night Richard's nightmare had returned and he had tossed and turned till daybreak. His last decent night's rest had been—a reluctant grin tugged at his mouth—in the hay back at the Mermaid.

Where was she? Geoffrey had said that she had been sighted with her escort.

'Hell and damnation.' Richard was a seasoned commander, he knew what was expected of him. He would pretend all was well. And not everything here gave cause for concern—he had inherited some good men from Martin. For their sakes, he would act as though nothing was wrong. He would win through.

But where the devil was Emma?

* * *

The door of the cramped chamber opened and Asa came in, bearing a tray of food. Bread. A jug of milk. Cheese. Some kind of sweet-looking pastry.

Asa set the tray on the coffer. 'Lord Richard is asking for you, Geoffrey says you are to go at once. I will remain here.'

Nodding, Emma squeezed past. 'Where?'

'Up the next twist of the stairs.'

At the top, Emma found herself facing a studded oak doorway, slightly ajar. It swung open on oiled hinges.

Richard was deep in conversation with Sir Jean and another man Emma had not seen before, but he smiled and gestured her inside. At sight of him, Emma felt a weight lifting from her shoulders.

'A moment, my lady.' He turned back to Sir Jean. 'My thanks, Jean, for escorting the ladies. You brought Roland?'

Sir Jean smiled. 'Of course, my lord, everything is exactly as you commanded. The hounds are in the stables.'

'My thanks. Your next commission will not, I fear, be as pleasant. I need you to take a full inventory in the armoury. From what Sir Hugh here tells me, many of the arms have gone missing since you left. He suspects someone within the castle is working for Alençon. See what you can discover, Jean.'

'Yes, my lord.'

'And, Jean…' Richard rubbed the back of his neck. Smudges under his eyes spoke of deep fatigue. 'Should persuasion become necessary, be sparing with the force. That is all.'

'Yes, my lord.'

Sir Jean and Sir Hugh bowed themselves out.

Richard and Emma looked at each other and the air seemed to fly from the room. Emma couldn't help but notice the way his eyes ran up and down her length, as though he was reassuring himself that she had not altered since Crèvecoeur. She had to stop herself looking him up and down in the same way. It had been just over a day since she had seen him but, oddly, it felt as though they had been apart for a lifetime.

She sucked in a breath. 'So, my lord, I see you have made another tower room your home.' The unstrung lute was leaning against a travelling chest, the sacking-wrapped sword and various other arms were leaning in a corner, and the crimson pennons already hung on one of the walls.

'Yes.' His brow creased. 'Have you had refreshment?'

'Not yet, my lord.'

'*Diable.*' Striding to the door, Richard stuck his head out. 'Geoffrey!'

'My lord?' Geoffrey's voice floated up from below.

'Bring us our supper up here, will you? I'll take mine with Lady Emma. Get them to bring hot water too.'

'Yes, my lord.'

She tipped her head back as Richard came to stand in front of her. He cleared his throat. 'You made good time. I thought that once you saw the delights of Falaise, you would be lost to me for weeks.'

'The delights of Falaise?

'The market.'

'Oh. No.'

He held out his hand. 'Come here, woman, greet me properly.'

Her heart began to thud. 'My lord, I…I have only just ridden in, I am unkempt—'

'I care not, come here.' Pulling her into his arms, he held her close. One large hand cradled the back of her head, not kissing, simply holding her and nuzzling her cheek.

She wound her arms about his waist.

He let out a great sigh. 'That's better. It seems I have need of you, Emma of Fulford. I have not slept properly since—' glancing up, she saw his smile was endearingly crooked '—our tryst in the stables at Honfleur.'

The lines of fatigue were clear, close to. 'That is natural, when you are concerned about possible attack.'

'Hmm.'

'And there is your wound, too.'

He flexed his shoulder and brought her head back under his chin. 'That was nothing.'

'Not all wounds are visible, Richard.'

He stiffened and stepped away, frowning. 'What do you mean?'

'You know very well what I am referring to, my lord. Something happened in the north of England, and it troubles your dreams.'

He grimaced. 'Are you a witch that you claim to read my thoughts?'

She narrowed her eyes at him. 'You do have

trouble sleeping, don't you? That is why you roam the stables in the early hours.'

'The dreams will pass. In any case, a dream cannot kill.'

She looked up at him through her lashes. Most likely he would not discuss it with her. Richard was a Norman lord, and no less a person than King William of England, Duke of Normandy, held him in high esteem. It must be hard for him to openly admit to weakness, even a small one like a little sleeplessness. Saxon warriors were trained to hide their shortcomings; it must be the same for him. 'You remind me of my father,' she said, giving voice to a startling perception. 'I know you carry many burdens and I would help you. I am sure, if you were to air your dream, its hold over you would weaken.'

'It is nothing.'

'It may be a slight wound, but something other than an arrow hurt you at the harrowing, and it had you in its grip that night at Honfleur. That is why you went to the stables.'

Eyes lighting, he reached for her waist. 'You had me in your grip that night and I slept very well, as I will sleep well tonight. May God forgive me, Emma, because I fear Adam will not. But I find I want to keep you. I cannot marry you, but neither do I wish to give you up.'

Good, Emma thought fiercely. *Because I do not want you to give me up.*

His grey eyes were looking deep into hers. The light in the room was fading fast, but Emma did not need light to recognise the warmth in his look. Drawn to that warmth, she swayed towards him. It was disconcerting, but the nature of her feelings towards him were changing. At the outset she had accepted his protection because she needed it, but now, now… God would have to forgive her, too, because she did not want to give Richard up. And not simply because of her problems with Judhael….

She *liked* this man, this Norman. Worse, she was beginning to feel a certain warmth for him. This man took care not to disparage her before Count Edouard, this man instructed his knights to—how had he put it a moment ago?—'be sparing with the force'. Affection was growing in her for him; yes, that was what it was, affection. It was no more than that.

A single knock and the door swung back to admit Geoffrey bearing a tray with a lamp and some covered dishes on it. He was followed by a procession of servants.

Emma's mouth fell open as a bathtub was hefted in. Several buckets of water, a ewer and jug, a pile of creamy linens…

A bath?

Watching her reaction, Richard's expression was amused. 'My thanks, Geoffrey, that will be all.'

'Until dawn, my lord?'

'Yes, rouse me at dawn.'

The servants tipped the water into the bathtub and Geoffrey followed them out. The door shut with a soft click. Emma couldn't tear her eyes from the bathtub. Her hair—at last she could wash her hair!

'A bath,' she said, longingly.

'You may go first.' He came towards her, smiling. 'It's a pity it is not large enough for two.'

'They could hardly carry a bigger tub up here,' she said. 'And think of the water it would need.'

'Quite.' He reached for the pins that kept her veil in place. 'We will have to wait until we can get to a bath house to share a bath.'

She glanced at him, scandalised, and tried to ward him off. *Share a bath with him?* Lord. Was she to have no secrets?

Richard brushed her hands aside. 'No, you won't deny me, I have been thinking of this ever since we rode out of Honfleur.'

'You have?'

Her veil sank to the floor and his hands busied themselves at her girdle. 'How does this thing—ah—I have it. Yes, *ma belle*, that straw was nothing less than an insult.'

'It was a little itchy.'

'And your clothes, the damn lacings. Turn around.'

Emma did as she was told. He was determined. Large hands moved caressingly over her while lacings were found and untied. He leaned forwards to kiss her cheek, bent to kiss her neck, then slid his hand into the back of her gown, peeling it slowly away. Unhurried but unstoppable. Fabric was tugged and pulled.

A rush of embarrassment heating her cheeks, Emma tried to hang on to the gown, holding it to her chest.

'No, *ma petite*, let me see you. I wanted to see you in the stables at Honfleur. I ached to see you that night at Crèvecoeur.I burned to see you last night when you were in Falaise. I have had no peace.' Wresting her hands from the gown, he drew it away, leaving her clad in her linen under-shift. He swallowed, his palm cupping a breast through the shift. *'Ma petite.'*

'Richard,' Emma murmured, surrendering to the inevitable. She raised her lips. His scent surrounded her, warm and potent and already familiar. She leaned in to him, pushing her fingers into his hair, holding him close.

'Emma.'

He was wrestling with lacings, undoing more ties and in a moment her undershift joined her gown on the rush matting. Outside, a blackbird was singing.

When he lifted his head, she swayed closer, overtaken by shyness. But instead of staring at her he released her, and gave her a gentle pat. 'Into that bath.'

He turned away, giving her space while he began to disrobe.

Emma scrambled into the tub. It was not deep, the water only reached her waist and she had to sit with her knees drawn up There was barely room for one in this tub, never mind two, and while she did feel shy, this was a luxury she had never known. A bathtub in a bedchamber? Sighing in delight, she loosed her hair and reached for the dipper.

Richard's boots thudded down, one, two...
Leather cross-gartering was thrown aside.

Luxury indeed. The water was fragrant with
lavender. Geoffrey had set soaps on a dish within
arm's reach, soaps fit for a queen. They had been
made with costly oils from distant lands and
scented with herbs. Soaps such as these were made
in England, but Emma had never used them
herself.

Quickly, she set about washing, watching
Richard out of the corner of her eye. He had been
eager to see her naked and she had to admit to
some curiosity herself. That night in Honfleur,
she had not seen him, either...

The last shafts of light from the window fell on
long, strong limbs. His chest was broad and its
muscled contours more intriguing than she had
thought possible. Dark hair vanished into his
chausses. Swiftly, he untied them and shoved
them down. Hastily, she averted his gaze—he
was aroused, magnificently so.

He made no attempt to approach her in the tub.
Snatching up a towel, he wrapped it about his
waist and, reaching for a taper, lit a candle by the
bedside. The light flickered over his skin. His
body, the set of his head on those well-built

shoulders, that narrow waist, the slim hips—Count Richard of Beaumont's physique remained imposing even when clad only in a linen cloth.

She let out a breath. Thank Heaven he was not intending to join her, for there was scarcely room for herself in the bathtub, let alone Emma *and* Richard.

'Hurry up, my lady.' He moved to close the shutter.

Emma was reaching for a drying cloth when he turned back, frowning.

'Emma, where are your belongings?'

'My belongings?' Holding the drying sheet to her, she stepped out of the bathtub. 'Downstairs in the chamber below.'

'How so? I gave orders that they should be brought up here.'

'But I…I thought Henri and I were to have the other room.'

'Henri and you?' His frown deepened. 'No, that room is for your son and the maid. From now on, I want you here with me.'

Emma found herself smiling as she approached the bed; she couldn't help it. *He wanted her to share his bedchamber, she was not to be relegated to a cramped storeroom!*

Moving past her, Richard dropped the cloth round his waist. Her gaze was drawn to the curve of his buttock. The muscles on his thigh flexed as he sank into the water.

'Never mind, you can send for your things tomorrow. I won't complain about your lack of a bedgown.'

Emma did not own a bedgown, most people in her station of life slept in their shifts, but she wasn't about to apprise him of that fact. *She could send for her things*! 'But, my lord—'

'You object?' A dark brow lifted as, with much vigour and splashing, Richard began flourishing a washcloth.

'No, of course not. If that is your wish.'

'So agreeable, my sweet. But…?'

'What about Lady Aude?'

His smile slipped a notch. 'What about her?'

'Won't she object?'

'Lady Aude will make no objection.'

Emma wound the drying sheet round her, tucking it in above her breasts. 'Have you spoken to her?'

'Naturally.'

'Did you tell her about us?'

'Of course.'

Emma stared. *Of course*. Was that all he had to say on the matter? *Of course*. 'Will you marry her?'

'I may have to.' He glanced across. 'I can tolerate her and I like her young brother. Despite the lack of stewardship at Crèvecoeur, Count Edouard's support may be important.'

'I realise that. But, but surely Lady Aude will object?'

Richard fished the washcloth out of the bottom of the tub. 'I shall deal with Lady Aude. She is not your concern. Now, if you please.' He flourished the cloth in her direction. 'If you wouldn't mind doing the honours with my back.'

Sighing, since he was obviously declaring the subject off-limits, Emma took the cloth from him and went to work. It was pleasant work, very pleasant, and infinitely preferable to scrubbing linens in the Itchen, she thought, as she soaped and scrubbed and rinsed. His skin gleamed in the candle-light. Lightly she touched the scar on his shoulder, where there was a slight depression, a reddish mark. 'It is healing well.'

'Mmm.'

Shaking her head, Emma began kneading his neck. Richard let out a sigh that was part groan and she could feel the tension that had lodged in his muscles begin to ease. His skin was surprisingly soft. She was careful to avoid the wound. Men. They thought themselves invincible with their strong bodies. They armed themselves to the teeth and clattered about in their armour, banging their shields together, riding their great horses. None of them facing the fact that underneath it all there was this, warm, soft flesh. Beautiful flesh and muscle which, while it was wholly male, remained vulnerable—male flesh could be hurt as much as it could do hurt. Men.

'I am hoping that you might be able to avert conflict in Beaumont,' she spoke softly.

'Hmm?' His voice was warm, having lost its sharp edge. He leaned forwards with his eyes closed to give her better access. 'Do not stop. That is… Yes, there.'

He was relaxing, perhaps for the first time in weeks. Emma decided not to pester him with questions. The man needed this—he was barely able to conceal his fatigue. Surely the tension he had been hiding could not have been wound any tighter?

Richard might be Count of Beaumont, but positions of high honour brought with them heavy burdens—Emma's father had taught her that. And this man, she was fast learning, did not take his responsibilities lightly.

'There, my lord.'

He caught her hand and pressed a kiss on it. 'My thanks.'

Emma retreated. Picking up her clothes, she hung her gown on a hook and took up her undershift.

'I trust you are not about to put that thing back on?'

She hesitated. 'Not if you don't want me to.'

'I most certainly do not.' When he stood a shower of water droplets arced across the room, gleaming like jewels. Briskly, he began drying himself.

Flinging her underskirt over the hook, Emma sank on to the mattress, the drying cloth wrapped firmly around her.

'And…' he grinned as he tossed the cloth down and advanced upon her '…I do hope I am not going to have to seduce that cloth off you.'

With a squeak, she backed into the middle of the bed.

Large fingers curled round her neck, his thumb pushed her chin up. 'Emma, look at me.'

Emma looked. His thumb was moving up and down her cheek, pulling on her lower lip. His eyes were soft, dark and fathomless.

'Emma,' he murmured, as his lips met hers.

It was a sweet kiss, the sweetest she had received in her life. It curled her toes and created a pool of longing in her belly; it made her groan with longing. She reached for him.

They shifted and moved closer, side by side on the big bed. And somehow the cloth was gone from her body and the bedcovers were pushed back. There was nothing in the world but his mouth on hers. His hands were at her breasts, stroking and teasing. Emma arched upwards, Richard giving a guttural murmur of approval and then his mouth replaced his hands and his hands moved on. Lower, across her belly, back up again. Lightly, he touched her face, her cheeks. His fingers tangled in her hair.

He lifted his head, a blonde skein curled round his fingers. 'It is still damp.'

'Yes.'

A tiny crease appeared in his brow as, carefully, he spread her hair across the pillows. 'We ought to dry it, to comb it,' he said.

That 'we' pleased her more than it should. Though she knew she was deluding herself, it seemed to speak of tenderness. Tenderness? In a man who had taken her as his mistress?

Tenderness was not a male quality. Emma must not let her desires run away with her; men were no more tender with women than they were careful with their own bodies. Her father had never been tender, and as for Judhael…

'My hair will be fine.' She understood what he really wanted.

Reaching out, she drew his mouth back to hers.

In the morning Henri was not in his room when Emma went to find him, nor was he in the hall.

Several long trestle tables were up from breakfast and a battalion of servants was clearing the leftovers. Asa was at one of the benches, biting into a slice of bread, gazing soulfully at a group of knights in animated discussion over a weapon stack. Of course, Sir Jean was among them. Soldiers were drilling in the bailey, someone barked an order, feet tramped. There was a pause, a hoarse shout. More tramping.

'Asa, if I might have your attention a moment?'

Asa dragged her attention from Sir Jean. 'My lady?'

'Where is Henri?'

'Henri?' Gulping down her bread, Asa looked blankly at her.

Emma clenched her teeth. The girl looked as though she had not the first idea who Henri was. 'Asa…'

Asa roused herself. 'Henri? Heavens, has he gone again? Slippery as an eel, that boy.'

A ball of anxiety formed in Emma's stomach, a fingernail tapped edgily on the tabletop. 'Asa, when you are caring for him, you must watch him *at all times.*'

Asa scrambled to her feet. 'Yes, my lady. I'm sorry, my lady.'

People were staring. Servants laden with platters and trays were looking her way. A guard lounged by the main doorway, picking his nose, eyes fixed on her. Someone must have spoken to them about her. Lifting her chin, Emma made a point of meeting the guard's glance. At once he straightened and gave her a smile. There was no insolence in his demeanour, nor, as far as Emma could judge in any of the servants. Some of her anxiety melted away.

A maidservant appeared, gesturing politely at a trestle. 'You would eat, my lady? I will fetch you warm bread.'

'In a moment, I thank you. But first I must find my son.'

'The little boy called Henri?'

'Yes.'

'There he is.' The maid pointed at a woman coming in from the bailey. A lady by her dress and veil, she walked with slow dignity, blue skirts trailing, fine white veil seeming to shimmer with each step. Her circlet had the yellow gleam of gold. The guard bowed his head as she passed.

Henri had fast hold of one of the lady's hands and in the other he was holding what appeared to be a toy boat. A deadly hush fell on the hall.

Emma went cold. 'Asa, who is that lady?' She strongly suspected she knew the answer, but she had to ask.

She was utterly beautiful. She had pale white skin, shining russet hair and full lips, but one glance told Emma that the core of this woman's beauty resided in her person rather than her features. She was poised in her carriage, and smiling, but nevertheless she brought an indefinable air of sadness with her into the keep. She drew all eyes.

'Why, that is Lady Aude.'

Chapter Thirteen

Lady Aude! Mouth dry, Emma managed a curtsy and forced herself to cross the rushes and greet her. Her heart slammed in her ears. Would Lady Aude acknowledge her?

'Lady Aude de Crèvecoeur, I understand?' Emma held her hand out to Henri, who skipped over and took it.

'Yes. And you must be Lady Emma of Fulford. Welcome to Beaumont.'

Lady Aude's eyes were arresting, with the glow and colour of amber. 'I thank you. I hope Henri has not been making a nuisance of himself.'

'On the contrary, Lord Richard finds him most diverting. But since the men have started their drill, he thought it best that Henri was returned to his nursemaid.'

'Henri has been with Count Richard?'

'Yes.'

'Mama, look! Count Rich gave me this.' Grinning, blessedly oblivious of any undercurrents, Henri offered the boat up for Emma's inspection. It was large and finely detailed, a world apart from the crude stick that had sailed out of reach on the Itchen.

'That's lovely, sweetheart. I like the blue-and-yellow sails.'

'Yes!'

Lady Aude was watching them, a pensive smile on her lips. 'Your son has made quite an impression on Lord Richard. In the midst of mustering the local knights and soldiers, he found time to have that boat made.'

Emma clung to Henri as though he were her lifeline. Lady Aude de Crèvecoeur bowed her head and drifted slowly away amid a flutter of silk.

This was Ugly Aude? This beautiful, sad, sympathetic woman? In any other circumstances, they might have been friends. But with matters as they stood… Lady Aude was right, careful politeness was probably the only course open to them. Emma would, naturally, follow her lead. But poor woman, to be grieving for one man, while another was suing for her hand in marriage.

But...*ugly*? Anyone less ugly, Emma could not imagine. Those eyes, that hair...

Emma had decided to spend the day exploring Beaumont Castle, subtly testing the servants in their attitude towards her. So far she had encountered no animosity anywhere, for which she suspected she had Richard to thank. She felt a rush of affection for him, an overburdened count who took time to ensure that both she and Henri were made welcome. She frowned. Affection? This must stop. Her feelings for him could not be allowed to grow; she was already indecently fond of him, and he wasn't even Henri's father.

The girl who had approached her in the hall was named Lisa, and Lisa was happy to show Emma everything from the watchpoints at the top of the highest tower, to the peculiar stone chimney in the hall that she had noted on her arrival. She was even shown the cellars and found herself gazing at row upon row of casked wine, of salt beef, of cheese...

All of this was, of course, Lady Aude's domain. Lady Aude had been chatelaine at Beaumont for most of the time since her betrothal to Richard's cousin. Emma had no intention of treading on any toes, but if she was going to remain here, she needed to find something with which she could occupy herself. Merely being Richard's mistress would not be enough. Life here was going to be a challenge.

In the evening, none the wiser for what she might find to do in a castle that was well regimented from turret to cellar, Emma and Henri returned to the hall where the boards were being set for supper. Lisa vanished into the cookhouse.

Catching sight of Richard's squire talking with others by the fireplace, Emma called him over. This was so awkward. 'Geoffrey?'

'Lady Emma?'

'Please would you ask someone to bring me food up on a tray?' It was one thing to exchange a few civilised words with Richard's fiancée, but quite another to sit at her table and break bread with her. Meals taken in halls were such public affairs. No woman, not even one with as saintly an aspect as Lady Aude, would find that easy to stomach.

'Of course, my lady.'

Emma ate with Henri in his narrow room and

sat with him until he fell asleep. Then, prising the boat from his fingers lest he poke himself in the eye with the mast in his sleep, she left the door ajar and went upstairs.

The upper bedchamber was full of shadows, but it was not yet dark enough to merit a candle. The blackbird was singing his evening song, a trio of notes followed by a trill. It floated through the window, over and over.

Geoffrey had told her that messengers had arrived from Count Edouard, so it was likely that Richard would be late retiring. Sinking on to the bed, Emma took time to absorb her surroundings properly as she had not done last night.

Her few possessions had been stowed in a storage chest that Geoffrey had indicated was exclusively for her use. This evening, Richard's lute, still unstrung, hung on a hook on the wall above it; and a discarded helmet lay next to the wrapped sword propped in the corner. The helmet had the most alarming dent in it.

Her gaze skimmed over the ewer and jug on one of Richard's large travelling chests, over the crimson pennons on the wall. She yawned and wandered to the ewer to wash.

The stiffness of the journey had not yet left her.

When her father had been Thane of Fulford, Emma had thought nothing of day-long rides across the downs. But since she had been living in Winchester, her body had had to become used to a different sort of exercise. Washing linen was back-breaking work, but it did not use the same muscles as riding. Her legs… Saints.

Drying her face on a linen cloth, Emma removed her clothing, save for her undershift and crept under the covers.

A clunk woke her. Soft light filled the room. 'Richard?'

He was standing by the window—it must have been the closing of the shutter that had woken her. The lamp on the bedside coffer was alight, a round glow that pushed back the dark.

'I am sorry if I disturbed you.' Crossing the room, he came to look down at her before turning away to undress. His belt fell to the floor. His tunic, shirt…

'The Count of Beaumont needs his squire, I see,' Emma said, raising a brow at his untidiness.

'Hmm? Oh, yes.' Smiling, he bent over the ewer. Water splashed. 'You could oblige.'

'I do not think so.' Emma pulled the bedclothes up around her chin. 'It is too cosy in here. I am not used to such a fine mattress and now I've got in I may never want to get out.' Too late did she realise the possible interpretation he might place on her words. Biting her lip, she focused on his crimson pennon.

Rustling. The mattress sagged and a warm arm snaked round her waist.

'Richard?'

'Mmm?' Gently, he bit her shoulder. Guilty pleasure shimmered through her. 'Why are you wearing this thing?' His hand slid down to the hem of her nightshirt.

More pleasure. Setting her mind against it, Emma pushed his hand away. Startled grey eyes met hers; he was not used to being rejected. 'Richard, there is something I must say.'

Strong fingers resumed their slow tracking down her thigh.

She caught his wrist. 'It concerns Lady Aude.'

Sighing, he drew back and rested his head on his hands. 'I heard that you met her.'

'Yes.' Emma leaned up on an elbow. 'But, Richard, you told me she was ugly. How can you call her ugly? That woman would put Venus in the shade!'

Those broad shoulders rose in a careless shrug.

'I am not drawn to her. She always did belong to Martin.'

'Richard, I think you should let me find my relatives. Aude de Crèvecoeur seems a kind woman. I do not want—'

'No.' His lips tightened. 'You are mine. I have battled with my conscience to keep you and I will not give you up.'

Sitting up, he waved at the coffer that had been set aside for her use. Emma saw that a pouch had been placed on the closed coffer lid, a fat pouch, doubtless bulging with coin. Anger began to simmer inside her, an anger that was only partly tempered when she read confusion and hurt in his eyes.

'That came out badly,' he admitted. 'I meant to give it to you as a gift, but there is more if you wish. You may go to the market in the village tomorrow, I am told that a pedlar from Paris—'

'Richard, it is no good. I thought I could do this, but I cannot. Lady Aude…if you marry her and keep me under her nose…' she shook her head '…it is not right.'

His mouth thinned. 'You were happy enough to throw yourself at me in Winchester. You were practically selling yourself—'

'Give me strength! The only person around here who is selling himself is you!' His jaw dropped. 'Yes, *you*, Richard! You are marrying a fine woman, but she does not attract you. You do not love her, either, do you?'

'Love?' A cynical laugh gave her an answer.

'I thought not. You are probably incapable of love. So explain, if you please, why are you marrying her?'

'It is politics, Emma, you would not—'

'I would not understand? How *dare* you say that to me! Politics such as yours robbed me of my father and brother. And, indirectly, of my mother, too.'

His chest heaved. 'Believe me, I am sorry for that.'

Emma's anger was at boiling point. 'Politics! It drives men to...to...' She glared at the crimson pennons. 'Were those fluttering at Hastings, Richard?'

The grey eyes became distant.

'Tell me, I want to know! Were they flying in the vanguard when the nobility of England was mown down like so much grass? I see why you chose that colour, lord knows why it didn't occur to me before. A crimson field, indeed! It is a field of blood, is it not?'

A large hand reached out; she batted it away. 'Our family chose that colour long before the Great Battle,' he said, with a sigh. 'Emma you should rest, you are overwrought.'

'Let me finish. You, my lord Richard, are marrying Lady Aude for gain. You need her brother's support and what is that but a gain? You are selling yourself. But I—' Anger almost choked her. 'Yes, I bedded you, and, yes, I took your purse at Honfleur, and, yes, I will probably take that purse tomorrow and it most certainly isn't because of your good looks.

'I *chose* you, Richard! I picked you out in Winchester long before I came to the castle in search of work. At first I picked you out because I…' she swallowed '…I admit it freely, I was drawn to you. But the reason I actually approached you was because Henri and I needed help and you were best placed to give it. The only difference between you and me, Richard, is that I know what I have done, whereas you…you are deluding yourself. You don't love Aude de Crèvecoeur. She doesn't love you. And it is worse than that. When I looked into that woman's eyes today, I saw someone who longs to be released from her obligations here. That woman is in a prison, Richard, and it is called grief. I suspect she loved your cousin. Yes, theirs was to have been a political alliance, but love was there, *love*. And you, my lord, do not have the slightest notion of what love is!'

Drawing a shaky breath, Emma glared at him, half-braced to ward off a blow. Judhael would certainly not have hesitated after such an outburst. Several heartbeats later, she realised the blow was not going to come.

'You do have some interesting views, *ma petite*,' Richard said, in so mild a voice he quite took the wind out of her sails.

Interesting views? That cool gaze was thoughtful. He gave her one of his lopsided smiles while she took another gulping breath, appalled at herself. What had she done? She must be mad, to shriek at the Count of Beaumont as though, as though…

'However, I am relieved to hear that you were drawn to me. And that I have at least one other redeeming feature,' he murmured.

She folded her arms. 'Oh?'

'You said you like my looks.'

'I do not, you are as ugly as sin!'

Shifting towards her, a warm hand moved suggestively on her thigh. 'I take it then that there's no chance of…?'

She pushed at his chest. 'Not a chance, not tonight. In any case, I am no longer certain that it is my safe time.' This was an outright lie and, judging by his expression, Richard recognised it as such.

'Truly?'

She glared. 'Truly.'

'Very well.' Shifting, he pinched out the candle, keeping hold of her all the while. Gently but firmly he pressed her head down on to his chest. 'I will leave you in peace tonight. You are not in the mood and far be it for me to force myself on you when you are unwilling.'

Emma lay rigid in his arms, not believing he would be as good as his word. Judhael would not have been. If Judhael had wanted her, Judhael would have taken her.

It was hard to nurse your anger though, when you were held warm and snug in strong arms and that wicked masculine scent was fuddling your senses. Emma frowned into the dark. The force of her anger had shocked her; it had driven the charm she had been striving for right out of the window. It wasn't like her to rant and rave, and it certainly wasn't in her interests to alienate Richard. She was lucky he hadn't flung her into the great hall.

With a sigh she relaxed against the muscled length of his body. So much anger, it was almost as though she loved him. She could not, must not begin to love Richard of Beaumont. This was meant to be a simple arrangement, one which was to have suited both parties equally.

Sweet Mary help her, she must not begin to feel more than affection for him. Misery lay at the end of that road: look at poor Frida at the Staple, look at Lady Aude. Any such feelings must be quashed. Instantly.

It had been the thought of him marrying Lady Aude that had set her off, that and the discovery that Emma might like the woman.

Was she jealous? Saint Swithun help her. This obsession with a man who wasn't Henri's father was positively indecent. Sinful.

She must guard her heart, for her role at Beaumont remained uncertain. But at what point had it started to feel downright humiliating to know that Richard would never, not even for one second, contemplate marriage with Emma of Fulford?

* * *

'My lady? Lady Emma?'

She woke with a start and stared past Richard's empty pillow towards the door. The window shutter had been opened and a shaft of sunlight slashed across the floor. Whoever was outside kept on knocking.

'My lady?'

It wasn't Geoffrey and Emma didn't recognise the voice. Throwing her cloak round her shoulders, she went to the door and opened it a chink.

It was Theo, the Saxon mercenary who had accompanied Godric on the crossing from Bosham. Unlike most of his compatriots, Theo had shaved his hair and his beard was short and neat. 'Yes?'

'Count Richard said I was to offer you my escort if you wanted to go to the market.' Theo's disgruntled expression told Emma what he thought of such a commission at a time when a man ought to be sharpening weapons or drilling with his comrades in the bailey.

A market. Emma was tempted, but thought of Judhael gave her pause.

'My thanks, but there is no need. Theo, isn't it?'

'Yes, my lady.'

'Theo, I am certain I can manage without—'

Theo shook his head. 'My lord was most explicit. You are not to leave the confines of the castle without my escort.'

Emma eyed Theo. He had a hard edge to him and looked more than strong enough to ward off any trouble. She would love to see Beaumont and the market. Why should Judhael rule her life? He might not even be there; even if he was, Richard had sent this man to look out for her. She stiffened her spine; there would be no more cowering in corners for her.

'I see. Well, thank you, Theo, I would like to go to the village, very much. I will meet you by the gatehouse in, say, half an hour.'

'Very good, my lady.' Inclining his head, Theo withdrew.

A bright sun had banished the mist, making visible what had been invisible on the day of their arrival. As Emma and Henri walked hand in hand through the gatehouse and out on to the drawbridge, Emma's eyes widened. The drawbridge spanned not a river as she had imagined, but a deep ravine. The drop was dizzying.

Castle Beaumont was perched on a rocky outcrop and Emma's first proper view of the county from the other side of the drawbridge took her breath away. 'So high,' she murmured, keeping fast hold of Henri.

Theo marched stolidly at her side with hand on his sword hilt as though, even up here by his lord's drawbridge, he feared attack. He was being over-cautious, Emma decided as she looked out over a wooded valley. Nevertheless she was glad of his company. Judhael might be about and, while she felt confident that she could deal with him, at least in public, she was thankful to have an escort.

A river wound through the valley floor. Oak and beech trees were coming into leaf and the riverbank was lined with poplars and alder, tiny at this distance. Here and there the forest had been cleared for farmland. She could see the orchards that Richard had mentioned. A few shreds of mist remained, refusing to give up the hollows. Farther down the valley, a buzzard was circling.

'The village is halfway down the hill,' Theo said. 'My lady, are you certain you wish to walk?'

'Yes, I don't recall it being far.'

Muttering under his breath, her reluctant escort tramped along beside her. At a crossroads there was a small shrine to Our Lady, buried in offerings. Primroses and wood anemones had been scattered over several pilgrims' lead tokens and for an instant Emma was whisked back to Saint Swithun's shrine in Winchester.

Past the shrine, the houses began. The village of Beaumont had a church and a smithy. Emma's heart twisted as once again she was put in mind of Wessex. How like Fulford Beaumont was, save that here there was no mead hall. A tavern faced a grassy square, there were a couple of prosperous peasants' cottages, and several humbler ones. Many of the houses were basic wattle and daub with thatched roofs, but some were planked. The only stone building in the vicinity was the castle that overlooked everything from its rocky escarpment.

There was another noticeable difference to Fulford, Emma thought, making a beeline for the market stalls set up on the grass in front of the tavern. Here, naturally, everyone was speaking Norman French. Two women were haggling amiably over the price of new season's eggs; a man sat on a log outside the tavern singing a marching song—he was off-key and drunk, but it was definitely French.

A fabric stall caught her eyes. It was groaning

with as tempting an array of materials as one could hope to see: soft silks in rich reds and dark blues; shiny satins; filmy fabrics and heavy homespun; velvets and damasks. Richard had mentioned a pedlar from Paris—this must be his stall. Emma smiled down at Henri. He was growing so fast always in need of new clothes. She was bound to find something for him here.

'Emma?' A voice hissed in her ear. 'Speak to me, Emma!'

An English voice? Here? She turned and ice skittered down her spine. 'Judhael!'

The world narrowed down to a pair of staring blue eyes. The spring sun lost its warmth, the hustle of the market quieted and the village seemed to vanish from her sight. Judhael. Emma braced herself. In her heart she had known that this meeting was inevitable.

Judhael was much changed. A straggling blond beard could not hide the fact that he had lost weight. His cheekbones were prominent, his eye sockets too pronounced. A livid scar cut diagonally across his jaw. It looked old, but it was not one Emma recognised. The stitching had been botched.

'Will you not speak to me, my lady?'

Theo made a movement, his knuckles

gleaming white on his sword hilt as he looked a question at her.

'It is all right, Theo.' The coming moments would not be pleasant, but Emma was confident she could cope. She motioned the mercenary to one side. 'I know this man, he and I are…old friends.'

Theo withdrew a few paces, obedient because in Judhael he recognised a fellow Saxon, but his eyes never left her for an instant.

A muscle twitched in Judhael's cheek. 'Friends, love, is that all? We were more than that once.' He jerked his head in the direction of the tavern. 'Come, share a drink with me, there is much I would say before we leave.'

'Leave?' Emma held her breath, it sounded as though Azor had succeeded in persuading Judhael to join the fight against the Eastern Emperor.

'Yes, Azor and I have a mind to go to Apulia.' Judhael glanced casually at Henri, and every nerve in Emma's body went on alert.

'Where is Azor?' she asked, in as pleasant a tone as she could muster. Had Azor told Judhael that he had a son? He promised he would not.

A shrug. 'He's around somewhere. Come, love, have a drink with me.' Judhael held out a pitifully thin hand, more claw than human appendage. It did not look like the hand of the man who had been her father's favoured housecarl.

'I think not.' She crossed her arms. 'Judhael, I am glad you survived the Harrowing, but I do not wish to speak to you. What is there to say?' Emma's mind was paralysed by conflicting thoughts. This was Judhael, her son's father, and she had dreaded him finding her for so long…and yet now that he was here, looking her in the eye, one thought emerged from all the others.

This was the man who had haunted her for years—this skeletal, beggarly creature?

Judhael's face, what Emma could see of it behind the beard, was nothing but bone and sharp angles; his shoulders sagged and his clothes were in shreds—beside them her Winchester work clothes would look positively pristine. The sour odour of stale sweat wrinkled her nostrils—Judhael's clothes needed washing; *he* needed washing.

Something within him had died. Judhael was a shadow of his former self. Was this what defeat did to a man?

He glanced again at Henri. 'Who is this? Looking after one of your lord's by-blows?'

Emma evaded his gaze. Azor had kept her

secret, bless him. Judhael might be a shadow of his former self, but she could well remember what the flat of his hand felt like. Much as she hated to do it, common sense told her she must lie, to deny that Henri was hers. She prayed that Henri would hold his tongue. 'He belongs to one of the ladies in the castle.'

Henri's eyes went wide. May God forgive her, she could see the questions forming in his young mind, she could feel his confusion. One day she would explain everything to him, but not today.

Please, God, let Henri keep silent.

Unfortunately, Henri took matters out of her hands, exactly as he had done in Honfleur. 'Mama?'

'Mama?' Judhael hissed out a breath. 'Holy Mother, the boy *is* yours! I thought you were nursemaiding for that lord.'

Emma drew herself up. What else could she do? 'Very well, I confess it. I am not a nursemaid. Henri is my son.'

Bending, Judhael caught Henri by the chin. Stared.

Henri whimpered and clutched Emma's skirts.

'How old is he?' Judhael snapped.

'Almost three.' She put steel in her voice. 'And have a care, I will not have him frightened.'

Judhael straightened and something of the old fire flared in his eyes. Emma's heart sank. Her chin inched up. She refused to flinch, but instead of lashing out or taking her by the shoulders to give her one of his teeth-rattling shakes, Judhael shook his head and stepped back.

'My son.' He rubbed his forehead; his nails were broken and dirty. 'I never thought—a son.' He stared at Henri, a man transfixed.

Emma fiddled with the purse at her belt. Had Judhael changed? Had she been wrong to conceal Henri's existence from him? She had done it to protect him, but it was impossible to conceal the truth any longer, Henri's age gave it away. 'Yes, Judhael, this is your son.'

Judhael's Adam's apple bobbed up and down. 'Name of Henri, I think you said?'

'Yes.'

Judhael inhaled deeply, his shoulders straightened. He went on gazing at Henri, expression softening. 'My son.' When he looked back at Emma there was no trace of his former arrogance, but that febrile brightness in his eyes was not entirely quenched. 'Emma, you have to let me speak privately with you. When I learned you had left Winchester in the company of that

Norman, I had already decided to try out the life of a mercenary. But I wanted to speak to you, to say a last farewell.'

Emma kept an arm firmly about Henri. 'We can say our farewells here.'

'Emma, *no*! Earlier I didn't know about Henri. But now that I do, it is imperative I speak to you.'

'Judhael, it makes no difference. I lost the desire to speak to you on Seven Wells Hill. We have nothing to say to each other.'

He caught at her arm, fingers boring into her flesh through the sleeve of her gown. Out of the corner of her eye, Emma saw Theo stiffen and edge closer. Judhael saw it, too. Releasing her, he made a point of retreating to give her space. His eyes were over-bright, staring. 'Emma, I am sorry. I have come to regret what happened that day. I made some bad mistakes, not least of which was to ride off without you. Blame my passion for King Harold's cause, which blinded me. Forgive me. Do not deny me my son.'

'Judhael, the past cannot be forgotten. Philip, Lufu—both were badly done. Besides, your recent actions make lies of your fine sentiments. What about those bruises I saw on Bertha's wrists? And that fire at City Mill—did you set it?'

Blue eyes bored into hers. 'At Fulford, Father Aelfric taught us the importance of a forgiving heart. Is there no forgiveness in you?'

'Don't preach to me! In the year King Harold was killed, my brother was a baby; he was a newborn and your ambitions almost killed him! And as for Bertha and Gytha—to threaten innocent women…' Emma shook her head. 'I do not think you have changed. And even if you have, there can be no going back for you and me.'

Judhael lifted his gaze to the castle on its rocky outcrop. 'You're hardly a saint yourself. I thought you were nursemaiding that man's bastard. But since you are not—what are you, Emma, his whore?'

Emma bit her tongue; refusing to let him goad her. It flashed in on her that in a sense it did not matter what she was to Richard because Richard—despite his impending marriage to Lady Aude—showed by his actions that he valued her. Their relationship might be an illicit one, but the Count of Beaumont treated his mistress with more respect than she had ever received in her life.

Judhael grunted. 'No going back, you say?'

'No.'

'Not even if our son might be legitimised?'

Emma's breath caught. 'Marriage—you are suggesting that I marry you?'

'Aye.'

She could hardly believe her ears. *Marriage? With Judhael?* A wedding between them would indeed legitimise Henri, and no one would be able to call him bastard again. Shamefully, one thought stood clear of the rest. It was a thought that made Emma ache, a thought she had no business thinking.

If she married Judhael, she would never see Richard again.

Henri's fingers were winding into her skirts. Emma folded them in hers. 'You are not serious. I am, as you have just pointed out, no saint—this child testifies to that. But at least I never risked the health of an infant—Philip was a baby, Judhael.' She turned away, grateful for Theo's watchful presence. 'I must go.'

Judhael's gaze was intent. 'Tell me one thing, Emma—your lord, the Count of Beaumont, will he marry you?'

'That is not your concern.'

A hand snatched at her, a hook-like hand with

dirty, broken nails. 'I do not like what you have become, Emma. I do not like it that our son must bear the stigma of illegitimacy.'

Pulling free, she gave him a steady look. 'We both knew what might happen in that autumn of 1066. It was my risk, as well as yours.'

At his sides, Judhael's fists clenched. 'Emma, we can make amends. Henri does not have to remain illegitimate. For the love of God, marry me. Come with me to Apulia.'

Chapter Fourteen

'No.' Emma's voice was steady, but her nerves were jangling. Being with Judhael had often reduced her to this state, she recalled. Only this time she was not going to be browbeaten. Judhael held her gaze, his expression steadier than it had been when he had been her father's housecarl. Doubts assailed her. He had always been so change-able—was it possible that he was trying to reform?

'Time,' Judhael said softly, glancing at Theo. 'Seeing me has been a surprise and you need time to consider. I will wait.'

'I will not change my mind,' she said. Henri shuffled. Realising she was squeezing his hand too tightly, she relaxed her hold. 'In any case, weren't you and Azor leaving for Apulia straight away?'

'I will delay my plans for you and our son, love.'

Firmly, she shook her head. 'Believe me, I will not come.'

'Think about it. And in the meantime…' Judhael eyed the purse that Richard had given her and put his hand out. 'I could do with a coin or two to tide me over.'

'Some things never change,' Emma murmured. Opening the purse, she tipped the contents into his grubby palm. The rank stench of his sweat hit her and it was an effort to hide her revulsion. 'I take it you sold the arm-rings you won from my father?'

'Eh?' Judhael looked blank.

'Never mind.' Thane Edgar's arm-rings, together with the ones she had given him, were doubtless long gone. She gestured towards the market. 'Buy yourself some new clothes, visit a bath house, get some fat on your ribs for the journey. But do not wait for me, because I will not come. Farewell, Judhael.'

It was pointless looking at the market stalls, since she was once again penniless, and in any case much of the brightness had somehow leeched out of the day. Nodding at Theo to accompany her, Emma turned her face to the castle. And even though she felt Judhael's eyes on her until she reached the shrine and must pass out of his sight, she did not look back.

As evening closed in, Emma retreated to Richard's bedchamber as soon as she was able. In the hall, Asa had badgered Sir Jean into teaching her the rudiments of some strange new board game. Since the girl was utterly absorbed—whether in the game or the man was an open question—Emma had given her leave to stay and had taken Henri to bed herself. Loving Henri as she did, it was no hardship.

As she sank on to the edge of the downy mattress on Richard's bed—would she ever get used to the softness?—her mind sifted through what had happened in the village.

Judhael was in Beaumont! He had seen Henri, he had learned that Henri was his son, and he had not fallen into one of his rages. Had time changed him so much? She would never have thought it possible. Yet today he had accepted her refusal with uncharacteristic calm. He must have changed. On the other hand, that wildness remained in his eyes. For his sake, she hoped that Azor's assessment of him was right. Apulia might be the making of him.

Emma loosened her braid and reached for her comb. She was hazy as to the precise location of Apulia, but it was far away, across the Alps, well outside the land of the Franks. If Judhael went with Azor to Apulia, she was not likely to meet him again. In Winchester she would have longed for such an outcome. But having seen him today, with the weight dropped from his bones, his muscles wasted…

As a mercenary, could Judhael last long?

Sighing, she ran the comb through her hair, found a knot and began teasing it out. More and more Saxons, thanes and housecarls who had lost their honour alongside their King, were becoming mercenaries. Which thane had Godric and Theo served under? she wondered. What had their lives been like before 1066; what ambitions had they buried?

But Godric and Theo were fortunate, they had landed on their feet when they had hired themselves out to the Comte de Beaumont. Richard treated his men with scrupulous fairness, and that went for his mercenaries as much as for those whose ties to him were feudal. Emma had not been here long, but that was already plain.

A sound on the landing drew her gaze to the door.

Richard. Shoving the purse he had given her, the *empty* purse, under the bed, Emma found a bright smile and prayed he would not remember to ask what she had bought at the market.

Outside the bedchamber, Richard leaned against the door for a moment, the metal studs biting into his shoulder. He was exhausted. He had put the guards through their paces; he had toured the estate at the head of his *conroi*, showing the flag; he had discussed tactics in the event of Argentan and Alençon joining forces. And still there was more to do. The armoury, the stores…however much he managed to delegate, there was always more awaiting his attention. There hadn't even been a moment to pay his respects at Martin's grave.

'*Merde.*' Lifting the latch, he went in. The air was filled with the scent of roses. His mood lifted.

Emma was sitting on the edge of the bed, comb in hand, smiling. Dropping the comb on the bedcover, she jumped up and came towards him. 'My lord!'

He reached for her waist and steered her back to the bed. 'You are a great blessing to me, *ma petite*. I need you tonight.'

'Do you?'

'Mmm.' Nudging her on to the bed, he settled himself beside her.

'No veil, good,' he muttered, threading his hands through a wild fall of honey-gold hair. 'Good.' The buckle on her girdle winked in the candle-light. He frowned as he began wrestling with it; it was not easy to undo. 'Lord, this is an ugly thing, you might find a better one in the village. Did you get to the market?'

'Yes, my lord.'

She flushed; it was most becoming. But there was something fleeting in Emma's expression that gave him pause. Guilt? Shame? He couldn't pin it down. 'My name is Richard,' he said softly. 'Have you forgotten?

'No, Richard, I haven't forgotten. I am sorry.'

She was watching him in that attentive way she had, with a hint of a crinkle in her brow. And there it was again, that fleeting thought he had had several times since meeting her, a wish that he was not honour bound to Lady Aude, a wish that he could offer Emma more than a half-life as his mistress. And there—again!—that sense that if he was not careful he might lose something of great importance. That there might be more between him and Lady Emma of Fulford, that he wanted more…

Lord, this woman muddled his mind. But roses, the scent of roses was filling his entire consciousness and all that mattered was that she was with him tonight. His Emma, looking anxiously up at him with those wide blue eyes. Her hair trailed out over the pillows like spun gold.

At last he managed to dispense with the girdle. 'Next time you go to the market, have pity on me and find one with a buckle that is easy to undo.'

'Yes, Richard.' Her eyes gleamed, unfathomable like the sea. Reaching up, she stroked his cheek. Her smile was back.

Richard closed his eyes as her fingers slid into his hair. 'Nice,' he murmured. 'Nice.'

There was only Emma in his mind and he could relax. 'You chase my worries away.' His eyes flew open—his need of this woman was surely a weakness, and he should be careful about admitting it. It was always a mistake to reveal weakness. His father had tried to beat that lesson into him more than once.

But her gaze remained steady, so did the smile. Could he trust Emma with his confidences? After his mother had gone to the convent, his father had become more stiff-necked and taciturn than ever, but he had found his mistress Lucie. Had his

father confided his innermost thoughts to Lucie?
'Richard, I think you should take your boots off.'

'Hmm? Oh, yes.' Glad that she did not seem to
have picked up on his slip, Richard levered
himself upright and dragged off his boots.

'And your belt. And—' her smile was warm
'—you may as well take off your tunic while you
are about it.'

He found a smile himself. 'Quite the sergeant
this evening, aren't you?'

'It seems you need it from time to time.'

As Richard tugged his tunic over his head, it
occurred to him that she might be right. But it went
against the grain, very much against the grain, to
agree. *Never confess to weakness*. So he merely
grunted and dropped his tunic on to the floor.

The room went dark as she snuffed the candle
out. He heard the rustling of bedcovers as she got
into bed. He felt his way back to her.

Warmth. Softness. Emma.

She drew the linens over him even as he was
pulling her under him. No gown, although she
was in her shift.

'That was quick,' he said, not displeased, as he
ran his hand over her, breast, waist, thigh. Hoping
she was not going to spout that nonsense about

it being the wrong time of the month, he pulled at the skirt of her shift.

She kissed his cheek and her fingers found their way into his hair, gently stroking the back of his head. She drew him onto her breast. 'Hush now.'

Hush?

'Sleep.'

Sleep?

The careful stroking went on and the scent of Emma, of roses, wound its gentle way into his mind. 'You need rest, Richard, quiet and rest. Geoffrey told me that many nights you have no sleep. It cannot go on, not when so many are relying on you to lead them.'

'Lead them…'

'Yes. Are your eyes closed?'

'Mmm.' *Leadership.* Her words had started an unwelcome train of thought, and rather to his surprise Richard found himself giving voice to it. 'That is what I aim to do, to command, to lead.' He raised his head from the cushion of her breast, but made no resistance when she pressed it back down again. She had lovely breasts, did Emma of Fulford, even if she did like to hide them from him by wearing her shift in bed. When this conversation was over—the woman clearly wanted conversation this evening—he would kiss every lovely inch of them. Come to think of it, he would kiss her everywhere…

'I am sure you are more than capable, Richard.'

'How would you know?'

'Your reputation in Winchester. When everyone realised that King William was not going to relinquish his claim to England, the whole of Wessex was in dread of who might be put at the head of the garrison.' Her voice became dry. 'King William is not known for his…charity or his kindness, and many of his commanders are of a like mind. But you, Richard…' She paused, continuing to play with his hair. It was very soothing. 'Wessex breathed a sigh of relief when command was given to you. You were known to be firm but fair. And I am certain that will not change simply because you are back in Normandy.'

Richard yawned and pressed a kiss on her collar-bone—the only part of her he could reach in his present position and he was disinclined to move. In a while though…

'Leadership. People think it is to do with ordering men about, but really I am carrying them, carrying them all.'

And there it was—that black thought he kept buried, that disloyal thought. Did King William always lead his subjects with love and care? Had it been good governance to stamp out every trace of life in those remote northern districts simply because some rebels had taken refuge there?

'Is it good government to kill innocents? Are there any circumstances in which it is justifiable?' Lord, he had done it again, voiced thoughts he should have kept to himself; perhaps she had not heard…

'You would not do that, Richard.' Her answer came softly through the dark, soothing and far more accepting than he would have thought possible given her father's allegiance to Harold Godwineson.

The calm certainty in her voice gave birth to a longing that was foolish in the extreme. Foolish, but…

'Emma?'

'Mmm?'

'There was a moment when I failed as a leader in York.'

Her fingertips were drawing tiny circles on his cheek. They stilled for a moment, then resumed. 'How so?'

Richard took a deep breath. 'We were deployed in the countryside outside York. Somewhere near a river, I forget the name. It was not as wide as the Itchen, and more thickly edged with reeds. The flow was faster. There had been much bloodshed and I was praying that it was over when I saw this child…'

'A child?'

'A Saxon boy. He was young, about Henri's age.'

'He was alone?' The stroking stopped. 'Where was his mother?'

'I do not know, I suspect she had been killed. Some of the troops—not mine, I hasten to add—had taken the command to rid the north of rebels rather too literally.'

He heard her swallow. 'Richard, you do not have to tell me this.'

'You don't wish to hear it?'

Her hand was back at his neck, soothing. 'If it gives you ease, Richard…'

'That child was running, running for his life. He had a trooper on his tail. There had been many dreadful sights that day, but that is the one that remains with me, the contrast between that poor innocent child and the fully mailed trooper.'

'What happened?'

Richard stared blindly into the dark. 'The trooper got him. I yelled out for him to hold, but he took no heed. Before you could blink, the sun was flickering along the length of his sword. Cold flame with death at its edge. It was over in a moment. The boy's blood soaked into the ground. Somewhere a rook was cawing—it is odd the ir-relevancies one remembers.' He gripped her shoulder. 'Emma, that trooper *was* one of mine.'

'But you ordered him to stop.'

'Yes.'

'He disobeyed you. Richard, you are not to blame.'

'I had the man disciplined, of course, but I cannot get that child out of my mind. He haunts my dreams.' Careful fingers were smoothing his hair, his neck, turning his head; Richard caught one in his teeth and gave it a gentle nip.

'Emma, I have also been thinking about our arrangement.'

'You have found time for that? My lord, you astound me.'

Up and down, up and down, the soothing touch of her hand in his hair. 'Emma, much as I wrestle with it, my conscience will not rest easy with my treatment of you.'

Her hand stilled. 'You wish to terminate our arrangement?'

'Lord, no.' The hand resumed its stroking. 'Back in Winchester I wanted you most... urgently, and I told myself that by offering to take you to Normandy I was saving you from yourself.' Her breast rose; sensing that she was about to speak, he put a finger on her lips. 'I am not done. I knew you had little means of support—your father having lost his lands.'

'He lost more than that, Father lost his *life*, as did my brother.'

'I am sorry for that, believe me, but that is the nature of war. What I am groping towards is this question. Last night you said you were drawn to me. I need to know—if circumstances had been otherwise, would you have accepted me for your lover, freely for yourself?'

'Are you trying to ask if I have a real liking for you, Richard?'

Richard frowned into the darkness; he would never have put it quite in those terms, but since she had mentioned it... 'Well, do you?'

Soft lips pressed a kiss to his cheekbone. 'Yes, Richard, I like you very well.'

Extraordinary. It was only a little phrase, yet it

lifted a weight from his shoulders. Richard couldn't fathom the power this woman seemed to command, he wouldn't have thought it possible.

'Emma, I allowed myself to get carried away in the stables at Honfleur, and I am sorry for it, although for myself I have no regrets. When I can, I shall start negotiations to put right the wrong I did you.'

'Negotiations?' Her voice was barely a whisper.

'I would like to honour in full the undertakings I made to you in Winchester. It may take time, however.'

'Richard, I am content with matters as they stand.'

'That may be, but I am not.'

Silence. What was going through her head? Emma had a mind of her own and Richard sensed she was not entirely happy with his decision. Not for the first time he found himself recalling Lucie, his father's mistress. Richard had been fond of Lucie, he had always felt that she had had a raw deal of it. 'You put me in mind of Lucie,' he said.

'Lucie?'

'My father's mistress. After Mother entered the convent, Lucie never left his side.'

'Did your father love her?'

'Lord, I wouldn't know, my father would never

speak of love. For myself, I doubt it exists, but I do know my father needed Lucie.'

'I see.'

'My father never believed the theory that chastity made a man's sword arm stronger.'

She gave a light laugh. 'You seem to agree with him.'

Conscious he was venturing on to dangerous territory, Richard chose not to respond. A man might relax in the company of a woman, and, from observing his knights, Richard knew that he was not the only one who found that the release of sexual tension could give a marvellous clarity of mind. Up until this moment, Richard had viewed the brothels that invariably sprang up near garrisons as mere conveniences for the soldiers. But Emma was teaching him that when men visited such women, they were not only taking advantage of someone else's misfortune, they were often compounding it.

'Emma?'

'Hmm?'

'Did *any* of the women who worked at the Staple enjoy their work?'

'Richard?'

If his question had startled her, it had startled

him, too. Richard was seeing the world in a different light. It was as if he had been wearing blinkers his entire life and Emma had ripped them from him.

'Never mind.' This evening, there was little Richard could do to make amends. But when Argentan and Alençon had been dealt with, then he would do his utmost to set things right with her. However, his present commitments—to his county and to Aude de Crèvecoeur—meant that for the moment he was honour bound to keep quiet about his intentions. 'It must not happen again,' he muttered. 'It will not happen again.'

'Richard, you are not making sense. It is time you slept.'

'Mmm.' He yawned; he *was* tired. Conversation with Emma had done the trick, though. Thank God he had found her, a woman who could drive away war demons not only with her body, but also, miraculously, by sharing confidences, by being there. 'There is so much to do,' he muttered.

'I dare say, but there will be time enough tomorrow. You have not been sleeping well for how long?'

'A few days.'

'Geoffrey told me otherwise.'

'Geoffrey talks too much.'

'Sleep, Richard.'

The soothing hand was doing its work on the nape of his neck, the movement lulling him. Richard had seen her caress her son in much the same way. 'Henri, is he happy here?'

'Henri is fine. Go to sleep, Richard.'

Emma lay staring into the dark. She knew the exact moment Richard slipped into sleep; his body went lax in her arms, his head became heavy, his breathing softened.

She pressed her nose against his hair and inhaled. Richard. A masculine scent that initially had meant protection and safety, but at some point along the road from Winchester to Beaumont had changed. Emma did indeed have a liking for him, a liking that was foolishly strong. She had entered into this relationship determined not to become another Frida, determined that emotionally at least, she would hold him at arm's length. It now seemed a foolish hope.

They had only been together a few days, but from the start Richard had got under her guard. He had got under her guard with that toy boat. And the gift of his purse? No, never that. It was more his behind-the-scenes insistence that no one should offer her insult. And those questions he had asked, trying to hide the fact that the great lord, Richard Comte de Beaumont, cared that she should like him. And she—idiot—she did warm to him, indeed she did.

Her lips curved as she nuzzled him. Richard needed this rest, and it was pleasing to think that she could comfort him enough to hold his nightmare at bay.

Her smile faded. The violence he must have seen. Richard was a warrior who had sworn to uphold his King and his Duke, but he was not by nature a violent man. There was no violence for violence's sake, where Richard was concerned.

Like Richard, Emma's father had been a warrior, but, unlike Richard, Thane Edgar had been prone to foul rages. Beaumont was blessed in its lord. It must be better that a man like Richard, someone in full command of himself—even-tempered and just—should take up the reins of government here. Emma had loved her father, but as a young woman she had observed that his rages often led to flawed judgements—witness his decision to force Cecily into St Anne's convent. And her father's temper... Emma grimaced; it had been fear of Thane Edgar's black temper that had driven her into becoming Judhael's secret lover.

Judhael. Who had proved to be another man of violence. Until Richard, Emma believed that most men, and certainly the warriors, were cast in that same violent mould.

Judhael's gaunt face, as she had seen it that morning, floated to the forefront of her mind. In the village, Judhael had not shouted at her, he had not forced her to talk to him. Was he finally trying to learn control? She wanted to believe it.

A lock of Richard's hair was curled round her finger. The dark in the bedchamber was total, but the exact colour of that hair was imprinted on her heart—dark brown, with a glint of chestnut when the sun caught it. 'Richard,' she murmured, as she lay pondering ironies. It did not seem possible that one of Duke William's most powerful knights should have come to England to wage war on England's subjects, and yet be a man of peace. The Norman commander of the Winchester garrison, a man of peace? Yet it was so. Why else would the death of one Saxon boy haunt him so?

Richard had a real desire to give good governance. His concern for justice must, of course, be the reason he wanted to make good the promises he had made her in Winchester.

Emma's heart contracted. It wasn't because he was developing a fondness for her. Richard was honourable, he had sworn to find her a husband and now he was going to match his word with deed.

It is too soon, she thought. *Our time together will be too short.*

Richard intended to find that husband she had asked for. She shook her head. She didn't want a husband, unless it was him. Richard had spoiled her for any other man.

Unless—longing was a pain that pierced her heart—could Richard possibly be implying that he thought her his equal? Was he saying that he wanted to court her?

No, that could never be. She was landless and dowerless. Not only were her father's lands in the keeping of a Frank, his friend Sir Adam, but Richard himself was committed to Lady Aude. Her brother's men were indispensable to him. Emma of Fulford had nothing to offer.

Richard stirred and mumbled in his sleep, but

his hold of her did not slacken. A tear slid down Emma's cheek; she rubbed it away in his hair. Her throat ached.

She was upset because she had been remembering her father.

She was worried about Judhael embarking upon the life of a mercenary in Apulia.

She sniffed back another tear. She was not upset about Richard, Comte de Beaumont—her tears had nothing to do with him.

Nevertheless, several questions held her back from sleep. Surely any man who married someone as serenely beautiful as Lady Aude would learn to love her, and then what would happen to Emma of Fulford? And what did Richard mean when he said he was working to uphold the promises he had made in Winchester? Emma had rashly asked him to find her a husband. Had Richard already picked one out?

Even before they broke their fast his army began mustering in the hall and bailey. Since neither place was congenial for Henri to play in, Emma took him up to the relative quiet of Richard's bedchamber.

Pushing one of the chests beneath the narrow

window, Emma climbed up and peered down at the horde milling about below the gatehouse.

A stream of soldiers flowed over the walkway bridging the ravine. There were men in chain-mail; men in old-fashioned leather tunics with metal rings sewn on to them; peasant farmers with little in the way of armour save their strength and a sharp billhook. There were shields of every description, round shields and long shields; there were spears and lances; short swords and long swords. The blade of a Saxon battle-axe caught the light. Boots thumped like distant drums, horses neighed and snorted, the dust rose. It was just as well, Emma reflected, that Richard had slept last night, for his wits would need to be keen today.

They had started pouring in just before dawn. Knights from Falaise, responding to Richard's call to arms; men from Bayeux eager to prove their loyalty to Bishop Odo's half-brother, Duke William; there were archers from Caen and Pont-l'Evêque. Billowing clouds of dust had announced the arrival of several columns of elite knights from Rouen, proving that even those at the very heart of the Norman Duchy were racing to arms in support of the new Count of Beaumont.

What with the tramp of the many feet, the shouting, the winding of a horn, the bailey was in uproar. There was so much noise that even as Emma was craning her neck to see, there was a fluster of flashing wings and the doves in the stable eaves took flight. They formed a white swirl that curled over the heads of the restless figures below. Seconds later they were gone.

Emma couldn't blame them. Watching what was happening in the bailey was making her nervous. She chewed her lip. There would be more fighting, more bloodshed. She willed herself not to remember those lost in the Great Battle, but of course, that was impossible; her father was ever in her mind. And what had happened around York?

If only there were some way of preventing this, Emma thought, turning away from the window. On the floor, Henri was playing with his boat, oblivious to the warmongering below. The rush matting was, Henri had informed her, the sea, and Richard's spare boots were doing duty as giant sea monsters.

'A battle of another sort, eh, Henri?' Emma said, stepping down from the chest and neatly avoiding Richard's old lute—no longer a lute in this game, so Henri had informed her, but an island in an otherwise vast and empty ocean.

Her brow wrinkled. Maybe Henri was not oblivious of what was going on in the bailey. Lord, who does protect the innocents, if not men like Richard?

Boat in hand, Henri roared up and down across the floor. The boat met one of Richard's boots head-on, Henri made his most ferocious gurgling noise, and the boot flew into the heap of disused arms stacked in the corner. A couple of sacking-wrapped packages clattered to the floor.

'Careful, Henri.' Emma went to set them to rights.

'Sorry, Mama.'

The boat soared over its choppy sea and Richard's other boot—er, whale—attacked and…

The sackcloth around the discarded sword began to come undone as Emma grasped the sword hilt. A garnet flashed, silver gleamed. She stared, mind blank with disbelief. The decoration at the pommel—beaten silver set with a chunky garnet—was familiar. This sword-hilt…slowly her mind groped its way towards the truth…she knew this sword!

Trembling in every limb, Emma wrenched the sacking aside. Henri had gone quiet. She glanced across, but he was fine, still roaring up and down the matting, round and round the lute-island.

She blinked at the sword, not believing what she was holding and yet, and yet…

This was her father's sword!

It had lost its sheath but this—she turned it in her hands and ran shaky fingertips along the blade—was the sword of a Saxon thane, the sword of a man who had gone off to battle in the company of his son. The sword of a man who had not returned: Thane Edgar of Fulford.

Tears blinded her. She thought she made a choking noise; she certainly swallowed to ease the tightness in her throat. Her mind seemed to have frozen. More tears, which she blinked away.

The sword remained in her hand, solid and very real. And there, it was still there, the pink ribbon she had wound round the cross-guard in that autumn of 1066 as a luck-token. It was stained with dirt and what looked like blood. Hot tears, more and more, like a dam bursting. She bit back a sob.

What was her father's sword doing stacked so neatly in the corner of Richard de Beaumont's bedchamber? And why hadn't these other arms been returned to the armoury? Were they trophies? Trophies of the kills he had made?

From her stunned brain one final question emerged.

Did Richard kill her father?

Chapter Fifteen

Emma's legs gave way. She collapsed on to the bed, wiped the tears with her sleeve and laid the sword across her knees.

Think, Emma, think.

The blade was shiny and sharp, it had been cleaned and oiled. Naturally. No Norman or Saxon warrior worth his salt could stand to see a fine blade ruined for lack of care.

And as for the pink ribbon plaited around the cross-guard...

Gently, she touched it. The ribbon took her back to a time of innocence, a time of hope. She and Judhael had only just become lovers; they had wanted to tell Thane Edgar of their wish to marry. Events had conspired against them when England had been plunged into turmoil. First Harold Hardrada, then Duke William...

Henri's boat nudged her foot and yanked her out of her memories. She watched him crawl back to the centre of his imaginary sea.

'You hadn't even been born,' Emma murmured, dashing more tears away.

'Mama?'

Henri was intent on his game, which was probably just as well. What good would it do him to see his mother in this state?

Had Richard killed her father?

She rested her fingers on the blade. It was cold. There was no escaping this. The presence of this sword in Richard's bedchamber implicated him in her father's death. *Not Richard, no. Not Richard.* She held down another sob and stared at the stains on the ribbon. Her father's blood? A bee blundered in through the window while Emma sat as though turned to stone.

Henri was merrily continuing with his game. A second boot met the same fate as its mate and shot at the wall. 'Sorry, Mama.' The bee buzzed, Henri chortled quietly to himself, while below them in the bailey and the hall, men were mustering for war.

'Richard,' Emma spoke under her breath. 'Not you, dear God, not you.'

She felt stunned, utterly stunned, although she could dimly see that in one sense there was no fathoming her reaction. Her father's death at Hastings was old news; neither he nor her brother had returned. But it was one thing to know your father had been killed fighting for his King and quite another to discover that the man you had chosen as your protector might have been the one to strike the fatal blow.

On the other hand, Richard might not have killed her father.

Emma chewed the inside of her cheeks and fingered the end of the pink ribbon. It was unraveling; her entire world was unravelling. Why should Richard keep this sword? Her breast heaved and the old prejudices and fears seemed to rise up and devour her.

At best Richard was implicated. At worst…

Delicately, Emma unwound the rest of the ribbon from the cross-guard. Setting it to one side, she put the sword back in its sacking and returned it to the corner. Nothing must seem out of place when Richard started looking for her.

What had he said last night? *That is the nature of war*. Did he know whose sword this had been? Pain sliced through her. She had been living in a dream world since she had left Winchester and it was time she woke up. Yes, Richard was noble in the best sense of the word, but she had been blinkered to think they might ever live in true amity. A Saxon and a Norman? Too much stood between them for her to continue as Richard's mistress for a single minute more....

The pain in her middle intensified, and she wrapped her arms round her stomach and sank back on to the bed. She must leave Beaumont, and it hurt, it *hurt*. What kind of a woman was she to feel real pain at the thought of leaving Richard? He had seduced her with his title and his strength. He had seduced her with that fine body and his apparent need of her. But what did she truly know about him?

He was gentle with her.

He ordered tiny boats to be made for her son.

He was a liar. He had lied about Lady Aude— 'Ugly Aude' indeed.

And as for his sleeplessness—it might not be wholly rooted in his concern for that Saxon boy his trooper had killed. His insomnia could just as easily suggest that there were other dark deeds in Richard's past, deeds that were coming back to haunt him.

The sacking-wrapped sword drew her gaze. Dark deeds. What else might Richard be hiding from her?

The bee flew into the whitewashed wall, buzzing frantically as it tried to find its way out. It lurched back into the middle of the room and dived at the wall again, before finally finding freedom and lumbering out of the window.

Emma cleared her throat. She could not sit here for ever. 'Have you overcome the sea monsters, Henri?' Her voice did not sound like her own.

'Yes, Mama!'

Pushing to her feet, she gritted her teeth. This should be easy, particularly since she had armed herself against caring for Richard de Beaumont from the outset. She held out her hand. 'In that case, come along. We are doing downstairs to pack your things.'

Large blue eyes stared up at her. 'Pack?'

'Yes. Later this afternoon we are going on a journey.'

Henri's face lit up. 'With Count Rich?'

'No, my love.' As her answer sank in, Henri's face lost its shine. 'But if you are good, Henri, *very* good, we may go in another boat.'

It was a pity she had given the entire contents

of Richard's purse to Judhael, but that couldn't be helped. She had survived on her own once in Winchester; she could do so again.

'I am sorry, Lord Richard,' Sir Hugh said, with a triumphant grin that revealed he was anything but sorry. 'The response has been such that I doubt there will be space for everyone in the hall tonight.'

The hall was certainly crammed past bursting point. The high table was raised on a dais, and from Richard's vantage point at the head of it, he should have had clear sight of the main door. The horde hid it from him.

It was organised chaos in here. Soldiers, servants, knights, squires and even his hounds were weaving round each other, tripping each other up, as they scurried about their business. His ears rang with noise. One man hailed another across the scramble, another dropped a serving platter, a manservant swore, a woman shrieked with laughter, a dog snarled.

No children though, Richard realised. He had not seen Henri since dawn, when he had looked in on the boy before breakfast. There was no sigh of Emma, either. Not that he could blame them; this mêlée was not for them.

'Do what you can, Hugh,' he said. 'I can see it will be tight.'

'We will have to commandeer the stable.'

Richard nodded. 'You might also use that storage barn next to the armoury, and tents could be raised in the herb garden behind the keep if necessary.'

'The herb garden?'

'Yes, Hugh. If there's an inch of space anywhere, use it.'

'But…the herb garden? Lady Aude will not like it, my lord.'

Richard sent Sir Hugh a meaningful look. 'It is not up to the Lady Aude. Between you and me, she may not be here for much longer.'

'Oh! I see, my lord, very well.'

Richard rubbed his face and looked past the maps and wine-cups on the table to the hall beyond. 'I have to confess I had not realised the response to my call to arms would be quite so overwhelming.'

'Your family have ever been loyal to Normandy,' Hugh said with a little smile. 'And Normandy looks after its own.'

'Hmm.' Richard tapped the map with the point of his dagger. 'What time are those envoys expected back?'

'They should return at any time, my lord.'

'Excuse me, Lord Richard?' The mercenary Theo was saluting at his side, his expression troubled. 'A word, if you please, concerning the Lady Emma.'

'Can't it wait?'

'No, my lord, I do not think so.'

Rising with a frown—Richard loathed being interrupted while in conference—he ushered the Saxon into a side passage. It was cool and dark, and when the door swung shut the babble in the hall muted. 'Yes?'

Theo swallowed. 'Lady Emma—I thought you should know—she has left the castle. With the boy.'

'She has most likely taken him to the village to escape the military havoc here.'

'I am not sure, my lord. She was dressed for travelling and carrying a bundle. I wouldn't mind betting that she and her son were leaving. Leaving the district.'

A cold knot formed in Richard's stomach. *Emma? Leaving?* Surely she would have said something to him if she had intended leaving Beaumont? Especially when only last night he had told her he was going to honour his promises to her as soon as he might. What was she about?

'You must be mistaken, man, she said nothing to me about leaving.'

'Nevertheless, my lord, Lady Emma did not have the look of someone who was planning to return.'

'When, when did you see her go?'

'They crossed the drawbridge not ten minutes since. On foot. They were headed towards the village.'

'*Merde.*'

In the hall someone yelled out an order—Sir Hugh by the tone.

'Do you want me to bring her back, my lord?'

Richard laughed. It was a bitter sound, but the thought of Theo dragging Emma back by her ears if she did not want to come struck him as oddly amusing. 'No, follow her.' He dug into his pouch. 'Here, take this. Watch over them, covertly, you understand. I need to know what she does. Make sure she comes to no harm, but above all, Theo, do not lose her.'

'No, my lord.'

'Hurry, man. And take a horse, you might need it.'

Theo turned on his heels and Richard watched him squeezing his way through the crush until the door swung shut. It took a minute to steel himself to return to his council. Emma, gone? *No!* He had hoped she had developed a liking for him; he certainly felt more than fond of her. Perhaps he could have expressed himself better last night. But that was not possible, not while he was still honour bound to Lady Aude.

Richard's nails were gouging into his palms. He flexed his hands. He had been an idiot as far as Emma was concerned—he had allowed himself to feel affection for her. And what was the result? Emma had run away, exactly as his mother had done. It was—he should have learned this lesson in boyhood—what women did.

They ran away.

In his mother's case he had come to understand it. His mother had been driven away by his father's repeated infidelities. But what had driven Emma away? She knew he was to have married Lady Aude, but from the beginning he had made it clear he felt nothing for Aude. He had grown fond of Emma; she must realise he wanted no other lover. Had he mentioned that sense of connection he felt with her? He had thought so, but last night he had been so damned tired. And now, Lord, this must not be permitted to delay him. He had a county to secure.

Richard stared blindly at an iron stud in the door, caught by a lowering suspicion. Last night, Emma had talked about his insomnia, she had mentioned that she had discussed him with Geoffrey. Last night he had accepted comfort from her. Had that been his mistake?

Had Emma fled because he had weakened himself in her eyes? Was he, in her view, no longer the strong protector she craved?

Mon Dieu, of all the days for her to take to her heels, she could not have picked a worse one.

Another bellow from Sir Hugh broke into Richard's thoughts. He squared his shoulders, set his hand to the door and ejected Emma from his mind. He had a battle to win, and win it he would.

Emma was heading for the village inn, on the chance of catching Judhael before he left for Apulia. As she hurried across the grass in front of it, the sun was sitting low on the horizon above a stand of trees in the west. The shadows were lengthening.

Pushing past a burly foot soldier in a leather gambeson and baggy chausses, Emma stepped over the worn threshold and led Henri inside. Almost immediately she regretted it. The inn was as thick with men as the great hall had been. Overspill from the castle, she supposed. Half the male population of the Duchy must have come to Beaumont.

A suggestive whistle had her back on home ground in an instant. It was as though she were standing in the Staple once again and Hélène was filling ale-jugs round the corner. She lifted her chin. She could deal with this.

Someone snatched at her skirt. Slapping the hand aside and giving the man—boy, really, he scarcely looked old enough to shave—a haughty glare such as she had often used back in Wessex, she elbowed her way to the heart of the room. It was stuffy and filled with blue smoke. More soldiers and yet more—each trestle was crammed, the benches bowed. Definitely over-spill from the castle.

'Emma!' Judhael stood before her, hand out-stretched.

'Judhael, I am glad you have not gone. I need to speak to you.'

'We'll go outside.' Judhael glanced at Henri. 'Let me carry you, lad.'

Thumb in his mouth, Henri's eyes were wide.

'It is all right, Judhael, I have him.'

They threaded their way outside and found a

bench that was catching the last rays of the dying sun. Judhael had taken Emma's advice. He had trimmed his hair and beard, and he was wearing, she was pleased to note, different clothes, clean ones. The sour smell had gone.

'You have reconsidered my offer,' Judhael said, a hint of complacency in his expression. 'You will marry me.'

'I am sorry, Judhael, but I have already given you my answer, I cannot…'

The words died on Emma's lips, as the truth hit home with the force of a thunderbolt.

She could not marry Judhael because she loved Richard! It had nothing to do with what Judhael had done in the past, nothing to do with her fears that he would never be entirely reformed. No, the main reason she could not marry Judhael was sitting up there in that castle at his council table in discussion with his knights. Richard.

Tearing her gaze from Judhael's, Emma blinked at the grass at her feet. How was this possible? From the start she had been determined to keep Richard at arm's length. And now he was implicated in her father's death. *I cannot love Richard, that would be…*

'It is impossible,' she said.

'Emma…'

The complacency had vanished from Judhael's expression. Gathering her wits, she touched his sleeve. 'I am sorry, Judhael,' she said softly. 'But it is as I said yesterday, I cannot marry you.'

He grimaced. 'No going back? Truly?'

'Truly. But I do need your help.'

'Name it.'

Braced for an argument at the least, Emma stared. What, no swearing because she had thwarted him? No shouting? Praise the Lord, it would seem that Judhael was at last trying to reform.

'I find I must leave the castle, Judhael.' She nudged her bundle with the toe of her boot. 'And I…I am sorry to have to ask you this, but I would like some of that money back. I gave you all I had.'

'What will you do, find your mother's relatives?'

'No, I shall return to Fulford, I should have gone there years ago. The money will be needed for the journey.'

Judhael patted his purse. 'You have it. And more than that, I shall accompany you, at least as far as one of the ports. I will not stand to see you wandering around Normandy alone with our son, particularly with the Duchy in such a ferment.'

'That is not necessary, I am sure we shall manage.'

'I insist.'

'But what of your plans—Apulia, Robert Guiscard?'

'Our plans will keep. I would have you safely back in England first. What kind of a father would I be to allow you and Henri to make such a hazardous journey alone?'

As Judhael spoke, the sun sank below the trees, tinting the sky with pink. Some rooks were flying back to their roosts, black dots against the glow. In the past Emma had always taken second place to Judhael's ambitions; it felt very strange to be put first. She smiled. 'You have changed, Judhael.'

'Time changes everything, in the end.' His hand came to rest on her arm and something in his eyes made her draw back.

'I will not marry you, Judhael. My mind is firm on that.'

'I have ears, love, I heard you the first time.'

Despite his words, Emma could see that he didn't believe her; he hoped to win her over. He got to his feet. 'Come, love—'

'I would rather you did not call me that.'

'As you will. We should go and wrest another horse from the groom here. It won't be easy with all this going on.' Judhael jerked his head at the endless files of soldiers marching towards the castle.

'No, it won't. But I should like to set out as soon as possible, even though it will mean travelling through the dusk.' Castle Beaumont stood on its escarpment glowing soft apricot in the evening sun. A cold blade twisted inside her. 'He might come after me.'

Judhael's eyes became slits. 'How likely is that?'

'I am not sure.' Emma waved at the massing troops. 'His mind is fully occupied, but really I could not say.'

Judhael nodded. 'We shall leave immediately. And I will twist Azor's arm to make certain he comes with us. Another sword arm wouldn't go amiss.'

Three days later, Emma, Henri, Judhael and Azor were back in the port of Honfleur. There had—Emma was trying not to care—been no sighting of Richard, Comte de Beaumont, although the whole Duchy was talking of no-one else. Emma might have fled his castle, but there was no escaping him.

At an inn near St Pierre, Emma eavesdropped on a conversation between two women sitting by the hearth.

'Quick to step into his cousin's shoes, isn't he?' one woman had said, poking life into the fire with a stick.

'He will have to be quick if he aims to keep the county,' came the pragmatic reply. 'He will need to be clever, too, and perhaps he is—Morwenna told me that envoys rode out from Beaumont bound for Argentan and Alençon.'

At a well-head in the town of Pont-l'Evêque, there was more discussion.

'Count Richard brought letters with him, letters from Duke William,' a young man said, while carrying a bucket of water for his heavily pregnant wife. 'Argentan and Alençon don't stand a chance. Even Count Remond has sent a troop to support him.'

The pretty wife had laid a hand on her belly. 'Count Remond of Quimperlé? I thought his face was turned in another direction?'

'Not this time. They knew each other some years back and Count Richard's reputation…'

Emma had not tarried long enough at the well-head to hear about Count Richard's reputation, she could not bear to. Whenever his name was mentioned her spirits sank. It was as though they were speaking of someone else, a stranger whom she had never met, and she did not like it. The Comte de Beaumont. Oh, Richard…

Every step of their journey was taking her further away from him, and as the miles passed Emma's heart got heavier. By the time she reached Fulford, it would be entirely made of lead. And that would be a blessing, because then she would surely stop hurting. She couldn't wait to get out of the Duchy.

At Honfleur, however, there was a minor setback.

'There are no ships for Bosham for several days, *madame*,' one of the ship's masters informed her, while high in the salt-laden air the gulls swooped and keened.

Emma pointed at another ship where porters were rolling barrels on the quayside and loading them into hoists. 'That one's about to set sail.'

'That one?' The ship's master stroked his chin. 'Bound for St Malo.'

'And that one?'

'No, my dear, that's a river barge, it will eventually be going upriver towards Rouen. If you want to get to England you will have to wait. The next ship for Bosham leaves in four days' time. A merchant vessel. In the meantime, should you require lodgings—'

'No, thank you, we have lodgings.'

Their inn, the Ship, was a flea-pit and could not compare to the Mermaid. The food was barely palatable and the mattresses were damp and likely verminous. *Soon*, Emma told herself, soon I will be home at Fulford. *What a prideful fool I have been. Cecily was right, I do belong at Fulford. It is important to live a life surrounded by those who love you. At Fulford there is Cecily and Adam and Beatrice and...*

'You will like it at Fulford,' she told Henri, preparing him for what was to come. 'You will be able to play with your cousin, and I have a brother a little older than you. Adam will find a pony for you both and...' Her voice cracked; she swallowed quickly. 'You will love it.'

One evening, as they were chewing their way through a gristly beef stew that had been salted with a heavy hand, Judhael, who up till now had kept his distance, touched her arm. 'Don't go, love,' he said.

Across the table, Azor's head shot up. His expression was wary enough to have the hairs lifting on Emma's neck.

'Please, Judhael,' Emma said, shifting away, 'I am not your love.'

'You are. I would marry you!' His eyes were unnaturally bright. 'It was always my intention, you know that. Please, Emma, reconsider.'

'I cannot.'

Judhael's mouth set in stubborn lines. 'You could do worse than marry me.'

Azor thumped his cup down. 'Lady Emma, married to a mercenary? What kind of life would that be for her?'

Judhael's eyes glittered in the torchlight. 'It would be a life where she was no longer a fallen woman. It would legitimise our child.' He took her hand. 'Emma, I implore you—'

'No.'

'But I love you!' His voice rose, heads turned. *Lord, hadn't they left all this behind them?*

Flushing, Emma jerked free and hid her hands in her lap. 'But I don't love you, not any more.'

Much to her relief, Judhael subsided into silence.

The day of departure arrived, their ship was to leave at noon. Emma had spent an hour in the local bath house so as to give Judhael time to make his farewells to Henri. God alone knew whether they would ever meet again.

The minute Emma walked into the inn yard, it was apparent something was wrong. Judhael and Azor were standing by a stack of hay, glaring belligerently at each other and Judhael had a reddish mark—a developing bruise?—on one cheek. His badly stitched scar was livid in the morning light. There was no sign of Henri.

'What's happened? Where's Henri?'

'Ran off,' Judhael flung at her, eyes never leaving Azor's. He was rigid with fury.

Emma's skin chilled; she had seen Judhael in the grip of anger many times and the outcome was never pretty. *Henri!*

'Ran off? Which way?' She grabbed Judhael's sleeve. 'For pity's sake, which way did he go?'

Judhael lifted a shoulder, his eyes as hard as glass. 'Ask our friend here. I was too busy being thumped to see anything but stars.'

'Azor hit you? Why?' Emma darted a glance up and down the street. Nothing. She left Judhael rubbing the red mark on his cheek and ducked her head inside the tavern. No Henri. Lord. Her insides writhed. Where was he? 'Azor?'

A muscle worked in Azor's cheek. 'I am sorry, my lady.'

Azor's brown eyes did look apologetic, which was more than could be said for those of her erstwhile lover.

'You bastard, Azor,' Judhael cut in, voice tight with anger.

'You should not have hit him, Jude,' Azor said, 'he was only upset.'

'Why was Henri upset?'

'An accident. Jude trod on some boat he had—it broke.'

Enlightenment dawned. 'Henri cried.'

'Yes, my lady.'

So much for Judhael trying to reform. Emma rounded on him. 'You hit Henri! I should have known! Violence has always been your way.'

'Sometimes—' Judhael's tone was ugly '—it is the only way.' Refusing to meet her gaze, he scowled at the wooded hillside overlooking the port.

'You are impossible!' Emma's stomach was churning and all she could think was that Henri had run off, crying, in a strange town and Judhael was more concerned with his pride. 'Blessed Virgin, you must have some idea where he went!'

Finally, Judhael was looking at her. 'Only if you marry me.'

Repelled by such callousness, it took a moment to find words. 'I know who the real bastard is, Judhael, and it is not Henri.' Picking up her skirts, Emma began haring towards the port, veil dragging at her scalp as it caught in the breeze.

Chapter Sixteen

Richard slowed the horse he had borrowed from Aude's brother to a trot as they approached Honfleur. He had enjoyed feeling the wind in his hair. It had been an age since he had cantered along the roads of Normandy so informally, with only a sword and a leather gambeson, and without a full escort. He had won this privilege, but worry was nibbling away at his enjoyment. Theo's report had made it clear that Emma had succeeded in booking passage on a ship that would leave for Wessex later than morning. He was determined not to be late.

It had started to rain. Feeling it trickle down his neck, he pulled up his hood.

Since Richard was riding *incognito* he was accompanied only by Geoffrey and the Saxon mercenaries, having left the rest of his entourage back at Crèvecoeur. Speed was key, which was why he had even left his hounds behind. He would have set out sooner, but it had been vital to await the return of his envoys and see negotiations through to a conclusion before he left Beaumont. Now, with his chain of command as secure as he could make it, he had come for her.

Ahead lay the outskirts of the port: a storage barn, its thatch dark with age; a dubious-looking inn, its door rotted so badly it looked as though a wild beast had taken great bites out of the bottom of it.

Theo had also mentioned Emma's travelling companions in his report. Two Saxon housecarls, he had said, one going by the name of Judhael. *Merde*. Theo's report raised more questions than it answered. Had Emma arranged to meet Judhael in Beaumont? Why else would the man be there? No Norman in his right mind would employ Judhael of Fulford. And surely Judhael couldn't risk returning to England?

'About half a mile to go, my lord,' Geoffrey said, dragging up his hood, too.

Lost in his thoughts, Richard nodded. Would he be in time? He prayed so. How would she react when she saw him?

'I am certain Lady Emma will be pleased when she sees you, my lord,' Geoffrey ventured.

Richard raised a brow. 'I beg your pardon?'

'I am sorry, my lord.' Geoffrey flushed. 'It was impertinent of me to comment.'

'So it was, but since you have, you might care to expand.'

'When Lady Emma learns what you intend…' Geoffrey's voice trailed off.

'You presume to know the workings of my mind, Geoffrey?'

'No, my lord, my apologies, of course.' Geoffrey exchanged glances with Godric and Richard felt his colour rise.

Was it so obvious? It must be. He had to have her back. He was a besotted fool, so entranced by his runaway mistress that he could not live without her. He had not breathed a word of his intentions, yet somehow these two had caught wind of them. Of course, they had been party to the meeting Richard had had with the Count of Corbeil on the way here and they knew he wanted her back. But he had not breathed a word of his real intentions regarding Emma.

Over the years, Richard had travelled many miles with Geoffrey and part of him, the part that was more man than count, would have been happy to ask Geoffrey for his views about Emma. But, no, despite his informal attire today, he must remain 'the Count'. He must be mindful of his consequence at all times.

If Emma would return with him, then he really would have someone to talk things over with. There was that link he felt with her, that sense that a real meeting of minds might be possible, if only…

Merde, why had she run away? Could she still have feelings for Henri's father?

The road was shiny with rain, the ruts were filling with water. A couple of magpies were scrapping over fish guts by the ditch. They went on squabbling even when his horse's hoofs passed within a foot of them. A nose-wrinkling stink of ripe entrails filled the air.

Ahead, a child suddenly ran into the street and came straight at them, his little face the picture of misery. Seeing him, the hair prickled at the nape of Richard's neck—*a running child, running as fast as his short legs would carry him…* The muscles contracted in Richard's belly, a black memory stirred and, for a moment, he was in another country, in a bleak and bloody landscape near York.

As the child stumbled towards them, Richard's gaze sharpened. Surely that was…?

'Henri!' Geoffrey exclaimed.

'So it is. Wait here.' Signalling the others to halt, Richard urged his horse forwards.

Henri tripped on one of the ruts and fell flat in the mud.

It was the work of a moment to dismount and pick him up. 'Henri?'

Sniffing, wiping his nose with the back of his hand, Henri's eyes widened. His mother's eyes.

'Lord Rich!' He gave a watery smile. 'Was looking for you.'

'Were you, lad?'

'Yes.'

'Come along with me, then, and tell me what's wrong.' Henri's face was streaked with mud and tears, or was it rain? It was hard to tell.

The child sniffed and swallowed on a hiccough. 'He broke my boat!'

'Did he? Hold tight, Henri.' Richard set him on the saddle and mounted swiftly behind him, pulling him close.

'Yes.' Henri twisted towards him, face puckering, fists clinging at his gambeson. 'And…Rich, Rich, I lost Mama!'

'It is all right, Henri, you are safe with me. First we will go and find your mama and then we shall see about getting another boat made for you. In fact, if Mama agrees, you shall have lots of boats. How does that sound?'

A small damp body pressed close to his. 'Yes!' A smile trembled into being. 'Count Rich?'

'Hmm?'

'Mama and Jude…'

Richard realised he must be scowling when Henri's voice trailed off. He schooled his face into a pleasant expression. 'Yes?'

A small hand touched Richard's cheek, as though the child was offering him comfort. 'Mama and Jude, no kissie, kissie, no kissie, kissie.'

Richard's jaw sagged. Of all the things Henri could have told him this was…this was…*thank God*. He felt as though the clouds had lifted, but, no, a flurry of cold wind hit him in the face and the puddles were spotty with rain.

Henri's blond head shook from side to side. Mud was running down from one of his ears. Absently, Richard wiped it away.

Thank God.

'No kissie, kissie,' Henri repeated, and the child's satisfaction clearly matched his. Almost.

* * *

The rain was pouring down in earnest when Emma reached the quays. Somewhere along the way she had lost her veil. Standing at the mouth of the harbour, gulping for breath, she put a hand to her eyes to ward off the wet and peered desperately towards the jetties.

The tide was coming in. Their ship was at last at its mooring, and one or two sodden figures were squelching towards it across boards that were dark with wet. One man was leading a pony to the broad gangplank, another was hauling on the bridle of a reluctant baggage mule.

No Henri. There was a cold stone where her heart should be.

The other jetties were quiet. The fishermen must have put out earlier or taken refuge in one of the taverns.

'Henri!' Emma ran a few steps and peered into a dank alley between two storage barns. *'Henri!'*

No response.

Hoofs clattered behind her, metal-shod hoofs that scraped the cobbles. She turned, and the world lurched sideways.

'Henri!' She stared up into the face of his rescuer. *'Richard!'*

Richard grinned. 'At your service, my lady.'

'Look, Mama, I found Count Rich!'

The relief weakened her. It was an effort to move to Richard's knee, but she managed it. She held up her arms. 'Come here, Henri.'

Her son was warm and soft and… She drew back. 'You're covered in mud!'

'Sorry, Mama.'

Her eyes met Richard's over the blond head.

'A little mishap on the Pont-l'Evêque road,' Richard murmured.

'He was on the road to Pont-l'Evêque?' Heavens.

'Apparently he was looking for me.'

Her eyes stung and suddenly Emma was pleased it was raining. She blinked like a mad thing. 'I see. Well, I thank you, my lord, with all my heart.'

Richard smiled and Emma's heart did a silly leap. He looked to be in good health, although perhaps a little tired and unshaven. And there was something different about him. She frowned. Of course! He was wearing a leather gambeson such as an ordinary soldier might wear. Where was his chain-mail, his shield, the crimson pennons? Where was his entourage? The dogs? Had matters gone badly in Beaumont? Her heart squeezed as she stared up at him. She ought not to care any more, particularly since she had found her father's sword in his possession. It was galling to learn that she did care, very much. She was going to have to be strong.

'I did not expect to see you again,' she said, in as wooden a voice as she could manage.

'I gathered as much, in Beaumont.'

Hugging Henri to her, Emma set her face towards the ship. 'Thank you for bringing Henri to me, my lord. Thank you. But if you will excuse me, I have booked passage to Bosham and we must embark.'

Richard sent her the most peculiar smile. 'Which boat, that one?'

Emma's gaze followed his pointing finger. 'Geoffrey!' A horrible suspicion formed. 'Why are Geoffrey and Theo talking to the ship's master?'

Richard's eyes glinted.

'Richard, have you taken it upon yourself to cancel my booking? Have you?'

'How dare you!' Emma hissed a few minutes later as Richard hauled her into one of the more prosperous merchant's houses overlooking the port. 'How dare you!'

Inside, Richard released her. Rubbing her arm,

she glared at him, grinding her teeth in her anger. With Henri's eyes on them, she couldn't make a fuss, at least not as large a fuss as she wanted to and Richard knew it, the brute. She took a steadying breath. 'Where are they?'

'Who?'

'The poor souls whose house your men have commandeered, where are they?'

'Visiting friends.'

Money must have changed hands. The house was large and lovingly furnished with clean, white-washed walls and a polished table. The subtle smell of beeswax lay beneath the smoky tang of a household fire. Bunches of lavender had been hung from the beams and a copper pot gleamed on the hearth. It was probably the best house in the port.

'I don't know why you have brought me here. I have nothing to say to you and I have no intention of going back with you.'

'Mama?' Anxious eyes were looking up at her. Henri did not like her tone, nor, judging by the expression on his face, did Richard.

'Godric?'

'My lord?'

'Take Henri out to watch the ships, will you?

And don't let him out of your sight, he can move like lightning when he wants to.'

'Yes, my lord.' Godric held out his hand and looked enquiringly at Emma.

Emma nodded her permission.

'Come and see the boats then, my lad. I wonder if there are any with red sails?'

At the door, Henri hung back. 'Count Rich?'

'Hmm?'

'You won't forget your promise?'

Richard's expression lightened and he ruffled Henri's hair. 'Would I forget something as important as that?'

Henri smiled and allowed Godric to lead him out. They were alone.

Emma felt the familiar awareness shimmering through her. Every nerve seemed to tingle simply being with him. Heaven help her, she had missed him.

Determined to resist, she strode up and down. 'Promise? What promise?'

'Later.' Richard came to stand in front of her, close enough for her to see that he did indeed need a shave. He smelt of horse and sweat and Richard, and his mere presence in front of her was shamefully weakening. It was so weakening she could hardly tear her gaze from his mouth. She would give her life to be able to step into those strong arms and let them stroke away the past… Lord, this was not going to be easy….

'I have a question for you, Emma. Two, in fact.' Those grey eyes were watching her as intently as a hawk watches his prey.

'Yes?'

'Theo told me some men escorted you here.'

'Theo saw me? I wondered how you knew where to come. You had me followed!'

Richard reached out and for a brief joyous moment, Emma thought he meant to enfold her in his arms, but he simply felt the woollen fabric of her skirt and frowned. 'This is wet, Emma, you should change.'

'I shall do nothing of the sort! What would I wear?'

His mouth twitched and he gestured towards a couple of bundles that lay unnoticed by the wall. Her bundle, hers and Henri's. He had had them brought from the inn. Emma glowered at him. 'You assume too much, Richard.'

'I assume nothing, I assure you. Change, Emma, you will catch a chill.'

Emma folded her arms across her breasts. 'I

will not!' Rain was getting in through the smoke-louvres, the fire hissed.

'Have it your own way.' His eyes held hers. 'Theo mentioned that one of the men…was his name Judhael? That was your former lover's name, as I recall.'

'I cannot say.'

'It *was* Judhael. Lord, Emma, the man abandoned you years ago and you insist on protecting him?'

She shook her head. 'Judhael did not abandon me, I walked away from him.'

'Did you arrange to meet him in Beaumont?'

'*No*! He and a companion—oh, Richard, what can it matter? I am trying to get back to England. J…my old friends escorted me. And all would have been well and Henri and I would have been safely on our way if you had not told the ship's master that we do not require passage on his ship.' She glared at him. 'You were wrong to do that, I am going back to England. There is still time. They will not sail until high tide.'

'I regret, my lady, but that ship will sail without you.' Grim-jawed and determined, Richard looked anything but regretful. 'We have matters to discuss before you may leave. After that…' he shrugged '…it will be your decision. You may leave then if you wish.'

'I have nothing to say to you! I would like to leave immediately.'

He drew closer, and his eyes were as frosty as they had been when she had first met him back in Winchester. Had Richard been defeated in Beaumont? Was she once again looking into the eyes of man made bitter by defeat? Since he was wearing the plain attire of a humble soldier, it seemed likely. Lord, hadn't she seen enough men destroyed that way?

'Later, Emma, after our talk.'

He had backed her up against the table, which was digging into her thighs. 'Richard, *please*.'

He took her shoulders. 'Why did you leave? If it was not because Henri's father had come for you, because you love him—'

'*No*! No, it was not.' His fingers were merciless, and his eyes—Emma really did not like that cold look. Curse her for her weakness, but she wanted to see those grey eyes lit with warmth again, as they had been in that tower room in Beaumont.

'Then why walk out? Why?'

Emma turned her head to avoid that pitiless

gaze and focused on the baggage across the room. 'The sword, it was the sword.' Her mouth was dry. Licking her lips. she stumbled on. 'I found Thane Edgar's sword in your room. *My dead father's sword.*'

His grip eased, he was frowning, eyes blank. 'Sword?'

Breaking free, tears blinding her so she could— thank God—no longer see him, Emma wrapped her arms about her middle. 'You can't even remember, can you?' Her laugh was harsh, cracking in the middle. 'Saints, you kill my father and you can't even remember!'

'The sword, the one from Hastings, the one I had Geoffrey wrap in sacking—it belonged to your father?'

Bleakly Emma nodded, conscious of him looming over her. That powerful male shape was shadowy, silhouetted by the light coming in through the shutters and blurred by her tears. Silence gripped them and it seemed they had both been turned to stone. Outside, a gull mewed, a sparrow chirped. The fire was no longer hissing, the rain must have stopped.

Richard broke the spell by running his hand across his forehead. 'Your father, Thane Edgar…by all that's holy, Emma, I did not know that man was your father. And I did not kill him.'

'I wish I could believe that.' More tears flooded her eyes.

He took her hand, his touch gentle this time, and ran his thumb over her fingers. 'I swear it, Emma. But now I understand why you fled.' Drawing her to a bench, he pulled her down beside him. 'If you will listen, I will explain why I kept that sword.'

She nodded. For some reason it had become impossible to look him in the eye, so she stared instead at a knot in the tabletop.

'I did not kill your father, but I did see him die,' Richard said. 'I will not burden your mind with details because they can come back to haunt you, but you should know that your father died bravely.'

Emma ran a fingertip over the swirls in the knot, round and round, round and round. 'Was he near the King?'

'Harold Godwineson? Yes, the owner of that sword was at the heart of things, in the midst of his companions. He died a warrior's death.'

The whorls in the knot wavered and swam, tears burned tracks down her cheeks.

'Emma.'

A large hand reached out and carefully turned her face towards him. Fingers smoothed the tears away. Fingers that Emma thought—but of course she could not see properly for the crying—were trembling. She bit back a sob. Hope, she was learning, could be as painful as despair….

'Emma, you *must* believe me. When…if we return to Beaumont I will put Thane Edgar's sword into your keeping. I saved it to remind myself that in war there is bravery and heroism on *both* sides.' His throat worked. 'I find I need you to believe me.'

Burrowing into his arms—oh, the relief—Emma pressed her face into leather worn soft with use and nodded. 'I do,' she choked. 'I do. I expect you would have killed my father if you had had to, but I thank God that you did not.'

They sat on the bench for some time. Shadows shifted. Richard stroked her head, and pressed warm lips against her temple. Winding her arms about him, she hugged him as tightly as she could and lifted her tear-blotched face to his. *If we return to Beaumont*, he had said. Events there must have turned out badly.

'Richard?'

'Mmm?' He pressed another kiss to her temple

and eased her plait from the back of her neck with a grimace. 'You are drenched. We need to get you dry.'

Sniffing like a child, Emma nodded and stood meek as a lamb while Richard of Beaumont began undressing her. It was very innocent, very chaste. She let the relief sink in. Her father had died a hero's death, as he would have wished. And Richard had not killed him, thank God.

Questions crowded in on her. 'Richard?'

He was frowning over the recalcitrant buckle on her girdle. 'Lord, I hate this thing, why on earth won't you get another? Ah, there!' The girdle clunked on to the table and he turned her about, searching for the ties at the back of her gown.

'What happened in Beaumont, Richard—was there a battle?'

'In a moment. First you will tell me. Are we reconciled?'

Emma blinked and, turning back to face him, reached for the solidity of that plain gambeson. Her fingers curled firmly into the leather. The tide must indeed have turned against him in Beaumont. Richard had come to her without his entourage, in the guise of an ordinary man. He was, apparently, no longer the powerful protector she had sought out in Winchester. But if he wanted her, he could have her. She no longer cared for the trappings—man or count, she would be content with either. She had dreamed of marriage once, but for this man, she would set those dreams aside, too.

'We are reconciled.' It sounded like a vow, which in a way, it was. Richard had had her heart in his keeping for some while, if he did but know it.

A smile lit his eyes. It was his old smile, the warm one she had seen in Beaumont and it took years off him. She thought he would kiss her, but he simply stood there, staring at her and smiling. She flushed, suddenly ridiculously self-conscious.

'Beaumont, Richard? *What happened?*'

He made her face the other way and returned to her lacings, 'There was no fighting, thank God.' His breath was warm on the back of her neck. 'With William's support and that of my allies, negotiations won the day. The Counts of Argentan and Alençon were after easy pickings. When they realised half the Duchy was up in arms against them, they came to their senses.'

'You won!'

'Aye, Beaumont is mine, and without as much as a sword being unsheathed. When two stags fight antler to antler there does not have to be bloodshed, but one must acknowledge the other has won. Of course, we may not rest on our laurels, they will always be probing for weakness, but we shall be ready for them should they return.'

'I am so glad,' Emma said, as he peeled the damp wool of her gown from her shoulders. 'You will give your people good governance, I am sure.' She reached for his hand, but he had turned away and was rummaging in her pack for a dry gown. 'What happened about the armoury and all those damaged weapons?'

He looked across. 'I forgot you heard about that. Jean found the culprit and is dealing with him. Will this blue one do?'

'Yes.'

She stood meek as a lamb and let him dress her. 'So, the Count of Beaumont is acting as my maid-servant,' she murmured.

'What?' His grin was lopsided. 'Desperate times! I can't have you catching your death, not when I have plans for you.'

'You do?'

'You, *ma petite*, are coming back to Beaumont with me. There is no escape.' His grin fell away, was replaced by a guarded look that might be called hesitant. It made her want to kiss him. 'You are, aren't you?'

Emma nodded. She could pretend no longer. She loved this man. She had known it before, but the finding of her father's sword had caused the past to rise up between them like a sea monster. It was time to put it behind them.

'The doves will have flown back to their roosts by now, so, yes, yes, I will, too.'

'The doves?'

'The ones in the stables, which the soldiers scared away.'

His hand came round her neck, caressed her nape. 'There will always be soldiers. I have my duties and sometimes a show of force is necessary, but since you are coming back with me…' his eyes became watchful '…there is a matter of some importance we must discuss.'

'Oh?'

'In Winchester, you asked me to find you a suitable husband. I am ready to open negotiations.'

He had found her a husband? No! 'But, Richard—'

'You will have to tell me if you think he is suitable.'

Richard, the established Count of Beaumont, overlord by inheritance and now by acclamation, went down on one knee before her.

'Emma of Fulford, will you consent to become my Countess?'

She gripped a broad shoulder. '*You?* You want to marry me?' She found herself watching open-mouthed as he stared up into her eyes.

'Marry me, Emma. I will cherish you as no woman has ever been cherished.'

'But…but…what about Lady Aude?'

'I escorted her back to Crèvecoeur on my way here. She never wanted me, we all know that.'

'But isn't marriage with her necessary to strengthen the alliance with her brother?'

'Edouard and I have established a good under-standing of each other without that. Besides—' his expression softened '—I have developed an inordinate fondness for a wench I stumbled across in a tavern.'

Emma put her hands on her hips. 'An inordi-nate *fondness*?'

Reaching for her, he slipped a warm hand under her skirt and moved it up and down her calf. 'A most distressing fondness, an uncontrollable fondness.'

'*Fondness?*'

He leaned his head against her thigh and sighed. 'Aye. It might be love, but I doubt it. She is the most terrible wench. If I do marry her, I expect she will force me to journey to Wessex for the wedding since her family live there. I have to supply her with fat purses. And her son is almost as bad, whole fleets of boats have to be made to satisfy him....'

Heart singing, for she was beginning to believe at last that Richard really did love her, Emma struggled to maintain her composure. She raised a brow. 'Whole fleets? Goodness.'

Richard pushed himself to his feet. 'Drives as hard a bargain as his mother, does Henri. Well, will you have me? I have dispatched Theo with a letter to the King asking for his blessing. He will need to know.'

'So that is what Geoffrey and Theo were doing by the ship!'

He gave her one of his crooked smiles. 'I confess it, Theo was stealing your place on board. Well? Will you come back to Beaumont as my bride?'

'Yes, I have developed an inordinate fondness for you, too.'

Grey eyes looked into hers, eyes that were full of warmth and dark with passion. Cold? Never. 'An inordinate fondness?' he murmured.

'Richard, I love you.' At his grin, she reached for his shoulders and offered her mouth to his, but he held back. 'Richard?'

'There is one condition,' he said, eyes serious.

'Condition?'

'You must swear not to run away again. Emma, please know that I love you, I adore you, but there will be times when I can't go chasing all over the countryside after you.'

'I know, and I promise, there will be no more running away. You and Judhael both have strong political ambitions, but I have learned there is a vast difference between you.'

'Mmm?' Wrapping his hands about her waist, he tugged her to him and nuzzled her ear-lobe. Desire pooled in her belly. She had missed him these past few days; she had ached for him. One look from Richard, one touch, and she knew her eyes were glazed with want.

'Yes.' It was hard to speak, her voice was as croaky as a frog's and her fingers were sliding into his thick brown hair. But this she must say. 'Richard, once I thought your ambitions were similar to Judhael's, but the two of you are worlds apart. Judhael had an unhealthy fixation, an obsession if you will. He is twisted by defeat.'

'Emma, in war no one escapes unscathed.'

'I know. But not all men react in the same way. Whatever battles you may face in the future, they will not warp you as they have warped Judhael. You are dedicated to…well, good governance is as good a phrase as any. You care about your men, your people.'

Richard lifted his head. He was fiddling with a ribbon on her braid, and she had the feeling that it would soon be undone, and that he had wasted his time in dressing her.

'Richard, are you listening?'

'Of course,' he murmured, lips moving inexorably across her cheeks, her temples…

'Wretch, you haven't heard a word I said!' She gave him a gentle punch and he caught her wrist.

'Enough talking, tavern wench, and give your lord a decent kiss. It's time for a little display of that inordinate fondness we have been discussing.'

Epilogue

Winchester Cathedral, England—one month later.

The Count of Beaumont and his new Countess stood hand in hand in the porch of the Minster, scarcely able to see the forecourt for the crowd of family, friends and well-wishers. Emma's heart was so full, she thought it might burst.

There was so much to take in. Not five minutes' since, in the incense-scented calm of the Lady Chapel, the Abbot himself had endorsed King William's blessing of their marriage. And now they had emerged from the Minster, to stand blinking at everyone in a burst of spring sunlight. Emma was wearing the pink gown; she must have regained her former figure since running off with Richard, for the bodice no longer gaped. The silk veil was secured with a golden circlet. At her side, Richard was magnificent in his gold tunic. Crimson pennons, each with its golden stripe, flew from a dozen spears.

The Cathedral bells were ringing and a cheer went up as they stepped into the Close. The entire garrison had gathered to see the woman their former commander had married. A Countess, Saints. And her marriage blessed in the Minster itself, in the shadow of Saint Swithun's shrine. Lord.

Emma caught her sister Cecily's gaze and smiled. Today was a day in which anything seemed possible, a day in which it seemed that the ancient hostilities might at last be buried, the old wrongs forgotten. Today her life was beginning anew. A Countess? She felt like a queen.

'Emma, Emma!' A figure in the crowd waved, and a posy of wildflowers landed at her feet. Someone retrieved it and thrust it into her hand.

'Hélène!'

Hélène was there on the edge of the crowd, jumping up and down, all smiles. Frida was with her, and Marie. And there, Gytha and Bertha and Aediva…

Richard's thumb curled into her palm in a soft,

secret caress. He was smiling, gesturing at one of the knights. 'Sir Guy.'

'Lord Richard. I wish you well.'

'They are all here.' Emma swallowed down a lump, as the Cathedral yard was lost in a mist of tears. 'Everyone has come to wish us well.'

'And why should they not?' Richard squeezed her hand, and began towing her purposefully towards the knight. 'Sir Guy, if I might ask a favour of you?'

'Lord Richard.'

Richard glanced swiftly at Emma, who was surreptitiously wiping tears away on the sleeve of her gown. Her face was lit with happiness, as he knew his was, too. 'Your chamber, Sir Guy...?'

'The tower room?' Sir Guy tried, not very successfully, to hide a grin. 'It is yours, my lord, for as long as you may require it.'

HISTORICAL

Large Print

TALL, DARK AND DISREPUTABLE
Deb Marlowe

Mateo Cardea's dark good-looks filled Portia Tofton's girlish dreams – dreams that were shattered when Mateo rejected her hand in marriage. Now Portia's home has been gambled away, and Mateo is the only man who can help. However, she has in her possession something he wants – so she strikes a deal with the devil himself!

THE MISTRESS OF HANOVER SQUARE
Anne Herries

Forever generous, matchmaker Amelia Royston will do anything to help others' dreams come true – yet will her own feet ever be swept off the ground? Then the charismatic Earl of Ravenshead returns to tip her world upside down! He finally declares his intention to marry her – but is he only wanting a convenient bride…?

THE ACCIDENTAL COUNTESS
Michelle Willingham

When Stephen Chesterfield, the Earl of Whitmore, awakes to find a beautiful woman berating him, he knows he is in trouble! He cannot recall the last three months of his life, never mind having a wife! What's more, someone is trying to silence him before his memory returns… Can he find trust and love before it is too late?

MILLS & BOON

HISTORICAL

Large Print

THE ROGUE'S DISGRACED LADY
Carole Mortimer

Lady Juliet Boyd has kept out of the public eye since the suspicious death of her husband, until she meets the scandalous Sebastian St Claire, who makes her feel things, *need* things she's never experienced before. Juliet finds his lovemaking irresistible. But does he really want her – or just the truth behind her disgrace?

A MARRIAGEABLE MISS
Dorothy Elbury

When Miss Helena Wheatley's father falls ill, she is forced to turn to one of her suitors to avoid an unwelcome marriage! The Earl of Markfield honourably agrees to squire her around Town until her father recovers. Then they are caught alone together, and their temporary agreement suddenly looks set to become a lot more permanent…

WICKED RAKE,
DEFIANT MISTRESS
Ann Lethbridge

When a mysterious woman holds him at gunpoint, Garrick Le Clere, Marquess of Beauworth, knows he's finally met his match! Alone, Lady Eleanor Hadley is without hope, until the notorious rake offers a way out of her predicament… Now Garrick has a new mistress, and she's not only a virgin, but a Lady – with a dangerous secret!

 MILLS & BOON